Stephanie Zia was born in Dorset in 1955. Before becoming a full-time writer she was a production assistant in BBC TV's music and arts department. She has written for national newspapers, women's magazines and interiors magazines. She lives in west London.

Keeping Mum is her second novel.

GW00370406

Also by Stephanie Zia
Baby On Board

Keeping Mum

Stephanie Zia

PIATKUS

Copyright © Stephanie Zia 2004

First published in Great Britain in 2004 by
Judy Piatkus (Publishers) Ltd of
5 Windmill Street, London W1T 2JA
email:info@piatkus.co.uk

The moral right of the author has been asserted

A catalogue record for this book is available from the British Library

ISBN 0 7499 3478 6

Set in Times by
Action Publishing Technology Ltd, Gloucester

Printed and bound in Great Britain by
Mackays of Chatham Ltd, Chatham, Kent

Acknowledgements

For essential encouragement and valued criticism, my grateful thanks to Judith, Gillian, Emma, Jacqui, Louise and Linda. Special thanks to Jacqui Hazell for introducing me to the wonderful world of interiors, Maria Torshall-Ayris for advice on all things Swedish, and Sandra Doling for her fabulous flamenco lessons. Thanks also to Rebecca Topley, Debbie McDonnell, Tonee Reid, Kate Harrison, Helen Rogan, Sandra McHugh, Jean Etches, Sue and John Haycock, Michael Gray, Kathryn McDonnell and Richard Cross.

For information on Sicily and the politics of embroidery I am indebted to *The Blue Guide to Sicily* by Ellen Grady and *The Subversive Stitch: Embroidery and the Making of the Feminine* by Rozsika Parka.

Finally, a big thank you to all at the Kew Bookshop and everyone who bought the first book and said such nice things. It meant a hell of a lot.

Chapter One

'Take a woman of thirty-six and a man of thirty-six.' Carla closed the wet-room window with an abrupt thud. Her husband, bouncing in his boxers on the trampoline below, turned to a satisfying abstract behind the frosted glass.

'Women who go for older men aren't stupid,' she muttered, kicking the soggy heap of pyjamas and damp towels into a corner before going for a tortuous profile-examination. 'It saves them untold years of body angst in later life.'

Standing as tall as 5′4″ could get in bare feet, she held herself in and pushed herself out in all the right places that were fast repositioning themselves into the wrong places. Facing facts that had to be faced head on. Full on. Full-length-mirror-on. Ignoring her best bits, of which there were many. She wasn't fat for a start. More – rounded. Though this did nothing to stop her feeling hippo-arsed when a bad body day felt like presenting itself. But then Tom did look twenty-five if a day, whilst she, dropping and drooping all over the place, and at that moment covered from top to toe in crimson Heidi Klein kaftans, was hurtling full pelt into a forties sag bag without a pause.

Giving herself one of her best Nigella pouts, she turned away from the mirror and squirted two tiny cool cream meringues of hand cream onto the backs of her hand. Her own deterioration butting up against her husband's ever-increasing resemblance to Peter Pan was something she'd have to deal with, as she did everything else, in a calm, practical, sensible, Carla way. That's all. She'd find a way. Carla always found a way. She splodged her hands together, twisting them round till the palms met, finger slithering over finger, hand twisting over hand. The familiar scent of Crabtree and Evelyn tea rose soothed her.

Carla had beautiful hands. Slender, smooth, olive skin with oval nails – not long, but filed to a bump in the middle. She mixed her own nail varnish, a rare kind of dusky pink, dull almost, but with an iridescent funky glow, a definite but not overwhelming presence. A bit like Carla.

After carefully applying her make-up she gathered the washing, went into the hallway, sat herself at the top of the slide and slid down to the day room below.

'Well fan my brow and slap my cheeks, this day's getting better and better, isn't it.' She held the cream card at arm's length for a moment, her head tilted to one side, looking at it in an abstract way.

Then she looked at the bin. Wishing it were that simple.

'What's that?' Tom snapped off a banana from the fruit bowl.

'Bruno's ready to show off his new home.'

'Already?'

Carla looked at the card. 'Well, not till November.'

'Getting his invites in early, isn't he?' Tom pointed the banana at the tall shiny silver rubbish bin. 'Wingardium Leviosa.'

The bin flipped open.

2

'It's supposed to be amazing.'

'I bet it is,' she said dryly.

The bin closed with a thud.

'Come on, there's no point being bitter about him Carl, you're just wasting your energy.'

He stood behind her, touching her shoulders lightly as he read the card.

She leaned back, breathing in his sweet musky sweat as his cold nakedness pressed into her back.

'Do we have to go?'

He let go of her a little too quickly, tugging his blue and white Japanese bathrobe off the door-hook before going for the coffee.

Neither of them spoke.

'You see him all the time Tom,' she said into the silence, 'and we'd only be going for appearances' sake, wouldn't we.'

'It's me they're treating like crap, Carla, not you.'

'Same difference. I just don't think I'll be able to stop myself giving him a tongue-lashing.'

'That wouldn't help Carla.'

'He could've stood up for you more. There'll be so many there, we wouldn't be missed . . .'

Tom stopped, mid-scoop of coffee. Pausing for a moment before turning round. They exchanged one of those coded looks all couples who've been together for a long time have.

'I know, I know, everyone'll be there,' she sighed.

He turned away.

'Want a juice, boys?' he called to the two silent figures sprawled in front of the TV at the far end of the large open-plan room.

They'd have to go. They'd have to say nice things about Bruno's fuck-off penthouse as well. Bought with the fuck-off money he'd made from the fuck-off buy-out.

'If coming, please tick box ...' she read out, 'what's wrong with RSVP like the rest of the world?'

'That's what everyone puts these days.'

'I am out of the loop, aren't I. And what's this?'

'What?'

'No presents!'

'Carla, why do you have to analyse everything to death?'

'No presents, indeed. As if! What arrogance.' She flung the card down on the table and set about emptying the dishwasher.

'He's deaccessorising, that's all.' Tom switched on the coffee grinder.

'What?' she shouted.

'Everyone's doing it,' he shouted back, 'you know – the preoccupation with possession prevents men from living freely and nobly and all that stuff.'

'Bruno IASSACI? Preoccupation with *possession*? *Noble*? Don't make me laugh. And since when have you started standing up for him, anyway?' She opened the dishwasher.

'Oh, he's all right ...'

'BrUno!!'

Tom shrugged and switched off the grinder.

He speeded up his movements, clattering the coffee cups as he took them out of the cupboard. 'He's no different from all the other big corporate bastards, is he? Giving you your start on the one hand and taking away your future with the other. Spitting you out at the end to make way for the next lot.'

'And making fat profits out of you into the bargain.'

'He gave us a bloody good start, didn't he?'

'And didn't you just give him his future? God, I hate

4

this job.' She picked out the knives one by one, wiping them down with a tea towel.

'You say that every day.'

'It's time to move on, that's all.'

'We've done all right so far, haven't we?'

'Not as well as Bruno has out of your designs...'

'Carla, while I don't want to spend the rest of my life twisting and turning into a bitter, foul-mouthed git always down the caff moaning about missed opportunities, neither do I want to fall out with Bruno Iassaci or snub him in any way when he might hold the key to yours, mine, all our futures.'

'He's a shit we can live without.' She clattered the knives into a drawer.

'He also happens to be one of the most important operators in world furniture and if you think our future lies in snubbing him when he happens by the way to still be my boss ...!'

'Also.'

'What?'

'Also. You said also.'

Ignoring her, he stood on the roundabout footplate of the kitchen island and spun himself round and reached up to the circular cupboard above.

'There's a packet already opened in the bottom cupboard.'

Tom swirled back again and slit open the new box. He pulled out the greaseproof-wrapped cereal and squashed it around until a shock of bright red and yellow plastic revealed itself. His frown only turned to a smile after dipping his hand in and holding up the figure triumphantly.

'It's the dog! What's it called, Carl? WILF? What's the Tweenies dog called...?'

5

He squashed the misshapen bag back into the box and shook it over a bowl, crouched in concentration.

'Fizz, that's it. That's it. Out out, you lot. Out you come. Arghahaaa I see a Milo, I see lots of Jakes and Fizzes. Where's Bella, we have a shortage of Bellas here, guys.'

Carla gave a motherly sigh.

'It's Doodles actually,' she said so quietly he didn't hear her. She picked up her sewing bag and took herself off to the sun-filled cushion pit at the garden end of the room.

Chapter Two

'What's up? Has she broken the lens?' said Tom.

'I hope so.' Carla pinched his thigh.

The photographer flicked his frown from the camera to Carla for a microsecond. 'Won't be long.'

There was a long silence.

'I'm off.' Wilf pushed his chair back.

'No, you don't.' Carla grabbed him by the elbow, relaxing her grip on Dyl, who immediately tried to wriggle free.

Tom grabbed the other elbow. 'Sit still and do as you're told.'

'Stay as you are please,' said the photographer.

'We'll be ready when you are.' She caught Dyl before he zapped out of reach.

Wilf and Tom slumped forward onto crossed arms.

Carla stayed sitting erect, with Dyl in a vice-grip on her lap.

'Sophie, come over here a mo, would you sweetheart.'

Tom visibly perked up as Sophie, dangling with light meters, hipster jeans and belt bags, arrived to assist.

Wilf smirked.

Dyl wriggled.

Carla gazed absent-mindedly at the words 'Calvin Klein' embossed in stretchy elastic around Sophie's tiny midriff.

'I'm hungry,' Dyl wailed.

Carla gave Tom her I-think-it's-your-turn look.

To her surprise Tom leaped up immediately, touching Sophie's waist lightly as he pushed past her to get to the cupboard. Surprise explained. He grabbed the biscuit tin and was back within seconds.

Sophie turned and smiled at him as he sat down. Tom sat to attention, grinning back at her.

'Oooh la la.' Wilf creased up.

Tom handed round orange Kit Kats, giving Carla's knee a double squeeze.

Sophie was stretching up now, wriggling her arse self-consciously and turning to reveal her belly button.

Carla held onto Dyl a bit tighter, turning her gaze to the heaving mass of stylists, art directors and make-up ladies, and their assistant and assistant assistants and runners and all their stuff: enormous leather shoulder bags, silver metal boxes, lights, clipboards, making even their huge living area seem squashed.

'I think I'd rather have the builders back than this.'

'You wouldn't.'

Carla widened her eyes into her 'no, really' expression. She would really.

Some of them had been around for so long, they'd become like part of the furniture, part of the family, some of them. Oh there'd been a few early disasters. Like kids, they'd run rings around her in the early days. There was nothing builders loved more than ignorance. But after thirteen years of turning their rubble of a building into the home it had become, Carla had become a bit of a pro. Enforcing strict penalty clauses and bossing dusty,

8

mouthy, bobble-hatted blokes about had become part of her routine. After a while they started to respect her. A grudging respect which had made it all the better, somehow. Something she'd earned.

'At least with builders there's something to show for it at the end.'

'What are you on about? We'll have a sodding great article in a mainstream glossy. Did you hear her saying she'll get us on her *Homes to Die For* show next. It's what we're needing ...'

'It's all right for you, you're used to it.'

'It'll settle down.'

'I don't like it.'

'Why not? You look fine.'

Fine?

'I'm not talking about me. It's the house.'

'What about the house?'

'Put it this way, I wouldn't be surprised if, coming back from the school run tomorrow, I found a gap in the terrace like a pulled tooth, and No. 22 had taken itself off for a holiday to oh ... Lanzarote, leaving a sign, "no more photos", dangling on a stick.'

'Lanzarote?'

'The Maldives, then.'

'We'd have to get it a snorkel.'

'All right Tom, you think of somewhere. All I'm saying is it's getting out of hand.'

'Don't be daft, Carl.'

'I'm serious. I've had enough. Keep those chocolaty hands OFF me, Dyl!!'

Tom looked at her as if she were mad.

'Why are you looking at me like that?'

'This is great for us Carl.'

'Why? We're not desperate. We don't need to show off.'

'Showing off's nothing to do with it.'

'We've been through this already and I know, look, I'm here, we're doing it, right?'

'Think how useful it'll be when we come to sell.'

It was Carla's turn to look at Tom as if he was the mad one.

'I'm not saying *now* . . .'

'This is a family home Tom, not a CV.'

'Deia!'

'What?'

'Deia – for the holiday home, the home's holiday I mean.'

Give him a line and he'd run for it, she thought wearily, knowing he'd be back on it for days.

They often talked about No. 22 like this. Like it was another child almost. A blend of Tom's playful eccentricity and Carla's calm, cool practicalness. 'A partnership that goes together like tongue and groove', according to the July issue of *Home from Home*, the glossiest of the glossies.

Its fame had started slowly enough, appearing in obscure oversized Italian and Swedish design magazines only available at the Whitechapel and Tate Modern. Tom himself was used to attention ever since Bruno pulled him out of his degree show and whisked him down to London, with Carla not far behind. But now, as the house nudged into mainstream TV and *Prima Home* territory, it wasn't "Tom Alexander award-winning furniture designer" any more, it was "Tom and Carla Alexander, creators of the amazing House on the Hill." TomnCarla, no spaces between.

'All right everybody, we're on again. Could we manage a few more smiles this time, please?'

A long, loud base thrrrrp note came from the photographer's bottom. There was a gaping silence. Everyone in

10

the room stopped what they were doing. Tom, Carla, Wilf and Dyl all looked to each other for confirmation, their cheeks emitting squeaks of repressed laughter before exploding into fits of giggles. The camera fired a machine-gun round of clicks.

To hide his embarrassment, Carla thought, but then she spotted his assistant discreetly removing a fart cushion from his behind. By the time she'd rearranged her face into her gorgeous Disney smile, the one she used to such effect on doctors' receptionists and PTA Chairs, the clicks had stopped and the assistant was packing up the gear; the boys had disappeared into the garden and Tom was chatting with Sophie, who'd forgotten about the job in hand and was giving him her full attention, picking at the strands of her long, dark curls.

'Sooowper darlings, thank you.' The large, lipstick-loud, gravely voice of one Tasmania Cunningham, the afternoon TV interiors expert, appeared from nowhere. 'Now, could I have you over here a moment Tom? A few more quickie q's, won't take a sec.'

Carla stayed where she was, her face folded deep into worry. Not because Tasmania ignored her. That was preferable. And not because of Sophie. Sophie wasn't worth the effort. She'd be gone and forgotten in a moment.

She'd known this would be part of their life together, right from the day she'd first set eyes on Tom. Every year in every college had one. The stellar. The intergalactic who had it all. Talent, looks and fun. A smile turned on her just the once in the queue for watery coffee on a Tuesday afternoon was all it had taken. And she'd known. And she'd waited. Watching without looking. A quiet noticing as he'd gone through the campus It girls. And then the prickles of a distant, almost spiteful pride as she'd

11

watched him tire of them one by one. Not through any vanity on her part, more a knowing. A knowing that had finally turned to knowledge one night at a long-awaited Smiths gig where, in a dark, sticky-floored bar, soft-eyed, talented Tom, his unavailable desirability more than a match for the man on the stage, fell for warm, round, pretty Carla from fabric design. An attraction which ran far deeper than skinny hips and easy smiles.

Sophie returned grumpily to her packing as Tasmania settled herself into Tom's orbit, smoothing down her flicky orange hair. 'So, Tom, tell me now, how did all this come about?'

Tom looked puzzled.

'All what?'

'This!' She swept her arms dramatically about, looking like a pink punk bat in her pashmina shawl.

'The house?'

'The house. You. All! Let's start with *you*, shall we . . .'

Tom looked at her like she must know the story.

She stared back, blank-faced, mini tape-recorder held towards him.

'From the beginning, you mean?'

Tasmania nodded. 'Your first chair, what was it called?'

'Out of the Blue.'

Tasmania nodded more vigorously.

'I, the prototype I made for my degree show in 1986, was picked up, I was picked up by Bruno Iassaci of Carliatti, he came to the show, and he took me on. And the chair. It went to Milan. . . you must know the story.'

'*So* unusual, Tom . . .'

'It won the best of show . . . and went into production . . .'

'*Unheard of* leap from graduate to the international arena, Tom . . .'

'It was, it was like having a number one record. An amazing time!'

'Amazing,' breathed Tasmania happily.

It was. He'd looked like a rock star too, with his shaggy, brown, Bolan curls. It was funny the way it still looked long, his hair, even though it was short now, coming to an abrupt curly end all the way round just below his ears. Like most designers, he wasn't much of a one for personal elegance, but he always looked scruffily good with minimal effort.

'So I've been at Carliatti ever since, really, and that's it. For the last year I've been doing a new range coming out next month, as it happens, Paranormal – have they sent you the press releases yet?'

'Yes – yes, yes, yes, so, I imagine that's the last you'll be making under the – er, Carliatti name. Tell me about the Speranza takeover? You seem to have survived. Will you be staying?'

Tom shrugged and grinned his broad Ewan McGregor grin. 'Why not?'

Carla took a deep breath. Good boy Tom, good boy.

'Your designs are always ahead of time but at the same time seem to exist in a timeless simultaneousness, wouldn't you say?'

Carla caught the quizzical frown, oblivious to Tasmania.

'At the same time, yes, of course.'

'QUITE!' she beamed happily.

'What would you say *encapsulates* your style, Tom?'

'You're the writer, what do you think?'

'Relevant, ethical . . .?'

'Mmmmm. I'd say it's all about staying true to the materials but at the same time putting the fun into functional . . .'

13

Carla smiled to herself. He'd said this a thousand times but always managed to make it sound like he'd just thought of it.

'So ... the house ... It hits you as soon as you step through the door, doesn't it? That utterly incongruous blend of primary colours and gorgeous tapestries, quilts and hangings.'

'Thanks.'

Hmm, thanks, too.

'Yes, tell me about the house Tom.'

Patronising cow.

'I was looking for a shell of a building to convert and it was luck, really. I saw this one in the *Evening Standard* and came out to have a look and knew, well, right away really, it was the one.'

'Why?'

I?

'Why what?'

'Why Richmond?'

'That was just where the house happened to be. It was years before the boom.'

'Before it became known as the Beverly Hills of London,' Tasmania tittered.

'That'd probably've put us off even coming. Actually, to be honest, it reminded us of the North, like nowhere else in London.'

Us. Better, thank you, Tom.

'The *North*?'

That first smell of wood smoke and the windy, fresh air, she remembered it well. Like the rows of tiny back-street terraces on the cold, northern slopes of Sheffield where Tom had grown up.

'As I said, we saw it in the *Standard*, came down and had a look and knew right away we'd found what we wanted.'

'Why?'

We. We.

Tom shrugged.

'Everything, really. You know as soon as you step in the door, don't you, when something's right.'

She remembered the first time they'd seen No. 22 Richmond Hill Grove, standing forlornly at the end of a small street of Victorian redbrick terraces. Its tall windows boarded up, its steep steps crumbling to a slope, a rusty red Anglia on bricks in the drive. Graffitti'd, uncared for and unloved, like it had been waiting through all those years of neglect for them to arrive.

'And the playground theme, how did that all come about?'

'There's the Memphis influence, of course, but here it started with the slide. I built it as a fun thing for my first son, Wilf, not long after he was born, as it happens.'

He'd barely been conceived.

Tasmania looked over at it. 'Extraordinary. Like a cross between a spiral staircase and a helter-skelter, isn't it.'

'At first it was a kids slide adapted. But before he'd grown old enough to use it properly . . .'

When he was barely three months old and the nursery still wasn't finished.

'. . . I noticed how much grown-ups wanted to go on it, so I had a tougher one specially welded and incorporated the helter-skelter thing. Funnily enough, the kids love going up the spiral in the middle as much as they love coming down.'

I? Puh! Whilst Tom had spent the past sixteen years designing for Carliatti, having cups of coffee brought to him by nubile PAs and working-out in his lunch hour, Carla had project-managed all of it, raising two boys whilst bossing around a constant turnover of builders with their sixty-four skips of hardcore, numerous decorators and slippery contractors.

'It also comes in handy as a laundry chute,' said Carla.

Tasmania jumped. They both looked at her like she'd popped out of the floor.

'It's actually quite a practical thing to have around.'

'If you've got the space,' said Tasmania with a new bitchy tone in her voice.

'And we've kept the real stairs,' said Tom, 'so, the theme grew from there really. The roundabout carousel there in the central kitchen area, the ball pond cushion pit behind it – that gets the morning sun. I should say the light was important too, when we first saw the place, that's all there was really, a few walls and a lot of light. It gets the full shade at the back and full sun at the front. My wife, she prefers the shade . . .'

'It is a combination, isn't it, really, of an enormous play area and a comfortable flop house. Breaking down barriers between generations, would you say that's been your theme?'

'Mmmm,' Tom nodded.

'Tell me about the dedicated play room.'

'That was the garage, or coach house, I should say originally it would've been. One of the last rooms we did. We laid the bright red resin pigmented floor, put in a climbing wall, table-tennis table, all the stuff, and got in the juke box and all the instruments, the drums, keyboards and electric guitars, soundproofed it . . . Again, the grown-ups use it as much as the kids. And the kids like to flop out in there. And then there's the play-pit down the end of the garden . . .'

'So, why do you call this room the Klounge?'

Obviously not *Household Harmony's* brief, gardens. Good. The gardening glossies hadn't got there yet and she

16

wanted to keep it that way. It was the one part of the house that hadn't become public property.

'It's what everyone's doing these days, isn't it, but no one's come up with a name really.'

'Kitchen cum living room?'

'You could call it that . . .'

Carla quietly stood up and left the room. She felt Tom's puzzled stare behind her. A quiet sulk, that's what she needed. She'd stay out of his way for a while. Let him think about what had made her mad. She moved slowly and assuredly as always, trudging upstairs to wash the gunge out of her hair that the stylist had sprayed in.

We. I. They. Why should she be bothered? That was how Tom always did interviews. What they'd agreed without ever having to agree it. The 'we' had only crept in lately and, much as she detested the limelight, it had felt good. She was still anonymous, but a little more of a presence. But – sell? She couldn't believe he could even *say* the word. He knew her love for her home was the same kind of love she had for him. She knew every tiny, dusty corner intimately. She loved them as much for their faults as for their virtues – his overwhelming energy, the leaking pipe on the children's sink; his over-the-top flirtatiousness, the damp chill in the back attic room; his blokey Northern chauvinism, the jinxed bed in the garden which wouldn't even take bizzy lizzies, his love of his family, his brilliance with the boys, the way the light fell into the rooms in the mornings, his playfulness, his obvious attraction to women only turned up her mother's pride. However much he flirted, at the end of the day, and the end of every day, he was with her. It had always been so, even before he was famous. Whether his flirtations ever went anywhere was something she didn't bother thinking about, knowing deep down that his hundreds of mini-conquests never went further than playful banter.

17

But selling the house? Even to mention it. Didn't he realise how that would affect her? Didn't he *know*? And not only the house, the Hill. She'd worked hard, damned hard, to fit in amongst the stick-thin fashionista of Richmond Hill and she'd done bloody well. As much as she felt she'd ever fitted in anywhere, it was here. She had her core of friends, Elle, of course, and Antonia and Cyn. There were some she could do without, the Bryonys and Hazels of the world, the cud-chewers as she called them, but then, they were in every playground across the land. No – he must have realised. Then, why?

She moved cautiously. The house felt different. It did. Like an old friend had suddenly, and for no fathomable reason, done something so completely out of character she'd never be able to look at them in the same way again. She crept into the wet room, as if there were something behind the door she wouldn't want to see, instead of the vast cocoon of Italian marble and shelves of folded white fluffy towels.

She slipped off her clothes and stood under the umbrella-sized showerhead.

For the first time in fourteen years, wondering who'd live there after them. What would they look like? Where were they now? What were they doing now, these strangers, totally oblivious they'd one day be there in that room, using that shower?

The steely hard pinpricks of water hitting her scalp soothed her. She squirted shampoo onto her hair. Whoever they were, these people, whose future was already part of her past, they wouldn't be getting their hands on it for a long, long time.

She began massaging.

If all was right in the world they wouldn't even be born yet.

She rubbed hard.

What if they miscalculated?

She screwed up her face and rubbed harder.

She had to think of the advantages, go forward positively with her husband and make the change as smoothly and successfully as she'd engineered every other aspect of their lives together.

If Tom didn't get out of Carliatti soon he'd be dead, she knew that and accepted that. Creatively dead, it went unsaid. For someone like Tom, a fate worse than. She ran her fingers through her hair like a thick comb. She wasn't daft. She knew no one had a job for life any more. If the business failed, then the house would have to go. And everything in it. But for Tom to think like that? That was different. That was new.

She turned off the water and dotted masses of creamy coconut conditioner all over her hair. White on black.

Why did these magazine journalists keep on wanting to know more? More, more and more all the time? More information. Who was Carla? Who were the boys? What did they wear? What did she cook with?

The *Telegraph* supplement had made her feel like she'd stripped naked for *Playboy*, the stir it'd caused in the playground. And she hadn't even been *in* that one! She could still hear guardian of the *Guardian* Hazel Macfernon ticking off another box in her suspicions about the Alexanders being nothing but frivolous, capitalist über-consumers. And in the *Telegraph* – what would you expect! It hadn't come out like she'd imagined at all. She'd taken the nice, chatty journalist lady round, pointing out all the subtleties of colour. The way ochre and purple lifted each other; the way the deep purple and pale lime of Tom's basement workroom brought relaxation and stimulation into the same space. And the woman had seemed so interested. It wasn't Carla's fault that they'd chosen to highlight the domestic side of things. That instead of the Memphis-inspired hallway, the over-enthusiastic stylist had dug out their embarrassingly mud-free Barbours and Wellingtons – a result of their too infrequent walks in Richmond Park rather than any regular cleaning regime – and arranged them in descending order of size; that instead of the textured, layered whites and creams of the master bedroom they'd gone for the clothes hanging in the dressing room, of all things – Tom's one short rail of his four suits, two sand-coloured for summer, two charcoal-grey for winter, two formal, two casual, next to racks and racks of Carla's dresses, skirts and tops, carefully organised through the colour spectrum from palest yellow to deep crimson – pointing out the absence of trousers and jeans and anything in black or white; that instead of the usual roundabout and slide, they'd done what she supposed was called in the trade an 'original angle' and gone for the food cupboard, the saucepans and the frying-pan arrangements.

And then what was it with Bruno? It wasn't like Tom to be defending him. Something was up. She examined it, twisted it and turned it around, rubbing the conditioner through till the strands of her hair slithered and parted, turning in seconds from matted clumps to silk-smooth order, every hair straight and slick next to every other hair.

She paused for a moment. Ever since a hairdresser told her that leaving conditioner in for two minutes was a waste of time, she always stopped and wondered. Had that girl been telling the truth, or was she strapped for time that day and keen to get onto her next client? She rinsed it off. She'd never known what to do in those two minutes anyway.

20

Advantages, think of the advantages. Getting Bruno Iassaci out of their lives for a start. Bloody Bruno. Bigmouth, preening, pain-in-the-neck Bruno. A candidate for spontaneous combustion if ever there was one. Though putting up with him had been a small price to pay for all they'd achieved, it would be wonderful to get him out of their lives.

She hummed to herself as she got ready for the evening. Humming worked sometimes. Changed the mood around her. And it annoyed the hell out of Tom. Elle and Otto were coming for dinner that night. A Gordon Ramsay tuna salad lay marinating in the fridge, all she had to do was dress and serve. Slowly and assuredly, she pulled out a healing, deep indigo blue, full, ankle-length skirt and a pale lemon top, lemon to clear her mind. Blue and yellow together, refreshing and cleansing, like a mouthwash to clear her head.

Elle and Otto had news. What was it? 'News' normally meant one thing. She kept coming back to it. That had to be it. And if it was, should they? Her mind raced on, as it had all day, wondering how a new baby would topple the symmetry of their friendships. Scoring as they did the double whammy of children the same age in the same school and nursery, Carla and Tom and Elle and Otto saw a lot of each other. A mutual love of pubs and fishing welded Tom's artistic wildness with Otto's Swedish methodical precision in a bond of mutual respect. Whilst Elle was one of the most gorgeous and upbeat yet kind and sympathetic people Carla had ever known.

Should they follow suit? The thoughts tripped over each other. Her time was running out; she couldn't not know it. Later regrets had to be addressed before they surfaced. Discussed, taken apart and put back together again.

The answer was still no. With Tom's work it'd be the

21

most disastrous timing imaginable. And there was still that feeling there, three years after Dyl's birth, a feeling of nothing but aghast amazement that anybody should ever want to go through childbirth more than twice. Dyl wasn't the placid toddler Wilf had been. He'd been a difficult pregnancy and a nightmare birth. But then everything with Dyl was more complicated. Wasn't that what was putting her off having a third? But then again, Tom did look after her well when she was pregnant. It was so nice to be looked after for a change. And then, maybe, if Elle and Otto were jumping in, Tom would be more sympathetic to the idea.

But, no.

But Elle and Otto? They'd be crazy not to.

But no.

No, no.

Then again, there were some things in life, not many, but a few, where caution had to be thrown to the winds or else.

NO!

She grabbed some tea towels from the airing cupboard on her way into the broad, square hallway, sat herself at the top of the slide, put the tea towels on her lap, crossed her hands in front of her like a prim Mary Poppins and slid away from her uncertainties down to Tom and the kids below.

Chapter Three

'I'm so glad it's over Elle. There's nothing worse than being pushed around in your own home.'

'Now you know how it feels.' Tom banged the glasses on the turquoise Egnell coffee table.

Glass cracked against gloss in the icy silence that followed.

All afternoon Tom had been keeping his distance from Carla's gloom until it had turned into a full-blown mutual ignore, both communicating with the children but not each other. One of their worst kinds of rows, a row without words.

Otto, a big, fair, polar bear of a man, heaved himself forward on the sofa and grabbed his glass and a handful of nuts. 'I'll drink to that,' he said, over-jovially.

Elle gave Carla a sympathetic look. Carla kept her expression stoical and resigned.

'Anyway, it's all over now isn't it. Come on, get it down you,' said Tom.

'Who's babysitting tonight, then?' Carla asked, soothed by the tang of vodka and fresh lime hitting the back of her throat.

'Bridget, and she's got news about the manny,' said

Elle, winking noisily at Carla.

'What's a manny?' asked Tom.

'A male nanny. Elle has the hots for him,' said Otto matter-of-factly.

'His name is Gabriel,' said Elle dreamily.

Tom laughed.

'What's so funny?' said Elle.

'Nanny Gabriel, I bet that goes down well in the play-ground.'

'Chance would be a fine thing.'

Carla went over to the roundabout carousel and busied herself pouring more Kettle Chips and olives into little bowls. She'd never been able to cope with Elle's direct-ness in front of her husband. Typical Elle though, to be lusting after another whilst about to announce her preg-nancy. She turned the dial on the splash-back lighting system which could be switched any one of a thousand colours, settling for a shade halfway between dark aubergine and translucent pink.

She arranged the bowls on the motorised coffee table she'd bought Tom for Christmas last year. She pressed a button and the table trundled smoothly across the French oak floor.

'So, come on then, out with it, what are we celebrat-ing?' Carla called across to them.

'Shall you tell them Otto, or shall I?'

Otto smiled indulgently at his wife. 'Go on, you.'

Despite her apprehensions Carla felt her breasts swelling with maternal wonder. She smiled happily and expectantly at Elle as she settled next to her. Her free hand began stroking the cushion nearest to her, the one she'd made when first pregnant. Carla hadn't had weird food obsessions, but a sewing mania. She sewed a lot anyway, but when pregnant she couldn't stop, the strange patterns and colours seeming to appear by themselves. With Wilf, it had been the repetitious, angular dark blues and iridescent reds of the Alhambra at Granada. With Dyl, it had been Borobudur – all curly oranges and browns, and much more complicated to bring off on a twelve by twelve tapestry. But then everything with Dyl had been more complicated.

Elle beamed beatifically round at them all.

'Come on then, out with it,' said Tom.

'Otto and I, we're—'

'We wanted you to be the first to know ...'

'We ...'

'We're splitting up.'

Tom and Carla exchanged their first mutually sympathetic look of the day. Carla swallowed hard. The vodka sliced into her throat. She clutched at the cushion, stroking the thickly embroidered Moorish pattern over and over, absent-mindedly with her thumb. Tom began pacing up and down.

Elle went over and sat next to Otto. He put his arm around her.

Carla's mouth wouldn't stop opening and closing as her brain searched for the correct response to such an announcement. There wasn't one.

What was going on?

All of a sudden it felt like her life was being held together with Sellotape that'd had lost its stick and gone all brown and curly at the edges.

'Elle!' she spluttered at last, 'I know that manny's attractive ...'

'Oh IS he, Carl,' said Tom.

'Not that attractive, Tom,' Carla sighed, 'but don't you think you're jumping the gun a bit, here?'

Elle laughed, 'It's nothing to do with him, Carla.

Though maybe now I am free – who knows what luck could bring.'

'We are very happy you both are the first to know.' Otto squeezed Elle's shoulder before standing up and grabbing Tom by the elbow on one of his return paces.

'They said year 4 is full of divorces,' said Carla, 'but we're only a few weeks into the term!'

'What about year 3?' said Elle.

Carla went mentally through the class list, pinned above the computer, 'Jo Salmon, Gina and Rufus, Orianna and Matthew . . . Antonia, but, no, she's always been single . . .'

'Alistaire and Julia . . .' said Elle.

'Ah, but that one was on the cards, wasn't it,' said Tom. 'How those two ever got together in the first place is a mystery that'll never be. . .'

Carla sat up straight. 'But that's ridiculous, just because it's some kind of year 4 "thing" there's no reason for you two to . . . to . . .'

'A pre-emptive strike, I suppose you could call it,' said Otto.

'Split up whilst we're still friends,' said Elle. They looked lovingly at each other. Otto's hand, dangling on her shoulder, began patting it affectionately.

'Why not *stay* friends, then!!'

'We will. That is the point! More than friends sometimes, I expect.' Elle beamed at Otto.

'So – who's moving out then?' said Carla, grabbing a passing ankle with her feet. 'Stop it Tom, you're annoying everyone.'

Tom looked from one to the other, his mouth in a little o, his eyes on stalks, before wriggling his leg free and setting off for the other side of the room again.

'Neither of us.' Elle beamed. 'It would upset the children too much.'

'For the sake of the children?' said Carla slowly. 'I'm sorry, but it's wrong, totally wrong and we won't allow you to do it, will we, Tom?'

'Listen.' Otto leaned forward. 'We've both played away from home and we've both been hurt by it. All right?'

'And you've survived it!' said Tom. 'Look at you!'

'Just,' said Elle. 'We don't want to risk the danger of us falling out and never speaking to each over some stupid affair. Then where would the children be? This way, no one moves out, no one gets hurt, most importantly, the children . . .'

'I've never heard anything so ridi . . .' said Carla.

'It's very common in Sweden,' said Elle. 'We call it divorce-lite.'

'I'm not buying it,' said Tom flatly.

Carla went to dish out the supper. She felt more comfortable with something to do. Her immediate need was to protect Tom, his shock running, as it was, deeper even than her own. Unlike her country-hopping, divorce and boarding-school diplomatic background, Tom came from a solid, two-up, two-down, two-parents community where the more unsavoury facts of life were either seen but not heard or known about by all but covered in a thick brown blanket of community spirit. A time and a place where love lay in many depths, and the deeper layers were thick and solid. She plonked the plates around the table, their thud thud thud echoing creepily off the back glass wall the way they did when they'd just had a row.

Drinks were poured more liberally than usual that night, and glasses emptied. By the time they'd got to pudding, Carla was the only one sitting erect, alert and button-eyed, still trying to take it all in, deciphering what it meant for her, for Tom, for them all.

'So ... are you going to tell everyone?' said Carla, scooping extra large dollops of Ben & Jerry's Full Vermonty into glass bowls.

'Of course,' said Elle.

'The children?'

'Not the children. They are too young,' said Otto.

'There's enough time for them to grow into the situation,' said Elle sensibly, like she was talking about changing swimming clubs.

'Look,' said Tom, trying to disguise his slurred words with convoluted sentences, 'what you haven't taken into consideration here, I mean I know you're both grown, consenting adults and all that but you're not teenagers ...'

Otto, who could drink anyone under the table and still sound sensible and right about everything, looked at Tom soberly and expectantly.

'... y'know I've got a lot of respect for you, Otto, mate, but you've got to realise life isn't about swinging from the chandeliers all the time.'

'As you do from what I hear...' said Elle raising her eyebrows.

'Swings aren't chandeliers...'

'And they're a decoration,' said Carla weakly. There must've been more wrong with Elle and Otto's relationship than she realised. People only looked outside, people only strayed if there was something wrong.

'Maybe you should give us lessons, Tom,' said Elle. 'Only joking, Carla.'

'What Tom means,' Carla hunted for words, anxious to take them anywhere but there, 'is there's immature love and mature love, and the one grows out of the other, that's what it *does*.'

Otto laughed. 'Love does what it wants.'

'And it's quite simple,' said Elle lightly. 'I'm thirty-one

28

and I'm not ready for maturity, and I don't mind to admit it.'

'So, so.' Otto shrugged and smiled indulgently at Tom.

'The older you get, the less shelfish you get,' said Tom, 'the easier it is to make it work. So long as you're honest with each other, that's the main thing.'

'This is exactly what we are being Tom – honest. We are facing up to it together, and working through it together.'

'Does it mean, I mean, does it mean you actually *get* divorced, on paper, then?' Carla asked.

'We agree we are not a couple any more.'

'What will a solicitor make of it?'

'It's easy,' said Elle, 'we share everything just like before, except the bed.'

'It's not a quick decision, Carla,' said Otto, seeing her face, 'though in Sweden it is normal for couples to stay friends when they split up. Because we are such a small society, everyone knows everyone . . .'

'Swedish people also hate to move house,' said Elle.

'Not only Swedish people,' said Carla pointedly.

'But for us here, with my mother in the basement flat, it would be impossible,' said Otto.

'And my studio in the annexe,' said Elle.

Carla pondered these practicalities. It couldn't be denied, a move wouldn't be without its difficulties, though a photographic studio would be one hell of a lot easier to move than a mother-in-law.

'All right, Elle,' said Tom, 'let's be hypop, hyop, hyper . . .'

'Hypothetical.'

'Thank you Carla, hypothetical here, let's say, what if you get to know that guy in the playground, what's his name?'

'Gabriel.'

'What then?'

'I only want to fuck him Tom, I don't want an affair with him.'

'See!' said Otto.

'No, mate,' said Tom straight-faced, 'no, I'm sorry, I don't.'

Otto shrugged. 'My work is going well at least.'

'What's that got to do with it?'

'Nobody, I think, has both going right together; you either have your work going well and your home life is in trouble, or your home life is going well and your work is in trouble. It seems to be one of those rules nobody has found a name for yet.'

Carla kept quiet. What if your home and your life were the same thing and they were both under threat, what then? She listened to Elle and Otto. Too cheerful, much too cheerful. Whose decision had it been? Elle seemed so damned happy about it all but that couldn't be real. But then Elle was so up all the time. Otto was the earth wire in their marriage as much as she was in her own. He'd always grounded Elle, however outrageous she was. He enjoyed his wife's flamboyance, her flirtatiousness. Rather like she enjoyed Tom's.

Otto poured more drinks. 'All right, I shall explain. There is a difference between loving somebody and being "in" love, yes? We all agree?'

'And ...?' Tom helped himself to more ice cream.

'In love is a mad stage and nobody can live in there for very long, we all agree?'

'That's what we're saying, Otto,' said Carla patiently, 'mature love's another word for unconditional love.'

'Love is not something that stays the same. It changes. Like everything, like your designs.'

30

'Tom's designs are timeless,' said Carla quickly.

'All right, like your taste does; it is part of nature like everything human. It has been scientifically proven ...'

Here we go. Everything had to be scientifically proven with Otto or it didn't exist.

'... It has been scientifically proven that love develops in sections. After the initial high, which can and often does last for a long time ...'

'So you have marriage ...' said Elle.

'Indeed so. Then, after the initial high, it has to plateau out onto an even keel. Lasting long enough for the infants, after which that kind of love isn't needed any more.'

'And that's when immature love grows into mature love,' said Carla matter-of-factly. 'You have to grow together; if you don't grow together you grow apart.'

Elle shrugged. 'So – there was something wrong with our growbag, maybe.'

'Whose decision was it?' said Tom.

'A joint decision, of course,' said Otto, beaming at Elle.

You should have seen that coming, Tom. Everything with Elle and Otto was a joint decision.

'All right, so what happens then,' Tom said, 'when one of you, if one of you meets someone who's more than manny Gabriel ... I mean, look at you, you're both attractive people ...'

'Thank you, Tom.' Elle grinned at him.

'... what happens then?' Tom kept his frown on a bit too dramatically for Carla's comfort.

'We've discussed it of course,' said Elle.

'And ...?'

'This is the best way for us to go forward.' Otto's voice rose angrily. 'We're all grown-ups, we can all stay

31

friends, can't we? As you can see, we're not suddenly going separate ways; I hope you'll treat us the same way as you always have done. That's part of the reason we're making it like this. It's really quite simple. Neither of us wants to lose our children or our friends, you are all a mutual part of our lives . . .'

'That's where it'll all fall down,' said Tom to Carla later in bed.

'It's scary.' Carla cuddled up close to him. 'I mean, up till now the only thing there's not to like about Elle is the fact there's nothing not to like about her. Now I'm not sure. I mean, it's always been you and Otto, and Wilf and Jon, and Dyl and Tallulah.'

'You've always got on really well, you two.'

'We do, but we're not exactly alike, are we?'

'She's a live wire all right.'

'What's that supposed to mean?'

'She must be exhausting. I expect Otto could do with a rest. Hey, maybe that's it.'

'What, you mean she's insatiable?'

'Hadn't you noticed?'

'Has he told you that?'

'No.'

'Do you fancy her?'

'CARlaaaa.'

'She's fair game now.'

She regretted saying it as soon as it was out.

'Don't start that. Come here, woman.'

'Tom?'

'Mmmmm?' he put his hand up her nightdress and stroked her back.

'What you said about selling the house today.'

'Mmmmmm.'

'What did you mean?'

32

He crooked her neck in his hand and began massaging it.

'You know what I meant . . .'

'I don't . . .'

'You know everything, Carl.'

'I DON'T . . .'

'Only as a last resort, you know that. I love this place as much as I love you.'

'So do I.'

'Mmmmm.'

He massaged her neck deeper, his other hand moved up, then down her back, tingling her spine as she pressed into him.

'Only as a very, very last resort?'

'Of course. We'll find a backer. Don't worry.'

'I do worry.'

'I know you do. Sorry I said it. Shh now.' He kissed her gently, his hands slid up to her breasts, tightening. Cupping one in each hand, he stroked her nipples with his thumbs.

Their eyes kept locked, his breathing deepened, long, tantric breaths in and out, she followed suit, making herself breathe slower, she explored his eyes as he explored hers. She felt him harden, she shifted, he found her.

He pushed in a little way, just parting her, and pulled out. He did it again, and again, nine times, before thrusting hard and pulling out.

He found her again. Eight times this time, slower, but further as she yielded. Then two deep, hard thrusts before quickly withdrawing.

He went in again, slower, seven times, harder three times. Carla's breathing quickened.

'Shhhhhhhh . . .' He put his finger on her lips, his clear

grey eyes holding her gaze. His face became a haze till it was just the force of him.

Slowly, once, twice, she could bear it no more, she moved against him, three, four, five six, on the seventh he rammed her four times, pulling out quickly. His breathing was deep, controlled, steady, but he was sweating now, deep breaths, in, out.

The *Tantric Sex Manual* had been another daft Christmas present, the only kind he liked. To go with his new t'ai chi classes, she'd joked. But after going unusually quiet for the better part of Christmas night he'd taken it so obviously, so desperately to heart she began to bitterly regret buying the damned thing. She had to reassure him she'd bought it on a whim at the remaindered bookstore in Chiswick and no, it wasn't one of her carefully thought-out gifts like the Free Wheeling Franklin coffee table she'd had to order in the middle of the summer.

He entered her slowly five times, hard five. Slowly four times, hard six. Their sweat mingled, as he grew, she softened and expanded, feeling him deeper.

They moved together, slowly three times, hard seven.

Sure, she'd had to reassure him. After sharing the same bed for fourteen years, their sex lives had slipped into a routine. The thrill of nearness tempered into acceptance and expectance, that's what happened, she felt comfortable with it. OK, she did sometimes – all right, quite often then – use the time to tick off the chores achieved and chores to be added to the following day's list, but that was how her mind worked. Her body was pleasantly enjoying itself down below, thanks very much.

From that Boxing Day onwards, bedtimes started to change. In little ways at first, like he stopped saying 'plug me in, Carl,' which she'd gotten so used to she'd long ago stopped hearing, most likely herself to be wondering if there was any Hovis Best of Both left for Wilf's packed lunch in the morning or debating where to go for Dyl's next pair of shoes, wondering if a children's shoe shop existed which ever had any more than two of any size in anything.

Slowly twice, hard eight. She squealed.

'Not yet, not yet,' he put his hand over her mouth.

'I can't ...'

'Shhhhhhh.' They kissed, whilst he slowly entered her once and withdrew, finding her again immediately, hard right in, nine times.

Tom looked up at the ceiling and roared, 'Ready or not, here I come!'

Carla smiled up at him through a loving, orgasmic sigh of acceptance.

Chapter Four

Tom's warm, soft body, snuggling into Carla's back, took in the movement as she leaned over to check the alarm.

06.37. Saturday. A full thirty-three minutes before Dyl and the preferred toy of the day were scheduled to appear. Bliss. She wriggled into the downy puff of pillow, tucking her arm behind her head, the gentle rhythm of Tom's slow, steady, dream breaths beside her. She felt stiff and tired. She could open her eyes, but there was a strain, a pain behind them like she hadn't slept.

She squinted at the flinty autumn light falling like steel through the big front bay, throwing a trellis of leaf shadows onto the walls. After the endless run of grim wet days this sun was a surprise. It was a different light – upfront, sharp and bouncy. All the softness of summer left behind on the other side of the rain.

Through drips of condensation she caught the first winter glimpses of brick on the upstairs window of the house opposite. The leaves of the big, old beech were thinning and looking wind-worn, droopy and ready to drop.

The early autumn cold was still a novelty. She usually looked forward to wintry things with a naive expectance. But even the tree's soft rustle had a sinister ring to it.

Carla hated the heat. Hated the way it stole all energy and clarity. She liked shadows, burgundy-cool, and coal fires backed by a thermostat she could turn to high or low.

On winter storm nights they'd come up just to listen to that dear old beech. Pulling the sash windows wide and popping a bottle to the swish of the tree and the crack of the fire. She felt wistful, like it was a distant, unrepeatable memory rather than something to look forward to, something, even, that might never happen again.

A car drove past, sounding all the louder for its solitariness.

A chill of guilt pricked her as she remembered the night before.

Was there more to it than they'd been told?

Did Otto have someone else?

Did Elle?

Were they in different rooms, then? Like, now? They had to be. No, God, no, it was terrible.

Like a death.

Not birth, as she'd thought. Carla closed her eyes for a moment, squirming at the memory of how she'd got it all wrong, so wrong.

A water pipe gurgled and the radiator clicked.

How had it all started then? Was it the result of one of their volcanic rows? She remembered Otto, standing on the scorched terrace of their villa, the blue slash of sea and sky behind him, a big, blonde, hairy man, as rock-like as the statues posing around the pool, a knowing half-smile on his face. At first he'd indulged his wife, letting her rant and rave and punch and scream at him, but when she'd calmed he grew even larger and simply blew up. That had been scary, really scary.

However outrageous she was he usually took her punches like a rock. She had to see Elle as soon as possible, sit her down and give her a good talking to. Couples were either together or not; they couldn't simply revert to friendship, to some pseudo *Friends* flat-sharing, there were too many – *layers*. Did she think there was something *better* out there? Someone who wasn't the father of her children who'd understand her better? Did she *want* to be understood? Did Otto understand her too well? Yes. That was it. She'd get Tom to speak to Otto separately. He should be less solid, more unpredictable, to make her realise what she'd got before she went and threw it all away. But then, if they were both staying together as friends, she wasn't throwing it away, was she? And what about Otto? She shifted uncomfortably.

Tom stirred, readjusted his arm on her stomach and snuggled in tighter.

What if she and Tom – ?

If, right now, he were upstairs in the attic room? It would unquestionably be Tom who'd have to give up the bedroom. More than any other room in the house, this was Carla's. He'd taught her how to be sensitive to the hidden vibes of a room. Its air, its feel, its light. Taking her cue from the tree, she'd used pattern, silhouettes, listening to the space around her, letting it set its own tone. A medley of light-absorbing white. Thick white blankets on the bed, a huge flokati beside the fire. Fabrics layer upon layer. Different whites in different textures, tones, patterns – linen, lace, velvet, cord, paper-white, cream-white, blue-white, yellow-white, all absorbing and reflecting in their own ways. White candles, their tapers lit and stubbed to black. In the centre of the marble mantelpiece a vase, dark stone, curved, sensuous, smooth. Nothing decorative. She hated decorative pottery. She stared sleepily at the tree shadow, the logs waiting in the grate for the first storm, chestnuts, wine and flames. In the far right corner, the old radiogram and Tom's crazy vinyl record collection, selected for their mad covers, full of kitschy-cool and scratchy easy listening.

A few minutes later, a clicking cluster of miniature silver ladders appeared at the door, followed by Dyl clutching his fire engine and his big brown bear, and then Wilf arrived and Tom was awake and the demands of the day began.

'What are we going to do today?'

'What do you think?'

'It's Saturday.'

'Wey Saturday ...'

'And daddy's here all day.'

Saturday mornings were Carla's. After a week of her turns to get the children ready, it was his turn.

'Can we go swimming?' said Wilf.

'Oh, no, Wilf, not today.'

'I'll take them,' said Tom.

Carla patted his legs.

All chill between them had gone. They were in a normal Saturday, like the row had never happened.

'Can we go to the water slides?' said Wilf, sitting on him, 'pleeeese.'

'Dyl's too young for the slides Wilf,' said Carla, distractedly picking at the fire engine's ladder with her fingernails, raising it up to its full height.

'You can come too mummy, if you like!' Dyl pushed and reversed the big red truck over her stomach and down her legs to her toes.

'Thanks, but no Dyl.'

'Awwww, go on mum. We can all go,' said Wilf.

'No.'

'Meringues, can we have meringues then?' said Wilf.

'One meringue, *after* you've done your homework.'

'Awww.'

'Mummy wants to rest. Come on, let's shoot. Swimming, football, McDonalds', how does that sound?'

'Tooommmm.'

'Forget the McDonald's then.'

'Fish and chips, get them fish and chips.'

'Yey wey, fish and chips . . .' Dyl bounced on the bed.

'Stop it, Dyl, or you won't be going anywhere.'

Ignoring hangovers, the way only Tom could, he leaped out of bed. 'Come on, race you to the cereal.'

Soothed into the normality and comfort of the day, with the whole morning to herself stretching before her, Carla turned her gaze from the abandoned fire engine to the piles of unread and half-begun books on her side of the bed.

There was no set pattern to her reading. Junk-shop Penguins were as irresistible as browsing the tables at Waterstones, picking up the latest lightest reads and Kaffe needlepoint books. Biographies were her favourite, though, particularly complicated love lives with lots of photos, like Larkin or Du Maurier. She'd save the photos till the end, staring for ages at their portraits, her imagined characters brought to life, all mixed and mingled into the real faces. Lives tucked inside a book which had a beginning, a middle and an end. She liked that. The end always the same. Lives lived and gone. She picked up a book of Italian mosaics she'd bought for Tom.

She stared at it for a moment before sitting bolt upright.

'Tom! Tom!' she yelled.

'What is it?' Tom came running.

'Sicily, Tom, what should we do about Sicily?'

This was a real problem she almost welcomed. A practical difficulty which needed sorting and acting upon. Soon.

Tom came into the room rubbing his eyes. 'What are you on about?'

'We should have it booked already.'

'It's not till next Easter Carl.'

'You always say that.'

'Book it then.'

'Elle and Otto, Tom. Elle and Otto!'

'What, you think they won't want to come?'

'Don't tell me you've forgotten what went on last night!'

'No, of course, no, but they said . . .'

'Carry on as normal . . .'

'That's what they said.'

'It's not as easy as that, is it.'

'If that's what they want then that's what we should be doing.'

'Is it what we want, though, Tom?'

'What do you mean?'

'Can we cope with spending a whole week with them as a couple but not a couple?'

Tom shrugged.

'And would they want to still come together anyway?'

'If they're stopping in the same house in Richmond, chances are a week in Sicily's not going to be an issue, is it?'

'Anything could happen by then.'

'I know that!!'

'Do we want them?'

'They're still our friends Carla – there are enough bedrooms, aren't there?'

'They could be split up – I mean properly split up.'

'Or back together.'

'Or with other partners?'

'Book it. They're both bound to want to be with the

41

kids on holiday, so no, no question. Double-check with Elle and book it.'

'You'll have left Carliatti by then, Tom. What if they change their minds? We'd have to pay for it all ourselves.'

'Thanks for your confidence in my future business.'

'You know what I mean. We have to be careful.'

'Carla love, holidays are for enjoying, not for worrying and fretting about.'

'Someone has to do the worrying around here. I have to book it now. If we don't book it, it won't happen. OK? Can you call Otto later?'

'Today?'

'Yes. Today. We *could* find somewhere smaller ...'

They looked at each other. The Villa Solalonto had taken years of finding.

'In the same area.'

'Or we could share with somebody else ...' They looked at each other '... who we like enough, whose kids have got the same TV, sleep and treat rules?'

'Why don't you ask Elle?'

'Think, Tom. If they really are split by then, at least if they don't come we know Otto will pay their share. Otherwise ...' She didn't have to finish. Otto had a peculiar mean streak which had taken them by surprise once too often.

'See your point. Okey doke, I'll give him a bell later. WILF, are you dressed yet?'

'And Tomm ...'

Too late. He'd left the room.

'Wilf! Come on, get a move on, I'm Sirius ...'

The dappled shadows had moved across to the bed, sunlit, warm and comfortable.

The morning sounds changed to full-animation swimming and football preparation. She lay listening to their

42

getting-dressed noises. Three bundles of pent-up energy waiting to be spent. Tom shouting friendly orders, the boys shouting back, arguing, punching each other, racing around in their red and white football shirts, squealing. It was the slam of the door that did it. All warmth and contentedness vanished. Elle and Otto, Elle and Gabriel, Otto and someone else . . .

Half an hour later, attuned to the arrival of the moment between reading in bed in the morning being an utter luxury one moment and sordid sloth the next, she flung the book down and went to the wet room for her shower and her first pay-off, the clearing-up after the boys. Maybe they should have another bathroom, she thought, picking up towels, pyjamas, a water pistol and the now soggy brown bear. Tom had no time for bathrooms, seeing them as cold unforgiving places which wasted too much space, and Carla had happily gone along with keeping just the one room housing nasty things like full-length mirrors and scales. Having the builders in would be preferable to this horrible, hollow emptiness she was feeling around and inside, and the space in the spare room was beginning to niggle.

She left her contact lenses in their little case, put her glasses on and went down via the stairs. Ignoring the mess, she sat down in her dressing gown to do her menu plan. She took a print-out from the computer drawer and mixed the meals around: chicken and rice, Tuesday, with Tom; soup, Wednesday, Tom & boys; Thursday... fish, rocket and raspberries; Saturdays were takeaways; Sundays a roast. Menu done, she began writing, visualising herself walking around, chucking the stuff in her trolley.

lettuce
tomatoes
celery
green peppers
olives
broccoli

She always did her list in the order of the supermarket shelves.

She couldn't understand why people laughed at her lists. It was so much easier. She could visualise herself walking around, chucking the stuff in. It saved so much time, and made it much easier to spot the seasonal arrivals and disappearances. She kept eggs and organics in a separate column, to be grabbed when spotted. The organic explosion had thrown her a bit at first, and she'd resolutely ignored it, preferring to keep to her straight lines, thanks very much. But gradually the zigzags became part of the normal pattern of things: after the Aspertame-free squash, came the organic meat, root veg and milk.

She got dressed. A peach linen skirt, full of pockets, and a russet cashmere V-neck, was as far as down-dressing went for Carla. Even her gardening shoes had heels.

She got out into the garden as quickly as she could. Her favourite place in the world. Outside but inside. She didn't mind the autumn chores of digging, leaf-clearing and bonfire-making. The hidden things were the most important. The preparation. Getting the soil right. Mulching through her thoughts, absorbed in the never-ending work of it. Comfortable in the way all the little jobs came around and went around, never finished, always needing her for the next stage, over and over.

She made use of the sudden sun to clear out the green-house. The last big job of autumn before winter set in. She busied on, ignoring the fear inside her. The clunking echoing feel of the spades and forks, scraping, unsure, unknown. The abruptness of the door-slam and Elle and Otto's unreasonable reasoning popping up behind the fuss and grit of her work. She put all the plants outside and cleared the dead flowers and leaves, picked the last of the tomatoes and swept underneath the benches. After washing down the glass with water and Jeyes, the water dripping down over her rubber gloves, she left the doors and vents open for the glass to dry.

Her robin came and perched on its favourite glass sculpture in the ferny, leafy corner by the play room. She liked to think it had been the same one over all the years, though she knew it couldn't be. Not with their short, brutal lives.

She moved on to the flowerbeds by the paved oval which spiralled between the lawn and the play-pit at the end of the garden. The robin flew up onto a branch and began to sing.

She stopped by the blue hammock slung in the row of trees flanking the right-hand wall. Stiff, soggy and out of place, it looked ridiculous now; in a few days it had lost all purpose. She poured the water out of its dip and untied it. Then she collected a few seeds, picking out the partly deteriorated ones, they always grew better, and took them inside.

The robin waited expectantly for her its treats. Enticing it closer and closer, she walked backwards towards the house, chattering and chucking titbits of crumbly cheese and sausage meat. She felt a delicate crunch beneath the ball of her foot, followed by a soft squelch. The door slammed again. She looked slowly down at the pieces of shell, crumpled into the flattened sticky mucus mess of what, moments before, had been a fully functioning mollusc. She threw the rest of the food on the ground and rushed inside, not bothering as she usually did, to watch the rest of the bird population fall down out of the sky, looking for the worms she'd turned for them.

Chapter Five

Carla's mouth tightened in concentration as she reached the gate of Richmond Hill Juniors and Infants, expertly manoeuvring through the buggy, buggy, double-buggy, cello, scooter, springer-spaniel gridlock.

Her playground anxiety was more knee-jerk than anything, like walking through customs. She'd even traced it back to its source via one of those found memories parenthood sparks into existence. A cruel mixture of sudden parental abandonment and the fickleness of early childhood friendships. A situation which had played over and over through her childhood. She was too young to remember the Japanese school but she did remember the next one in a close-knit suburb of Rome. She worked hard at fitting in, and they were friendly enough when she'd learned the language, by which time it was time to leave. It's easy to feel lonely in Italy, her father had explained in a rare tender moment; it wasn't her fault, the place was one big family, that's how it was.

Playgrounds all looked the same, that was part of it. They had an atmosphere all of their own. The same scattering of low buildings and bossy signs. The same large windows stuck with stuff surrounded by lots of gritty grey, criss-crossed with red lines and white numbered squares, half buried by puddles, waiting to trip, to trap, to scrape new knees bloody. The high-frequency shouts, calls, cries with the songs, always the same songs, lingering in the air: 'Ip dip dip'; 'The big ship sails,' mysteriously reappearing ready-formed in the mouths of the unfolding generations.

And, ever-present, on the other side of the glass, teachers lurking, ready to pounce; 'Could I have a *word?*'

By the time she'd found Wilf in the steaming, rubbery stink of the cloakroom, Dyl had escaped his pushchair, racing off through the autumn drizzle to the climbing frame. Either that or to the road outside. She quickly kissed Wilf goodbye, turning to throw a guilty, tinkly wave at him, sitting in a crumpled lump on the floor, battling with his shoelaces.

Over by the slide in the far corner, next to Marcus Dowe, the beak-faced TV weatherman, Carla was pleased to see Antonia and Cyn. She went over to join them, burying deep the irrational fear she'd be found out one day and they wouldn't let her play today. Cynthia Jay, tiny, bouncy and pink-pretty, and Antonia, tall, brown, and piss-elegant, looked like they belonged among the designer-clad, polished and buffed women of Richmond Hill while Carla felt she always had to work at it.

She passed by the gaggles of women gathering themselves into their coffee groups, committee groups, jog groups, dog groups, lingering whilst the smart-suited workers, talking into their mobiles, walking in straight lines, couldn't get out quickly enough. In and out and away, already at work. Talking intensively to their children then leaving quickly, with trains to catch, people to see, money to make. Carla belonged to neither group.

Managing a home and a husband? They all did that, didn't they. The ones that still had husbands. It didn't gain her even a provisional membership to the angular hair and suits crowd.

'Come on Dyl, we've got to get moving!'

'Why so grumpy today Carla?' Antonia darted around the squiggly slide in a pole-dance half-twirl before crashing into the platform full of shrieking, delighted toddlers.

'It's first thing on a Monday morning Antonia, stop scrutinising me.'

'I'm not, you always look great Carla, and you know it.'

She did. She kept her insecurities well hidden behind her clothes and make-up, her big smile and confident voice. With the House and the famous husband, Carla was seen as pretty cool. Someone who had it all worked out.

The bell rang.

'Come on Dyl, we've got to get going.'

'Oh boy, oh boy.' Cyn's almond eyes sparkled mischievously. Antonia and Carla turned to follow her gaze towards the school gates, as did many other eyes.

'What timing is that,' said Cyn admiringly.

They watched him walking over to the separate infants gate which led from the playground to the back of the school, the departing, slack-jawed mums and nannies parting in his wake.

'And look who's right behind him!' said Carla, watching Elle following him a few steps behind like a puppy dog.

'That woman, she has no shame,' said Antonia.

Carla laughed, wondering if they knew yet. In a 1940s dress, her hair in a pony-tail bobbing out of a white Viking baseball cap, her son beside her eating an apple, neither of them in any hurry, Elle looked like she hadn't a care in the world.

Seeing other people's children eating fruit always irritated Carla, immediately making her feel like hers weren't getting enough. As Wilf definitely wasn't, since he'd point-blank refused to eat apples for the past six months, blaming his wobbly teeth. They probably had porridge for breakfast too. Instead of licking out the insides of a Marmite sandwich. And cleaned their teeth without being screamed at.

A big-chinned, mole-shouldered woman, her blonde bob pushed back with her ever-present padded hairband, clipped across the playground and pulled her buggy up next to Carla's.

'Did you *see* that Reception kid's nanny dropping him off outside!'

Carla stepped back, out of her minty breath. Bryony Baxter liked to stand in other people's spaces.

'No *way* is he old enough to go in by himself! I'll have to tell his mother, though...!' she paused, a painful thought visibly crossing her brow, '... I don't know who she is! Do you know who she is! Who is she! Look, there he is, that boy there!' She pointed to a small child walking happily across the playground.

'You're slipping up there Bryony,' Carla said overcheerily, catching Bryony's children's-TV-presenter way of talking. Annoyed at her horrible habit of being drawn to people who didn't like her. Wanting to make them like her so much she'd even fall into their way of talking. Even with Tom, she still unconsciously slipped into a Sheffield accent when they were together for any length of time.

Tank Commander Baxter, as Antonia called her, Bryony was one of the Scrummy PTA hardcore who could dredge up all Carla's insecurities merely by her presence. Sometimes Bryony was friendly and other times outright ignored her. This made Carla try even harder with her.

Like the big girls at her boarding school, who sometimes would let her play but then as soon as she felt she was in, would gang up on her or send her to Coventry. That was the cruellest one, the Coventry one; she'd hated that, and even now she sometimes wondered what Coventry had ever done to earn such an image. Bryony also triggered a horrible awareness that she had much in common with her *Groundhog-Day*-in-advance kind of a nightmare life. Whatever it was: tutors, tennis, brownies, riding, swimming lessons, the *Lion King* at each cast change, it was all booked and marked up there on their wall calendars aeons in advance. Though Carla didn't quite go as far as taking skiing brochures on their summer holidays, she did sometimes sneak in a bit of Christmas shopping in the summer sales. And though she knew it was logically the best way to go about things with two small boys and one big boy to organise, she wasn't beyond recognising that her inability to sleep at night if there was as much as one photo lying around which hadn't yet been stuck into an album was a little scary. That they might be there to remind her she had a past, a happy recent past at any rate, so entrenched in the future was her day-to-day existence.

Hazel Macfernon skidded her Purple Parker Über-Groove Jogging Pusher to a halt next to Bryony with an expert swivel and break of the front wheel. The only mother Carla had ever seen who actually jogged with her pushchair, Hazel was tiny, freckled, with a fiercely cropped hairstyle which frizzed at the top like a toilet brush. The Pocket-Sized Battleship, Ant called her. The only thing which separated her from the teaching staff was a classroom of her own and a pension scheme. It was rumoured she even had her own mug-hook in the staff room.

Posh Paloma's move over to the Cartwright orbit was

Carla's cue to get away. One on one she could do, but she was starting to feel the weight in the air of the presence of the three of them.

'DYL! Come on,' she shouted.

Then Elle arrived with Jo Salmon, no less, the dusky American actress. This was a rare playground appearance. Jo was normally only spotted on TV commercials, movie billboards and a reserved front-row seat at the Christmas nativity play. Carla had nothing but admiration for Jo; they'd all followed the story avidly as it played out in the tabloids: her German film-director husband leaving her so soon after the birth of the second child; the photos of him with his new lover, a young Russian actress with enormous boobs; then the little photos of Jo, inset into the page, thin and dark, with a twang of bravery in her smile. You'd never know it to look at her now. Carla lurked a little longer, relaxing her body as Tom had taught her, breathing deeply, smiling broadly and confidently. It was slightly odd, seeing the baby in its limited edition McLaren Titanium buggy, snuggled into the black sheep-skin lining of its leather seat. Normally it was driven by a uniformed nanny, escorted a few steps behind by a slidy-eyed bodyguard.

'Nanny sick again, would you believe it!' she said easily, handing out much-coveted invitations to her Halloween party. 'Only I could get a nanny who needs more looking after than I do.'

'Why doesn't she get the bodyguard to bring Arabel?' Cyn whispered.

'Probably not in his job description,' Carla whispered back.

It was a playground unsaid that everyone else organised their own parties around Jo's. Elle got an invitation, of course. Carla had a mild panic attack as Jo shuffled

52

through her cards. A split-second jetting back to her six-year-old self again before gratefully taking the silver and black envelope.

Behind her, she could hear Dyl arguing with another little boy.

'It was my turn.'

'No, it wasn't.'

'You pushed in.'

'No, I didn't. I DIDN'T.' Thump.

'DYL, stop it at once.'

'It's not fair, he started it . . .' Dyl threw dagger looks at the boy, about twice his size.

'We're off then,' said Carla, grabbing hold of Dyl and clicking him swiftly into his pushchair before he'd realised what had happened.

'It's not *fair*.' Dyl kicked angrily.

Elle caught up with her. 'Aren't you coming to Cyn's?'

'Cyn's?'

'Christmas fair meeting.'

Carla looked at her in astonishment.

'Don't worry, Carl, it's not a crime to forget a school meeting.'

Carla had always taken Elle's ability to be everywhere at once, to be doing her job and always being there for her children and for all the PTA meetings, as how Elle was. Now, there was more than a mild feeling of irritation. How could she have missed that? She ran it back through her head. The wall calendar got written up from the school newsletter every Friday at 6 as soon as the boys had settled in front of *The Simpsons*. It was then checked for the week on Monday morning, and every day before they left the house.

'When is it?'

'Ten, oh ha loh ha, here we go again.' Elle grabbed her

arm, screeching them both to a frozen halt in the middle of the playground.

Carla, still put out, frowned.

'What?'

Elle nodded towards the Infants gate.

'Look!'

'Where?'

He was loping across the playground from the Infants gate, holding his jacket around his chest.

'Oh – Elle.' Carla studied him; he didn't look like a nanny at all. Lean and slinky hipped, with a casual, purposeful confidence in his long stride, nothing like the normal nanny shuffle.

Elle squeezed herself. 'It feels fantaaastic,' she whispered, 'to think, to think if he looked at me ...'

'We have to talk more about this, Elle.'

'There's nothing more to say.'

'Is Otto as up as you about all of this?'

'Of course! Shhh,' she nodded down to Tallulah in her pushchair, chattering away to Dyl, who was blithely ignoring her, chewing at his beanie tiger.

They fell into silence as they followed a little way behind him. She was still shocked by it all. Like Elle really had stepped outside that conspiracy of marriage which says you don't say how it's all going, good or bad, you simply get on with it, the good bits and the bad bits, patching it here, mending it there. You don't share these things like girlie gossips about boyfriends.

At the end of the street he turned left up Hill Rise and Carla and Elle turned right, heading for the nursery in the centre of town and four hours of precious freedom.

Chapter Six

Cyn Jay's kitchen was an echoey, high-ceilinged, mock-Victorian conservatory kind of a kitchen with long stretches of oak country-style units too new to look old or country. Though it jutted out into a forest of trees bordering Richmond Park it was, like Cyn, bright and sunny.

Carla sat at the white marble table surrounded by ferns flickering in the air-con, hiding her nerves, her emotions ping-ponging between supreme pride and unutterable embarrassment.

'Tom and Carla Alexander's home is a triumph. A place of beauty and tranquillity yet full of surprise,' read Antonia, proudly. *'It is minimalism in a new light, working alongside maximalism hand in hand to great effect ...'*

'What's maxmamalism?' said Cyn, her chin resting on her hands.

Antonia flicked her eyes over the top of the magazine. 'Opposite of minimalism?'

'It means a cluttered mess, Cyn, like my home is most of the time. Full of junk like everyone else's,' said Carla flatly, wishing she'd never come. She felt as uneasy as she'd thought she would.

She smiled weakly at Antonia, whose infectious confidence was all the more draining. She meant well. It simply wouldn't have occurred to her that she wasn't actually doing Carla any favours here.

The well-intentioned enthusiasms of Antonia, Cyn and Elle couldn't mask the fidgets and exchanged glances between the cud-chewers down at the other end of the table. Posh Paloma was sitting grim-faced, Hazel Macfernon was writing on her clipboard, and Bryony Baxter was fiddling with her hairband, visibly gagging as always to get on with all things fund-raising.

'Listen to her! A cluttered mess? Nonsense, woman, there's not a thread out of place here.' Antonia held up the double-spread picture of the Klounge.

'That's because I get in an army of cleaners to give it an industrial clean and tidy.'

'All tax-deductible.' Cyn grinned. She had that rare kind of smile that lit up everyone else's faces as well as her own. Even Hazel's tiny, freckled frown softened for a moment. But then, Cyn was always smiling. Married for eight years to Rick Sick, the larger than life lead vocalist with the heavy metal band Scud. Rick was a fixture in his absence, always touring or in the studio, which seemed to suit Cyn fine.

Hazel stood up noisily. 'We must move forward, there's a lot to get through.'

'All right,' said Elle, sensing Carla's embarrassment. 'What have you got in store for us in year 4, rep?'

'Fund-raisers,' said Hazel.

'Christmas term, bizzy bizzy time, and we've got a big push on this year to get the new library stocked!' said Bryony.

'We need some ideas for the Christmas fair,' said Hazel.

'How about asking Relate to set up a counselling booth,' said Antonia dryly.

'Too late for that,' laughed Cyn.

So, she must have told them. Carla managed an amused smile. In spite of all appearances, she was beginning to feel that Elle's divorce, light, heavy, whatever it was, was having more of an effect on her than it was on Elle. With Tom's insistence, she'd booked Sicily as if nothing had happened. As if everything was as before. Which it wasn't. If Carla brought it up with Elle, she always brushed it off lightly, like there was so nothing to discuss.

Elle would survive, of course she would, but at what cost? At least she had her work to get lost in. In all the gives and takes in any marriage there was usually one who gave way more than the other, who adapted more to their partner than their partner adapted to them. Like her friendship with Elle? Tom adored Otto, but she'd had uneasy feelings about Elle before; she didn't like having them, but they were there and they were surfacing now.

'Buy one get one free!' said Antonia. 'Now, let me finish this, I'm nearly there. *'Carla's passion for, and considerable expertise in, antique and tribal textiles is much in evidence...'*

Paloma shifted in her chair. Bryony and Hazel, putty in Antonia's elegant hands, silently gave in.

'... fabrics and hangings skilfully chosen to blend, often incongruously, but always perfectly, alongside Tom's trademark fun and fantasy edge of cutting-edge designs, create their own energies and make every corner of this house buzz with a reason to celebrate all that's good about twenty-first-century design. Warm, satin-smooth Arts and Crafts originals sit on rubber floors where soft folds of exquisite fabric and Tom's famous Carliatti furniture pieces brush up against the latest plastics and concretes as

elegantly as any Tate Modern hanging. Ideas which seem madness on paper, in the hands of Tom and Carla, come off brilliantly.'

Cyn's Aunt Minnie, a curve of bosoms and arse straight out of Ribeiro, refilled coffee mugs. Glad for something to be doing with her face, Carla immediately began drinking hers, even though the coffee was too hot and burned her tongue. With Rick away so much, Cyn had wasted no time filling their big, stuccoed, white mansion with varying close and not so close relatives. Inadvertently launching her own black-market cleaning and babysitting agency and enjoying universal popularity into the bargain. It was one of the reasons year 4 parent meetings were always held in her kitchen. A neutral zone where the likes of Hazel Macfernon and Elle Olsson could be in the same room as each other for longer than five minutes.

'Tom *and* Carla,' Antonia repeated, smiling around the room.

'As it should be,' said Elle defensively.

'I'm sorry but I've a couple of items I want to flag up at this point,' said Hazel. 'The Christmas fair, we know about, and I've had some ideas in from some of you which need discussing. From Elle – a, erm naked calendar ...'

'*That* won't get past Mrs Armstrong!' beamed Bryony happily.

'Naked! Who!?' said Cyn.

'You'd do it, wouldn't you?' said Elle.

'ME!'

'I can see you now, Cyn,' Carla joined in.

'I don't think a children's photographer should really ...!'

'Oh, I'm sure it would all be in the best possible taste,' said Paloma, touching up her hair.

'Now, *Paloma*!' said Elle. 'I can see you as Mrs March.'

'Good GOD no!'

'Oh, go on . . .' Antonia chivvied.

Carla gave Paloma a diplomatic, neutral smile. Behind it, trying to imagine Paloma out of her beige riding trousers and muddy Barbour.

'A few horsewhips and dog-leads, you'd look great!' said Elle.

'And Pearl could be your handmaiden,' said Antonia, glancing over at the young girl playing with Cyn's cat on the wickerwork sofa. She didn't look up. Paloma was shocked but hiding it well behind a dignified you-must-be-joking smile. No one knew if Elle was being serious or not.

'. . . moving on, we'll take up your offer to organise the parents' Christmas party, Elle. . .' said Hazel, marking up her clipboard '. . . and Cyn here has suggested a recipe book.'

'*Cyn,*' said Paloma, looking relieved, 'do tell!'

'My friend, she'd made this stir-fry, my kids love it, so I got the recipe and she said her school got all the mums' favourite recipes, the ones their kids love the best, and put them in a book. I've got it somewhere . . .'

'Can you have it ready by December 7th?' said Hazel.

Cyn shrugged. 'Sure.'

Hazel stood up and sat down quickly, like an MP at Question Time.

'I'd like to praise Paloma and her team for the mini-tennis last term which the Reception children benefited from enormously. We shan't be repeating it next year. Now, Paloma has news of her major fund-raiser for the term. Over to you, Paloma.'

Paloma cleared her throat. There was a lot of it to clear. She spoke in a deep, whispery, throaty way, a cross between a sixty-a-day man and Joanna Lumley. 'I've had

59

an, erm, off the record, agreement from Mrs Armstrong that, after the tremendous success of the masked ball last year, this winter we'd stage an auction of promises.'

'Super!' beamed Bryony, 'with so many – talented – people on the Hill, it's bound to do well . . .!'

An even smaller, Kylie-sized version of Cyn brought over a tray of cakes and biscuits.

'Could I please finish this now?' said Antonia.

'We haven't time, Antonia . . .' said Hazel.

'No time . . .!' echoed Bryony.

'Antonia, I think they've had enough,' said Carla. But she knew there was no stopping Antonia. Overruling was her stock in trade.

'Tom *and* Carla,' Antonia repeated, smiling around the room. '*. . . in the hands of Tom and Carla, come off brilliantly. The whole house is a cross between a big play area and a comfortable flophouse. . .'*

Carla tuned out, hoping her uncharacteristic feebleness didn't come across as smugness. Like the holiday, another positive turning into a negative.

The suddenness of it had been a shock. She'd only popped in to the paper shop for a pint of semi-skimmed and had come face to face with a strangely grinning and bouncing Mr Panjani, beaming at her indulgently like she was Sharon Stone or something. She didn't know why until she put her pound coin down and jumped right up out of her shoes. She'd plonked it right on top of Tom's face. There they all were, on the cover! Frozen in unreality, surrounded by texts and headlines, sitting around the Klounge refectory table, laughing their heads off at that dumb photographer's fake fart, in between the *Evening Standard's* ever-changing headlines and another of Mr Panjani's locals, Sir David Attenborough, cuddling a rat on the cover of the *Radio Times*. All this two doors away from Richmond Hill Juniors and Infants.

Antonia's voice rumbled behind her thoughts. She'd read it a thousand times already and, yes, she was proud of it. She felt she should throw in a comment or something, at least stop sitting there like a dumbo. She sat up and tuned in.

'*The kitchen-cum-living room, known in the Alexander household as the Klounge, covers the whole of the raised ground floor. This enormous space is divided into three distinct areas. The relaxation bay at the front is very much Carla-influenced, swathed in her own embroideries and cleverly sourced textiles, whilst the funky funfair central kitchen area couldn't have been designed by anyone except Tom Alexander. The colours subdue towards the dining area at the rear, which, in fine weather, is transformed into an extension of the garden via a sliding glass wall running the whole width and height of the room. From here, an enclosed corridor leads to the converted coach house, which, with its bright red pigmented resin floor, full of musical instruments, drums, keyboards and electric guitars of all sizes, is as much for the grown-ups as for their two children, Wilfred and Dylan . . .*'

'They haven't been called that since their christenings!' Carla smiled, then frowned immediately. Hazel and Bryony were both going through papers on Hazel's clipboard.

'Antonia, I really think . . .' she added with, she hoped, as much feeling.

'Nearly there . . . *The children also have a pit full of rope swings and a tree-house at the bottom of the Japanese-inspired garden.*'

'Isn't Dyl a bit *young* for a tree house?' said Bryony.

'It's not, it's only a shed, risen a couple of feet above the ground . . . You know, you've seen it, Toby's played in it often enough.'

61

'Oh – *that* . . . that is a shed, isn't it!'

Carla smiled brightly at Bryony, extra brightly. Bitch.

'Last bit . . . *This house is perfectly geared for contemporary family living. It is not only a spectacular design showcase but works on all levels as a functional family home . . .*'

'A triumph, Carl, total triumph.' Antonia threw the magazine on the table.

'Let's get on . . .' said Hazel, standing again. She opened her mouth and closed it again as there was a flurry of movement by the door.

Cyn's Kylie-sized relative was now swamped by a coat and being followed by a large woman in a baggy dress with long, red hair tied halfway down her back.

'Sorry I'm late,' she said, settling herself next to Elle. This was Hannah Hargreaves' standard greeting because Hannah, owner of the Space Gallery on Hill Rise, was biologically incapable of being on time anywhere.

'Can't stay long I'm afraid, I've got a buyer coming in at 12 . . .' Elle moved her chair a little sideways to give Hannah more room as she began rummaging in an enormous carpet bag and plonking a blue thermos flask on the table.

'Well, I've got a meeting at 11.45!' harrumphed Bryony.

Carla breathed again, glad there'd been no post-mortem audible or dissentful mutterings of disapproval about child exploitation in magazines from the tank commander's end of the table.

There followed a discussion about what could be offered and who they could lynch for the auction. Embarrassed at having taken up so much of the meeting without actually volunteering for anything, Carla promised to make a customised cushion to the bidder's brief. The

62

meeting disintegrated into collective admiration for Antonia's new leather bag and gasps of amazement when they found out it was from M&S.

'All very fine but they'll all get them now,' Elle said as they crossed Queen's Road. 'I wanted to ask you, Carl.'

'Mmmm.'

'Tom.'

'Mmmm.'

'Do you think he'd help with the calendar?'

'In what way?'

'You know, with the design, backgrounds and things?'

'Aren't you an expert at that?'

'It's a bit different, Carl.' She sounded hurt. 'We have to shoot outside the studio, it'd be a big help to have an extra eye . . .'

'He's got a lot on his plate but . . .'

'A bit of advice really, it wouldn't take time. A couple of hours at the outside.'

'Sure, why don't you ask him?'

'Thanks, I thought I'd better check with you, I mean . . .'

'Sure . . . No problems.'

Chapter Seven

Snow on the hills, the radio said. It was talking about the Scottish hills, not their gentle, Surrey slope with a great big comfy town at the bottom of it, but even so, it was good to get some real weather at last, snuffing out the stalemate that'd been in the skies for days.

Carla pulled on her Chanel, black, quilted, knee-high boots, welcoming the solid warmth of them against her legs like an old friend. She looked out of the bedroom window. Tom wouldn't miss the signs; even in the middle of London, he'd be making excuses to get home early.

'Let's go Dyl,' she said, snapping down his plastic cover. 'Let's go and get Wilf before he gets blown across the playground.'

At the end of Friars Style Road, the sky opened up, jerking her umbrella away with it. As she turned to go down the Hill, she quickly dipped it down in front of the pushchair, catching it before it collapsed.

The noise of the trees hid Dyl's squeals, the ice in the wind hit her face, lifting her lenses and making her eyes water. But Carla didn't mind. She thought of the Scottish hills covered in snow, of Siberian plains and unseen seas all blowing in that wind around her safe,

Surrey skin, making a laughing mockery of those now distant hot days when even walking was reduced to a flip-flop stagger.

She liked being in high boots again, her step solid and assured as she kicked through the swirling leaves, past the mansion terraces on her right and the wide open spaces with all that weather in it to her left, heading into the shelter of the valley and the school below.

She'd made sure she was late so she could get in and out of the playground quickly without having to go through any surface conversations, but the children still weren't out and the parents and nannies were all there, huddled in groups, waiting and grumbling. She chose a small circle of brollys, flapping scarves and hoods hovering outside year 4 over the claustrophobia of the crowded shelter. The sky darkened a shade. She could smell the metallic smell of the rain before it came. Moments later it was falling out of the clouds, in hard, solid sheets.

'It's all elemental,' Hannah Hargreaves said ominously, looking up at the sky, a transparent red and black ladybird brolly held incongruously above her cloak blustering dramatically around her.

No one was listening.

'What's that?' Carla said to be friendly.

'It's all linked, linked with the moon and the tides.'

'Just the winter coming in a bit early, that's all. It does that sometimes.'

Hannah turned towards her. 'You mean you haven't noticed?'

'Noticed what?'

'The way the weather changes at 3. Every day. It's the power of the female, all moving at the same time, gathering together in playgrounds.'

Carla didn't say anything for a moment. Then she said,

'More to do with it being the only time we look up to see what it's been doing with itself all day.'

'That's what I mean! All of us, looking up, shifting, moving ...'

Rescued by a swirl of waist-high activity of boys, bags and lunchboxes, Carla left the playground quickly.

And then the best bit of all the bad-weather days, the getting home and out of it and into the warm again. Hearing it all going on outside. More opportunities for covering things up, for creating warm insides. She made the boys hot chocolate and let them curl up with the TV and went upstairs.

She threw the throw across the bed and stood back to admire it. She only got it out in winter, on their windy fire nights, a patchwork of antique saris, deep blues, warm browns, creamy whites, ochres and purples. She smoothed the fabric out, letting the roughs and smooths of the patchwork silks caress her hands. Thinking about all the things they'd talk about that evening, the ritual argument about what they'd do at Christmas, agreeing on the open invitations to parents which were never taken up. She listed in her mind the other things to tell him. How Wilf had earned his half pen licence. The school's policy of giving out half licenses, then full licenses, allowing children to write in fountain pen for some of their work, then all of their work, always made Tom laugh. He'd been looking forward to giving Wilf half a fountain pen as soon as he brought his certificate home. She stood back. Amazed at how the power of colours could change the whole feel of a room. It was snoozing now, softly, slumbering and stirring, its whites turned to creams, ready to be warmed. Absorbed by the quieter light, settling and softening and turned off.

Candles already in place, she bent down and opened a

little door in the surround. Humming quietly to herself, she put on her gardening gloves and took the grate from the little cupboard and slid the gas-fire fitment into the space before sliding it shut again. Gas effect for cold spring and early autumn, but for winter only a real fire would do. She opened the firelighters, breathing in the kerosene as she scrunched up newspaper balls and laid the coal on the top. She brought out extra candlesticks and was fitting them with long, thin white candles, lighting each wick in turn before putting it out with finger and thumb, when the doorbell went.

'Terrible weather to be out here this evening, madam.' He already had his suitcase open, one arm pressing down on piles of dusters and ironing-board covers to stop them blowing away. 'But I've come with a special deal here today...' he thrust the plastic card dangling round his throat into Carla's face.

'No, thank you.'

'Well, you can fuck off then.'

'So can you.' She slammed the door.

'Muuuum?' a voice called from the play room.

'I'm busy.'

'Come and see this! Pleeease, mum.'

She went into the play room.

'Weeeee.' A squealing, soft, flying missile whizzed past her ears. Then another, squiggling round and round to the floor.

'Mithhhed,' shrieked Dyl.

'Very funny.' She and Wilf made a dive for the yellow and red shrivelled bits of rubber. They knew she hated balloons. The ones that really annoyed her were the helium-filled ones. Adored and played with as long as it took to buy them and get them home. Then there they'd lurk, getting carried around every so often, to surprise

67

her, hidden behind doors, swaying like living things. At the first sign of a shrivel they were quietly knifed to death and binned.

'It's fun, mum.'

They glared at each other, eyes locked, as he blew the red one up again and let go. 'Weee, like a willy farting!'

Carla pounced on the balloons, Dyl swivelled back to *Mugging Monkeys 4* and Wilf set off up the kitchen climbing wall.

'Can we play something together, mum, please, together, just us?' Wilf peered down at her.

Carla jumped backwards as he detached himself, landing on the floor with a cracking thump. 'Have you finished your homework?'

'Nearly. Blind Man's Bluff? Please. Blind Man's Bluff.'

'Then homework, bath, teeth, bed. OK?'

'Oh kayyy.'

'Come on upstairs, then.'

She knelt down. 'Mind my mascara.' She felt his little fingers, eagerly tying the scarf behind her.

She loosened the front.

'Cheat!'

'Don't be cheeky.' She stood up and he twisted her round. His little hands firm on her hips, round and round and round in the dark.

She put her arms out ahead of her and walked forward, crashing straight into the bunk bed.

Stifled giggles erupted out of the darkness.

She spun round quickly. Swiping her arms out and grabbing at space as the giggling swish of clothes moved away.

A light but frantic fluttering sound above her head made her jump.

'What's that?'

'A dragonfly in the shade,' said a little voice behind her.

'Arrgggh, gotchya.' She turned and grabbed a handful of air.

A squeal of laughter moved to her other side.

She turned quickly, stopping to listen to the rustling silence.

'YEOWWCH.'

Hysterical giggles.

'And WHO was that pinching my behind.' She spun round, to be grabbed by a pair of arms and squeezed tight.

'It's the creeping monkey monster, GRRRRRRRRR.' Tom buried his face into her neck.

'DAddy!'

'Get away!' she laughed. 'I didn't hear you coming in.'

'Daddy's go, daddy's go.'

'Wilf, I said one go.'

'One go it is.' Tom took the scarf and put it to his eyes, waiting for it to be tied. 'And remember Wilf, upstairs is out of bounds.'

'Like the third floor on the right-hand side,' they chorused together.

Tom crept along the landing, exaggeratedly slowly, picking each leg up high, his arms in front of him like paws, stopping and listening every few steps like a pantomime cat. Carla went back to the bedroom.

She put a match to the scrunched-up newspaper. The paper blackened into red and the room filled with the liquorice smell of wood burn.

She went to get changed.

Tom had remembered. He was home early enough to put the children to bed while she prepared the food.

The coal all burned, Tom threw the first log on the fire

and Nat and Natalie Cole on the radiogram. She leaned against him, watching the smoke curling round a log, enveloping it, caressing it, waiting for the first flame to flicker up and lick around it.

'When's the final day then?'

'December the thirty-first.'

'December the thirty-first,' she echoed.

'A nice round date for you, Carl.'

'It's a bank holiday.'

'All right, Christmas. I won't be going back after Christmas.'

'Except for the leaving party.'

'Except for the leaving party.'

There was a silence Carla didn't go down. There was too much else to worry about.

He squeezed her. 'You've got to look at it like we're moving on, Carl, not back.'

'We've really got to find backers, and premises and . . . Having a date. It makes it, so *real* . . .' said Carla.

'It is.' Tom picked up his whisky glass. 'We've got to keep positive, that's the half of it, you know.'

'At least it gives me something solid to be scared about.'

'What do you mean?'

She grabbed the tongs and picked the chestnuts out of the fire.

'I don't know, I've – ever since Elle and Otto – I've felt uneasy, really uneasy.'

'So have I.' He picked up a chestnut from the grate and dropped it, shaking his hand. 'Yeowch, they're hot.'

'Have you?'

'Mmm.'

'At least we can be uneasy together.'

'Yeah.'

'And they seem all right. Elle does anyway. You still haven't seen Otto, Tom, you must, you must must talk to him.'

'When I get time. I've a lot to tie up before I walk out of that door.'

'So, how did everyone in the office take it?'

'They all knew, of course. The girls were a bit upset.'

'They *knew*?'

'Yeahh.'

'*How*?'

'Like us, I suppose, they worked out I was pretty unhappy and wouldn't be hanging around much longer.'

'So they didn't mind!'

'I didn't say that, did I?'

'But did they?'

'What?'

'Mind! Didn't they beg you to stay and all that stuff after...'

'After all I've done ... I made Carliatti, Carl. Carliatti doesn't exist any more, it's all Speranzaspeak now.' He fumbled for a cigarette. 'And, well, er, actually ...'

'What?'

Carla waited, listening to the logs hissing and popping and the old beech knocking at the window.

'What, Tom?' she repeated gently.

'What do you mean?'

'What – actually ... Come on, out with it.'

'There's a possibility, I'm not saying it's definite or anything like that, but there's a good chance I might have someone interested.'

'In backing you?'

Tom nodded.

'Tom, this is big news. Who? Go on!'

'You see, Bruno, he ...'

'*Bruno!*'

'Hear me out, Carl.'

Carla sat up, put her glass down and slowly turned towards him. 'One of the biggest, one of the only at the moment, I have to say, plusses in all of this is to get out of the hair, the shiny balding bonce, should I say, of that man and you're telling me ...!'

'Carla, listen to me,' he said so sharply she was shocked into silence. He took a deep breath. 'There's this dealer, an art-dealer friend of his.'

'Art?'

'An art dealer who's picked up on the designer-maker trend. They think it's where it's going to be, now Brit Art is so established. It's all moving away from conceptual and back to objects again, apparently. Anyway, this company's looking to invest in design big time, British design, Carl, and they're willing to take risks.'

'You're not a risk, Tom, you're a household name!'

'That doesn't mean there aren't big risks Carl, you know that. Bruno thinks ...'

'What's in it for him?'

'What?'

'Bruno Iassaci doesn't do anything unless there's something in it for him, you know that Tom.'

'Well – he'd, he'd be a ...'

'I can't believe I'm hearing this!'

'He'd be a *sleeping* partner Carl. He'd have no direct involvement.'

'Do you really want to watch Bruno Iassaci make another fortune off our backs?'

'He wouldn't! Well, he would a bit, if we do of course, which we will of course, but the opportunity is there Carl, and we have to look at it.'

'Who says?'

'We haven't been offered anything yet but we have to investigate it at least. We'd be insane not to.'

'But why does it have to be Bruno?'

'You keep on about not wanting to lose this place, don't you. And besides, you'd never see him. *I'd* never see him! I'd be working with these people ... whoever they are,' he added lamely.

'And how much of a "bit" would Bruno be biting off this time? Have you discussed that with him yet?'

'Who else is going to help us, Carl? Bruno's the most connected man in the business; it'd be well-nigh impossible to do anything without him anyway. Come on, at least let's see what they're offering.'

'Who are they?'

'I don't know, do I.'

'Do you have a *name*, Tom?' Carla pulled the cellophane off the chocolate box.

'I can't remember, foreign-sounding names, Danielle del something, and two others – with those funny Eastern names that go on and on, Fidjesk somethingorother ...'

'You're hopeless,' Carla sighed, picking out a chocolate, 'Get me the names on Monday and we'll give them a Google.'

Tom grabbed her shoulders. 'So you agree!'

'I didn't say that; I said we'd put their names into the Internet and see what information comes out.'

'I knew you'd see right sense!'

'I said, we'd *see*.'

'Oh, well, actually, there is something else –'

Carla took another chocolate and looked up at their shadows shuddering on the ceiling in the firelight, waiting for it.

'We won't need to – you see, I've, I've invited them on Sunday. I thought it'd be the perfect time – don't look at me like that, I had to Carl – they're only in the country a few days . . .'

'You invited them on Sunday!'

'Yes. Hey, where's the caramel cream gone?'

'But it's a first Sunday! First Sundays are strictly no business days . . .'

'You complain about not being involved then when I involve you, you don't want to know!'

'First Sundays are for friends, Tom. For friends to drop in. . .'

'It was either that or tonight, Carl. How would you've liked that? I knew it'd be a windy fire night, didn't I? And besides, it's important you meet them as well.'

'Why didn't you call and ask me?'

'I took the decision.'

She spoke slowly. 'The whole point of first Sundays is anyone can drop by so long as they don't talk about work! That's always been the *rule*!'

'Then I'm afraid it's a rule that will just have to be broken for once. And I expect a few others before we're out. You've got to go with me on this Carl, you've got no choice on it. Besides, what are you doing taking my caramel?'

'They've changed the shapes. Try that pointy one with a squiggle.'

'That's orange cream!'

'It's not, Tom, here, try it.' She gave him the chocolate and leaned into him.

'Hey, you're right!'

She leaned back into his arms, her legs in her sheerest black stockings stretched out before her, listening to his quiet munching.

A strong gust of wind rattled the window and snuffed out a candle. He stroked her leg.

'But then, you're always right Carl, aren't you?'

He turned her cheek and gave her a long, warm, choco-latey kiss.

Chapter Eight

'Leech. Hairless, great, parasitical, .foghorn-mouthed leech.' Carla banged the saucepan on the hob. She tipped in a cup of flour, a cup of water and a half-cup of salt, a spoon of olive oil, a teaspoon of cream of tartar, a few drops of vanilla essence, grabbed a wooden spoon and stirred. The radio pipped the hour.

'What colour, Dyl?'

'Blue.'

She waited.

'No, green.'

She waited.

'GREEN!'

'Green it is – too late now.' Three drops of green pierced the dull beige dough. She stirred it in.

Tom went up behind her and put his arms around her.

She wriggled away and pushed him off.

'Ooooh la laaa,' said Wilf, racing off to the play room.

'No boardroom conferences, I promise.'

'We didn't talk about Christmas.'

'We'll have another one.'

'There might not be another one.'

'All right, we'll talk about it tonight, or tomorrow night ...'

'And I forgot to tell you, Wilf's got his half pen licence.'

'Yeah, I know, he told me.'

'Oh.'

'What?'

'You didn't tell me he'd told you.'

The theme tune to *Desert Island Discs* came on the radio. She turned it up.

Tom picked up a strawberry.

'The strawberries were a mistake.'

She was annoyed he'd taken the pen licence news so lightly. Had he forgotten how she'd watched and listened as one by one all the other children in the class were given permission to write some of their work in pen? Some of them, like Hadley and Claudia, had won their full pen licences terms and terms ago.

'They look good.'

'I know. I was seduced. They even smelled a little. But here, taste.'

Tom screwed up his face. 'Like bitter sawdust.'

'I'll throw them out.'

'Leave them out. We don't have to eat them.'

The mixture in the saucepan gelled into a creamy lump, streaked with green like a big, molten humbug. She tipped it onto the surface and kneaded the dark inky greens and creams, blending them into a lump of elasticy, warm, sweet-smelling dough.

She plonked it onto the mini-work surface, next to Dyl and Wilf's mini-sink, cluttered with modelling tools and play dough shapers.

Humming away contentedly to himself, Dyl scraped up his mini-chair. She stood back and watched him proudly.

He might have the temper of Zeus on him, but, given the right toys, he was good at sitting in one place for a long time. He'd stay there, making psychotic creations for hours if Wilf let him.

Carla shrugged and raced on. She always cooked the same, a quick and easy to prepare in advance Nigella. By *Just A Minute* the beef was resting on the side, the quiche was warmed, the salad was made and the cosy fug of Sunday roast filled the air.

'You should be happy the clocks've gone back, it's given us an extra hour.' Tom took a wodge of supplements out of their cellophane.

'Us?'

Tom made a face at her, put his feet up on the table and flicked through 'The Culture'.

Bang on the last round of *Just A Minute* Wilf appeared like a cow coming in for milking.

'Pop corn, pop, pop corn pop, Pop pop pop pop ...' Wilf reached for the bag of kernels; she grabbed them off him.

'*Wait*, Wilf.'

She went upstairs, leaving the three of them watching the microwave like a TV, Dyl in Tom's arms, making kerpow and splat noises as the nut-hard kernels cracked, zapped and shot into squiggly white froths.

Without having to think, she picked out her purple floor-length skirt. She wore lots of purple. It was calming but gave off good power vibes and enhanced her perceptions of undercurrents and moods, all of which she'd need in spades that afternoon. The indigo top with black spaghetti straps was quietening without being energy-draining. This was as much black as Carla ever let near her. White, all colours, and black, the absence of colour, were no good to Carla and she never wore them.

Cama Chameleon Carla, Tom called her. He'd come up with it on one of their first dates, sprawled in front of an African art movie at the college one night. 'They look adorable with their large eyes, and their soft padded paws feel wonderful to the touch,' the film had said solemnly, 'but wise Africans never touch the chameleons.' 'Good job I'm not an African then, isn't it,' he'd whispered as he slid his hand to touch her somewhere he shouldn't. 'It's bad luck,' the film added, with perfect timing. He'd jokingly taken his hand away quickly at that.

She phoned Elle. 'Just to remind you about the clocks.'

'Why don't you just come out and say "don't be late, Elle, I need you".'

'All right – I admit it, I'm nervous.'

'You'll be fine.'

'Do me a favour and get here quick, can you, before they arrive.'

'Give them your warmest welcome and that's all you have to do. Let Tom do his thing. Think of the pay-off.'

'That's what I am thinking of.'

'We can hang out in the garden. Let Tom deal with them.'

'It's raining.'

'It'll stop.'

It did, but not until Bruno and his friends had arrived.

'Carla, this is new.' Elle sounded false and forced.

'Do you like it?'

They were both tuned into the action at the other end of the room.

'*Thomas – this space, it's incredible...*'

Thomas?

'*... of course I have seen pictures in the magazines but – Thomas, it's so big.*'

Bruno, the only person who was ever indifferent, to the

point of rudeness, about the house, was talking to the two men with funny names, both in matching grey suits, standing erect like bodyguards, as dumb and grim-looking as Gilbert and George in full-on performance mode.

'*. . . of course what we're after is the stamp of individuality missing from mass-produced goods. . .*'

'It's fantaastic, Carla,' Elle piped up woodenly. 'So different from your normal style . . .'

'Yes.'

She watched Elle fingering the fabric, stroking it. There was a sudden silence between them, the silence in which Carla should have leaped in with the offer to sell as she often did.

'It's not for sale, that one, I'm afraid.'

'It's lovely, though.'

A thin ghost-like figure in a long, baggy, cream silk dress, fishnet stockings, silver socks and ballet pumps detached itself from the group and drifted up, bending like a poppy in the breeze.

'Any more Badoit for Bwuno?' She craned her long neck towards Carla, exposing a network of purply veins through her powder-pale skin.

'Yes Chlorene, of course.'

She introduced Elle, who admired her dress.

'It's a handbag dwess, look,' she turned out the folds to reveal little zippers, 'so we don't have to carry our woombs on our shoulders any more . . .'

Elle looked at Carla.

'I think she means wombs . . .' Carla whispered to Elle, following Chlorine to the fridge.

Elle picked up the *News of the World* and settled into the sofa.

'Who did *this*?' Chlorene handed Bruno's glass to Carla and pointed to a picture on the fridge.

'It wasn't Tom.'

'Oh Carla, I see it, I see it's *you*, isn't it?'

'Good, isn't it,' said Carla, not missing a beat that Chlorene should have recognised her in the yellow llama with brown spots standing underneath a rainbow surrounded by hearts. 'Some psychological art class, they had to think of their mother as an animal – I think I got away quite lightly if you think of all the horrors he could have drawn!' She was warming to Chlorene slightly in the way any praise of one's child does.

'Wwhewere *are* they all?' Chlorene looked out into the garden.

'Oh, on the play station.' She looked at her watch. 'About another half hour before we see them.'

'How luvely. Your garden's looking swo good, Carla, even in the rain.'

'Especially in the rain.' Carla slammed the fridge shut.

'Do you have any Evian?'

'I thought you said Badoit.'

'Bwuno's cocktail? Half and half?'

'Of course, silly me. *Exactly* half and half, is it, or. . .'

'I'll say when, shall I?'

'Yes Chlorene, You say when.'

'How's the embroidery?'

'Going well.'

Carla didn't offer a polite enquiry after Chlorene's art into the silence that followed. She'd be stuck then, for hours. She decided, though, to foster the conversation. It would be her contribution to the afternoon. When Tom blamed her later for staying away from them all she'd have a definite moment to point back to.

'Did you know, gardening and embroidery have a lot in common?'

Chlorene frowned, puckering her fish-like lips.

81

'The very first gardening books used the language of embroidery. Look, I'll show you ...'

She went over and took down a heavy old book from the shelf above the computer, right by where Tom and the others were standing. 'Tom bought it for me for our first wedding anniversary,' she said extra-loudly, making even Bruno stop talking for a moment, 'soon after we bought the house.'

'Wreally?' said Chlorene, bending over beside her to turn the pages.

'... *Tom, here, has completely rationalised the intimate connection between form, function and beauty,*' Bruno piped up again to Danielle's two sidekicks like he was talking about a favourite dog, '*and put it into twenty-first century sustainability without losing the old art with life, life with art William Morris integrity...*'

'*Shall we sit down somewhere*,' Tom was offering now, arm half behind Danielle's back, steering her away from Carla and Chlorine.

'... And then it all turned about, you see? The embroiderers were hot onto the explorers coming back from the New World, itching to get their hands on each and every new plant discovery.'

'Giving them the contemporary edge of the time ...' said Chlorene, turning the pages without looking at them. 'Embrroidery must be so satisfying, Carla; it must be a little bit like being an artist, in the slow unfolding, at the same time thinking of nothing, but everything ...'

Chlorene was off. Carla, pretending to listen, tuned into the gathering, getting her first good look at Danielle del NoNo as she sat herself at the refectory table, Tom holding her chair, smiling stupidly.

Whilst Chlorene looked as though she could topple over at a puff of wind, Danielle del NoNo, all dark and angular, was all presence. Layered and flicked long dark hair, fast, dark eyes and the kind of unbelievable figure that made women's heads turn as much as men's. Carla glanced down to inspect her hands, as she always did. Thin, bony fingers weighted down with rings, and long, painted nails.

Go over, go on, go over, get it over and go and join them, she told herself; stake your claim. But her feet wouldn't move.

Feeling like a gooseberry in her own home, she went and sat with Elle. Elle immediately put the paper down. Her sympathy only confirmed and made real what was going on.

'Where's Otto?'

'He might drop by later, he's taken his mother to a Christmas fair.'

'In Richmond?'

'Bruges.'

Tallulah and Jon and Wilf and Dyl raced in, grabbed handfuls of popcorn and juice boxes and raced out to the bottom of the garden.

'It must have stopped raining.'

'I'll give them a proper tea later,' Carla said.

'I'm hungry too.' Elle stood. 'Come on, let's get it over with.'

'Yes, sorry ...'

'Who's betting she goes for the quiche,' whispered Elle as they clattered to and fro offering plates of milky warm beef, bloody and rare, jacket potatoes, a vast wooden platter of Little Gem and walnut salad, and a cream oval Le Creuset of tomato salad.

They sat with Chlorine at the unbusiness end of the table. Danielle smiled at Carla and Elle, like a diner might smile at their waitresses for the evening. Normally people helped themselves, that was part of it, eat when you want

83

to eat, come when you like, leave when you like, no pressures. Not this. She could never, would never, be absorbed into Bruno's orbit. She felt like a doll, a dull doll, a dull wife; how Bruno saw her was correct. That was what she was. Useless.

Danielle turned to Tom and whispered something.

Elle flashed a look at Carla. She whispered! How rude was that?

With the pudding came the children. There followed the agonising polite Sunday afternoon small talk between interrupted adults and reluctant children before they could escape with their ice cream.

Danielle's was the best.

'What's your favourite subject at school, Wilf?'

'Inset days.'

Good one Wilf. Carla gave him an extra dollop of ice cream.

'Insedaze, it's a new kind of science,' Carla explained.

Elle's sympathy wasn't doing her any good. Carla suggested she leave the children and go and do some shopping. When she got back from seeing Elle to the door, Tom and Danielle were in the garden. Smoking together now, in that intimate way only smokers who've just discovered each other could. Their puffy breaths mingling coolly as they talked, Danielle completely absorbed in what Tom was saying.

She tried to play it down. That was the effect Tom had on people. People found him interesting company. That's all. Nothing at all new there. But feeling like a stranger in her own home? Unable, even, to run for the garden. She stayed in the conservatory, wanting to be visibly visible. Visibly waiting. They were only talking. Tom looking so damned innocent, grinning and nodding away. Normally he barely noticed if he was being flirted with.

'Carrla, I wanted to give you this?'

Chlorene unzipped her silver bum bag and handed Carla a coloured postcard.

'I hope you can come.'

Carla looked down at the picture on the card, turning it over and back again several times before looking up at Chlorene with genuine puzzlement.

'I don't know what to say!' she said, not knowing what else to say. She turned the picture away from her again, trying to wipe the image of a bloody white cross wrapped in blue string from her mind.

'I'm not the only artist, it's a new perspective collective, but it's at the Serpentine, it's such a bweak for me.' Chlorene was standing really close to her, fixing her with her bulbous, pale blue eyes. Carla felt ill.

'A crucial factor I've got to get Tom to take on board is speed . . .' boomed Bruno's boardroom-speak from behind.

'I'm not sure I can . . .' Trying to ignore the dizzy feeling, she studied the card.

Chlorene was already bending, preparing to turn away. 'It's not until next month. It's more a girly thing, I suppose . . . Come on your own, or bwing a girlfriend.' She glanced meaningfully out of the window. 'Leave him behind.'

She drifted off. Carla glanced out and quickly away, avoiding all eye contact as Tom and Danielle returned from the garden and joined the table.

'Ah Tom, here you are,' said Bruno. 'I was just saying, to be commercially viable you've got to stick to your schedules.'

'What's new about that!' said Tom indignantly, drawing up a chair to join them. 'You should see the way they work us at Carliatti, one deadline after another,' he said chummily to Danielle.

'Turnover, Tom,' said Bruno, 'turnover.'

'But Thomas is an artist,' said Danielle settling down next to him. 'He has to take the time he has to take.'

'I'm not an artist.'

'And he's not a Thomas,' said Carla pointedly. It might sound childish but she could bear it no longer.

'But you *are* an artist, Thomas,' said Danielle, ignoring her.

'A designer's never an artist,' said Tom.

'But excuse me,' one of the suits spoke for the first time. 'I understood this is what you wanted to be doing.'

'He does,' Bruno snapped.

'You're a creative, Tom,' said Bruno.

'My chairs are to be sat in, not looked at!'

'On the one hand you're right, Tom, on the other you're wrong,' said Bruno. 'What we need to do here is set up, begin, begin the fusion, the fusion,' he repeated as if he'd just invented the word, 'between art and craft.'

'Rubbish,' said Tom flatly. 'Art is a one-off, original, never to be repeated. Craft is repeated, over and over ...'

'Excuse me,' said Gilbert, 'but I thought your wish was to make bespoke chairs.'

'Sculptures!' said Danielle.

'And they will be portrait chairs? One-off chairs for each individual. I'm sorry I think you'll find that's art.' said Gilbert.

'Everyone will adore them, Thomas, they'll be begging you to have their chairs done.'

'Chairs! Not bloody paintings or bloody lights going on and off or anything else. Chairs. Simple as that. Straight down the line. CHAIRS! They might be unusual, they might be one-offs, but they're still for putting your bum in, all right?'

'And you'll be getting your market range off the ground first, of course ...' said Bruno.

'Does anyone sit in the Margaret Thatcher chair?' asked Tom.

'Probably not – why?'

'Because it's probably in a museum somewhere, that's why. My chairs won't be in museums, they'll be in people's houses and people will sit on them.'

'He doesn't know his own worth!' said Danielle proudly.

'Let me take over here,' said Bruno, giving Tom a dagger look that could kill.

Haven't you just, mate. First windy fire night hijacked and now first Sunday.

'No – you all hang on a minute!' Carla boomed. 'Would someone mind telling me what's going on here?'

They looked up at her. She stood firm and stern, feeling like a piece of dogshit blown in on the wind.

Danielle gave Tom a sympathetic glance. Then smiled sweetly at Carla, 'I am so sorry, it is so rude to talk business in the home, no?'

Carla let her silence confirm this.

'Let's finish this talk now, you can come to my office next week, Thomas. We carry on there. I do apologise about this.' She said it with such sincerity Carla knew it wasn't true.

'Excuse me a moment.' Tom, who'd turned a lighter shade of dark purple, stood up, took Carla's elbow and led her out and to the side of the garden by the play room.

'What the bloody hell are you playing at, Carla?'

'I might ask you the same thing.'

'Don't make me look a fool, Carla. Shut up for a bit and we'll talk about it later. Those guys in there are big time.'

'You don't seem to be exactly encouraging them.'

'I'm making myself clear, that's all . . .'

87

'I'm sorry but I can't cope with it, it's worse than I expected it to be. It's not going to work. We'll have to think of something else.'

'Keep your voice down.' He grabbed her shoulders. 'Listen to me. You said we needed an absolute bastard on our side when it comes to business. And let's face it, better the devil you know, hey? Look – I'd better get back to them now, this is getting embarrassing.'

'What about her?'

'What about – her ...'

'It doesn't look like Bruno'll be the only sleeping partner.' She couldn't help it, it came out all by itself.

Tom gave her a gormless, not-you-woman look.

'All right, we'll talk about it later, but it better be good.'

She watched Tom going back into the house, feeling like all her curly c's had turned to kicking k's in a few short weeks. She thought back to Otto's rational theorising of love and friendship. Perhaps she'd been lucky, too lucky. She'd had all the good sides of love. She'd willingly surrendered to the significance of it, lived with the strength and the comfy, carpet-slipper acceptance of it. Now she was finding out about the other side. The vulnerability of it.

The house might be the only thing she got to keep if this deal went ahead. She'd better get on with accepting this new thought, full on, and draw up some contingency plans in case it became the case.

There was a rustle of movement by the dining area. She peeked around the wall. Tom and Danielle had come outside again. For *another* cigarette.

She panicked. What did she do now? Stay where she was? No. They were going further down the garden this time. Almost to the children's den.

She watched. Danielle wasn't even pretending to hide her interest in Tom now. But look at Tom! He wasn't responding at all. She wasn't getting anything back from him. This should have been a comfort to Carla but it wasn't.

With her back flattened against the wall, she slithered around the side of the house and slipped inside. She shook herself out quickly. Without as much as a glance at Bruno and his friends, she purposefully walked through to the klounge with a casual preoccupied toss of her head.

She stopped next to the bowl of strawberries, sitting untouched like a still-life on the side.

She looked down at the beautiful, bitter-tasting fruits, then up out into the garden.

'Yesss,' she grabbed the bowl and rushed outside.

'Go on with you, shooo,' she said over-dramatically. For the first time in her life, she was pleased to see Petra – next door's pesky, incontinent balding black cat – on the prowl for a poo.

'Such a pest, that cat!' she said jovially, striding up the garden, 'Now, Danielle, would you like one of these lovely strawberries?'

Not looking at Tom, she held out the bowl.

She avoided Tom for the rest of the afternoon. Only coming forward again when it was time to say goodbye.

As soon as the door had closed behind them, she at last allowed her smile to fade and made a dive for the computer.

'What are you doing?'

She tapped into Google and typed Danielle's name in the little white box ... It came up with 3,054 results.

Tom stood behind her.

'It's like spying, this, Carla.'

89

'Research, Tom. Research . . .'

There was a silence as they both read.

'So, she really is a countess . . .' said Tom.

'What?'

'She told me she's a countess . . . Look – there, see – she's got galleries in Rome, Siena, Milan . . . She's the real business.'

'And wants to invest in Thomas.'

'In us Carl, we've hit it here, we've been and gone and hit it . . .'

'She's an art dealer.'

'She wants to expand.'

'I bet she does.'

Carla clicked down the list, hoping for a magazine-type profile. She'd had a ring on, but then she had lots of rings on.

'Is she married?'

'I don't know, do I?'

'And where do Gilbert and George come into it?'

'I'm not sure.'

'Didn't Bruno *tell* you?'

'You know Bruno, he only tells me what he wants me to know.'

'Tom, you're hopeless! You've got to find out, what were their names, did they give you cards?'

'No.'

'To–oomm. . .'

'I don't think either was her husband, do you?'

'No Tom, no I don't think so. Make sure you find out.'

'All right, all right . . . I need another drink.'

She clicked off the computer and picked up the seca-teurs. The light was getting low but the last of the dahlias needed cutting back. That was the trick. After all the care and attention and love, what separated the poor gardener

from the good gardener was having the ability and tough-
ness of heart to recognise the moment something had
peaked and it was time to help it on its way.

Chapter Nine

Schools in the dark were strange, Carla thought, smiling around the hall of Richmond Hill Juniors and Infants as she settled herself down at table 12. All the usual benches, plastic chairs, gym equipment and clusters of music stands had disappeared, replaced by eighteen tables, seventeen round and one rectangular for the VIPs, decorated with the best from the dining drawers of Richmond Hill: thick white tablecloths, silver cutlery and candelabras, ribbons and helium balloons. More balloons, streamers and fairy lights dangled off the walls. Gathered around the tables were night-time versions of the playground groups, all straps, shoulders and DJs glittering with jewellery, and spouses neatly attached in boy-girl-boy-girl circles.

Andrew Hargreaves poured her drink. With half an eye and ear on Tom settling next to Elle on the other side of the table, Carla sat back in her seat, crossed her legs and flipped casually through the Order of Ceremonies. Furious, still, with herself about what she'd said to Tom about Danielle, she consciously worked at making sure not a flimsy shard of possessiveness revealed itself to the other side of the table.

Carla didn't do jealousy. Jealousy was ugly, immature and childish. And, now her cards were played, Tom was using it against her in the Bruno argument. He was playing up to Elle for all he was worth, more, much more than usual, to annoy her, she knew, and she wasn't going to buy into it.

This row had a different shape to it, though. The worst usually took the form of a three-day sulk until one of them eventually got bored and made a gesture, a small present, a kiss, an apology even, sometimes. They were already into the eighth day, with Tom disappearing to his work-shop every evening, shrugging off any accusations of sulking, only 'busy', to the point where touching had stopped altogether. He was still daft and bouncy with the boys. In bed, he showed his back, grumbling if she made any query – no, he's tired that's all, a lot on his plate, she must understand, now go to sleep.

'Hey,' said Antonia. 'What about this: weekend skiing in Chamonix. Lot 37, sleeps sixteen. We could do a table bid and share ...'

Carla looked at her as if she was mad.

'Nothing doing with us Ant,' said Tom without having to catch Carla's glance. The idea of skiing with Anne Frost's ghastly pink husband Jonathan, who looked dangerously like endorsing Antonia's idea, was unbear-able. After everyone had checked out who owned which holiday home and where, the talk soon got onto February half term. February half term, it seemed a lifetime away. They'd be into the second month by then, the second month of no cheque from Carliatti popping itself into their account all by itself. She could already feel the draughti-ness of it.

Andrew, a sharp, witty art dealer, strangely unlike dreamy Hannah, was banging on about St Petersburg and how they were going to buy a little flat there. Carla listened with a strange kind of detachment, a detachment she'd taken on ever since last Sunday. Reverting to the only thing she could trust in herself or in others at the moment, her gut instinct. Her knowing. And her knowing was telling her to stand back a little. A wrong move now could easily drop her in it even more, therefore she was making no move.

'Isn't St Petersburg full of mafia?' asked ghastly Jonathan.

'It's a city like any other. They're around but you don't spot them, except in the places like casinos of course.'

'**Lot no. 45 – Football Crazy**,' she read. 'An English football shirt, signed by Paul Gascoigne. Donated by Paul Gascoigne.'

Hmm, funny. She'd never heard Gazza was anything to do with the school, she thought idly as she put a cross next to **Lot no. 23 – A Bird's Eye View**. This was to remind herself to hide Tom's bidding paddle as soon as bidding started up on the helicopter ride over London. She wondered if Tom had seen it yet. A few weeks ago, she'd have been marking it up to buy it for him. Getting Tom used to seeing that money wasn't simply numbers you jiggled around wasn't something she looked forward to. She glanced through the lots.

BAFTA tickets from an absent Jo Salmon. A fabulous three-course meal to be cooked and delivered to your door by Paloma Laurance and Anne Frost. Since when had Anne been so pally with Paloma? Carla turned the page. There wasn't much that she fancied anyway.

Personal trainer sessions?

Oh no, not yet. Please. She took another sip of rosé.

'It's not what the children want, is it though – history, art galleries, and brrrr – co – oooold,!' she heard

94

Jonathan saying sneerily. *'We'll stick with La Manga, thanks all the same.'*

'Ice skating on the river, Tissa adores it.'

Trumpet lessons?

Nope.

French lessons?

For kids. Double no.

But, wait it got better. A weekend in a thatched cottage in Devon? She could do with that. Go off on her own to find herself?

A gardener for a day?

She could have offered that.

Have the use of a red E-type for the weekend?

Hmmm, possible. She nibbled at her canapé. A picture was forming. Mystery woman, scarf tied round head, a windy drive across Exmoor to an isolated thatched cottage, music blaring.

Someone to sew nametapes onto school uniforms?

Hardly the life's break she was looking for . . .

A rich fruit cake laced with brandy cooked especially for you?

Hmmm, she could take the cake with her in the E-type and scoff it all weekend in front of thatched cottage's log fire.

A week in the Wye Valley? Donated by Leticia McCarthy. So that's where the McCarthy's hung out in the holidays, was it?

Carla had never wanted a second home. Oh, the buying of it would be fun, she was sure, the falling in love and all that, but then, what happened when it came to leaving it behind? It'd be like leaving Dyl in the Kingston maternity wing. And then all that two-timing? How did all these people cope with the worry about it when they weren't there? She'd always felt a bit sorry for second homes. Like elderly aunts never visited often enough. Full of second-best, second-thoughts furniture and that slightly musty smell of gas, and always paved gardens, and letterboxes which only ever offered up bills and pizza menus.

'D'you know that Baxter boy's racket . . .' Hannah's husband Andrew was talking across her to Jonathan.

'I do.' Carla tuned back in. 'Unfortunately Wilf thinks he's his best friend . . .'

'After smashing every other child's conker in the playground it turned out he'd dipped his in wax and covered it with nail varnish!'

'Sounds like Toby.'

'He's a demon, that kid.'

'You should've had girls,' said Jonathan smugly.

'Oh, wait until later!' said Andrew and Carla together.

They were called out table by table to collect their main course. As she stood in the queue, Carla glanced across at Bryony's table. The husbands all in black ties, Bryony in a midnight-blue sequinned dress with a matching tiara-like hairband, nodding seriously. She looked vaguely around the room. With Cyn's husband on tour, and Ant, and Elle, their table was girl-heavy. Her eyes came to rest on the table in the back corner of the hall. The manny. She looked over at Elle, engrossed with Tom. Had she not noticed him? She looked back, curious to see who he was with. People she didn't know, new Reception parents. Like him, dark Italian looks, but smarter. Too much gold jewellery, lots of shining black hair and flagship designer clothes.

'Anything catch your fancy then?' said Andrew, already tucking into his char-grilled tuna niçoise when she returned.

'Not sure, how about you?'

96

'Hah, look at that.' He pointed a chubby finger at Carla's programme. 'A day on the set of *Blue Peter* . . . Tissie would love it. That's the one we'll get.'

'Carla, Tom's agreed to help a bit with the calendar,' said Elle, across the table. 'That OK?'

Carla smiled. 'Of course, that'd be lovely for Tom.'

'Have you got the go-ahead then?' asked Antonia.

'We'll get it.'

'You could do the costumes, Carl,' said Tom, a glimmer of kindness in his voice, the first for nearly a week.

'Thanks, Tom!' Carla said brightly.

'We won't be needing those, will we,' said Elle.

'No! No – course not!'

'It's models we'll be needing,' said Elle, looking wickedly at Carla.

'Go on, Carla,' said Cyn. 'It'll be a laugh.'

'My idea of hell on earth, Elle, and you know it.'

'Makes *Household Harmony* look tame, doesn't it,' said Tom.

'Think of it, you'd be exposed all over Richmond,' said Antonia.

'And beyond!' said Cynthia. 'If I'm in it . . .'

'Oh, you are . . .' said Elle.

Carla went back to studying the programme. What was he thinking? He had the most stressful period of his whole career ahead of him, he didn't even have the time to speak to her, and there he was committing himself all over the place.

'Carla, have you seen the last lot?' said Elle.

'I haven't got there yet.'

'Have a look.'

Carla turned the page. '**Lot 94. Last But Definitely Not Least.**'

Hmmmmmm, she tickled her chin with her finger and poured herself a glass of wine.

'I have to have this one, please, no one else bid against me,' said Elle.

Carla read, and looked up again at Elle and looked down again at the programme.

'I didn't know you were interested in dancing, Elle?'

'Read the small print, girl.'

Donated by Gabriel Fernandez.' Carla read.

Flamenco. So, he was Spanish was he?

Elle shrugged her shoulders. 'I was thinking only the other day he is a bit tall for an Italian.'

Carla chattered politely to Andrew about his gallery and then to Jonathan, not really tasting the food in between speaking and nodding and sipping, keeping Tom in her peripheral vision across the table.

Where was Otto tonight then? She wondered, nibbling at her mango and passion fruit pavlova. Elle was the one who was supposed to be feeling like this, not her. How would she be if it were her? On the surface no one would know. Like Elle, she could be confident, funny, smiley, in complete charge. Could she really retain that if she didn't have Tom? If she suddenly lost him? No, she'd be nothing, a blubbering blob of crushed roadkill-looking meringue.

After a loud banging on the VIP table at the front of the hall, there was a murmur of anticipatory plate-shifting and glass-filling as the auctioneer introduced himself.

'Here we have, ladies and gentlemen, lot 1, an aromatherapy massage in the privilege of your own home, courtesy of Paloma Laurance.'

'I didn't know she was a masseur,' said Cyn.

The gossip was under way.

Jonathan reached into his jacket, stood up, and waved

his mobile. 'I got a phone bid here . . . from Rick Sick . . .'

There was a smattering of laughter. Cynthia smiled brightly.

Carla worked hard at passing the salt, pouring drinks, sipping wine, smiling, laughing. Whatever else, she mustn't lose her strength. That was what Tom so loved in her. If she lost that she'd lose everything.

The bidding started modestly but rose as the evening progressed until silly money was being paid for almost everything. Carla's offer to sew a bespoke tapestry cushion went for £320, to a young, smart-looking woman she didn't know sitting on the 20-something bankers table.

Carla felt increasingly isolated but tried not to show it. She let Tom keep his paddle for the football shirt and the helicopter lot. Fortunately he didn't seem interested. Until. . .

'Lot 51,' the councillor announced, 'a night's B&B at the Richmond Heights Hotel, what am I bid?'

'How about it?' Tom said to Elle, thrusting his paddle in the air.

And he kept going through £60, £100, £140. . .

'£160, thank you, sir.'

The whole room was looking at him.

Even for Elle this was too much. She was shrugging her shoulders at Carla. Carla laughed.

'£180!'

Elle pushed Tom's paddle down and put her own up.

'£200. Any advance on £200, sir?'

'Sold to the lady here.'

'I will keep it for a rainy day.' Elle giggled at everybody except Tom.

In retaliation against Elle for losing her a making-it-up night away from home in a squishy hotel, Carla felt like bidding for the flamenco lessons but kept her senses about her. Bidding was furious as a large percentage of the female population of the school fought for the prize.

'What Elle wants Elle gets,' Tom said as they waded through the cinema crowds, and a queue of teenagers and bouncers outside the nightclub.

He put his arm around her protectively, the first sign of a thaw. She was pleased but didn't want to show it straight away.

'Do you realise you barely spoke to anyone else all night?'

'I was being friendly that's all . . .'

'She was all over you.'

'Now don't you start that again . . .' She felt Tom's arm go limp across her back.

'All right, all right, I'm sorry.' Maybe she said that a bit too quickly. 'And have you thought about how much time helping Elle will take?'

'What Elle wants Elle usually gets,' Tom repeated.

Carla put her hand to her mouth.

'What?'

'Nothing.'

'No, it's something, come on . . .'

'I was thinking – maybe she's going to try and persuade the manny to be in it; can you imagine the sales?'

'Maybe she's going to get him into that hotel for the night.'

'Yes! Tom, of course, I bet that's what she's up to.'

'You don't fancy him too, do you?' He gripped her tight again.

'How could I when I've got such a gorgeous husband,' she said, without missing a beat.

Chapter Ten

'I think they're just as happy here as in Legoland.' Elle dangled Tallulah over the Sheen rec swing and gently lowered her into the rubber caging, manoeuvring her tiny fat legs through the gap.

'Whichever,' said Antonia looking longingly at her watch. 'These places bore me senseless as soon as I'm through the gates.'

Wilf's favourite subject at school, the Inset teachers' training day, had come around. Sudden days off in the week geared by the local authorities to throw spanners at even the best-laid childcare plans.

'However many times I come I always think they'll simply go away and play and I'll get away with a break, but it never works out.'

'Children nagging their mothers to play with them all the time, mothers waiting for some horrible accident to happen. . .' Ant lifted Fizz, her three-year-old onto the metal horse.

'And I always want to go to the loo as soon as I get here,' said Carla. 'I don't know why.'

'So does Tallulah,' said Elle. 'Were you all right the other night Carl?'

'Yes, of course.'

'You seemed a bit quiet.'

Carla pushed Dyl in a gentle rhythm. Her annoyance had shown, of course it had shown.

'Not really. No, I wasn't.'

'It wasn't me, was it? I'm sorry if I monopolised Tom a bit.'

'It was more Tom being all over you, Elle, I hope he wasn't too much of a pest.'

'You'd've had a face as long as hers, Elle, if you'd had Jonathan Frost ear-holing you all night,' said Antonia, pushing the back bum seat of the red metal horse.

'So it was something, then.'

Carla pointedly looked down at Dyl and up at Elle.

'Everything's a bit up in the air, that's all,' she said matter-of-factly.

'So when isn't it!' Elle smiled, then stopped. 'Are you sure it was all right to ask him to help with the calendar?'

'What's a few hours here and there? All *right*, Dyl, hold your voice, will you?'

Dyl had done one of his shifts from happy swingy contented child sitting on toy horse to demented let-me-out-of-here caged monster son of child-murdering mother.

'Let's get them in the sandpit and go and sit down,' said Elle, lifting Tallulah out of the swing.

'It's that woman, isn't it,' she said as soon as they were out of toddler earshot.

'I'm still mad at myself for showing how she got to me.'

'You're too hard on yourself, Carla' said Antonia.

'I've taken it for years with Tom, it's been no problem before, so why did I go and open my mouth?'

'Because you needed to?' said Antonia.

'I don't do jealousy, Ant. . .'

'It's good to reveal your feelings, you have to let things out sometimes.'

'I've managed perfectly well until now.'

'Better than the rest of us, Carl.' Antonia raised her eyebrows at Elle.

Oh no, she thought, they're going to start teasing me.

'My perfectionist psychosis is my way of dealing with doing twenty jobs at once all the time, that's how I work, I can't help it!'

'All I'm saying is perhaps it's done you some good to reveal how you're feeling to Tom, instead of bottling it up all the time.'

'I don't bottle anything up! I've never had to! We tell each other everything, when we need to. Most of the time I don't *have* to reveal how I feel to Tom – he *knows* – just as I know how he feels.'

'A mystic link,' said Antonia darkly.

'It is. I don't mean to sound smug, but that's how it's been. Anyway, I'm feeling far from smug at the moment, aren't I.'

'It'll work out,' said Elle.

'He thinks the sun shines out of the arses of these people, that they're offering him all he's ever wanted, and so is putting my protestations down to an irrational dislike of this Danielle woman. I mean, *you* saw it, didn't you, Elle?'

'He *was* pretty mesmerised, Ant,' said Elle.

Carla's stomach flipped.

Wilf leaped off the speeding roundabout, his arms spreadeagled to balance himself before spinning Jon, holding on for all his life on the whirling platform.

'Wilf, *care*ful!' Carla called. 'My big worry isn't her; there've been hundreds like her before and will be hundreds like her in the future, that's how Tom is. It's the

103

Bruno connection that really scares me. Here's our one chance in life to get away from him and will we heck, but Tom won't see it, he simply won't see it . . .'

'He doesn't know his own value,' said Elle.

'That's it! If – I mean, when, he puts himself out there, he'll get offers pouring in but he doesn't buy it, says it's unnecessary, that we'll never get anything as good. Meantime he's steaming ahead with all these – meetings – and barely talking to me about it.'

Barely talking to her at all, despite their making up on the way back that night.

'I imagine it's one of those "worlds" isn't it, the furniture design business, where everybody who's anybody knows everybody else and what they're up to and what they're not up to and who's in and who's out,' said Antonia.

'Too right.'

'Is it just her then?' asked Antonia.

Carla shrugged. 'Oh there are these two sidekicks, European art dealers. But she's the main man, there's no doubt about that.'

'You never know, it could be good,' said Elle.

'Elle!'

'Sorry.'

'All I do know is Bruno Iassaci doesn't do people favours out of the kindness of his heart.'

'He'll still be at Carliatti though, won't he?'

'That's what worries me. If Tom hasn't been happy at Carliatti since the takeover, maybe Bruno feels the same and wants to get out and muscle in with Tom more than he realises.'

'Push, puuush, puuuuush,' Dyl and Fizz screamed from the horse, fighting for the superior front seat.

They stood up.

'Even with his fortune pay-out?'

'Now, hold tight.' Carla gripped Dyl's hands onto the peeling metal bar and gave the horse's mug-ugly red face a couple of hefty shoves. 'I don't know, it's a pretty big regime change and Bruno's used to holding the whip. He'll want in on it one way or another, that's for sure.'

'It does make sense though. If Tom's Bruno's protégé, he's not going to let him go just like that, is he?' said Antonia.

'Tom would have made it, eventually, without him.'

'It would have taken a long time, though, and even then there'd have been a different version of Bruno somewhere along the line, several different versions,' said Ant.

'Believe me, there's only one Bruno, Antonia.'

'All right, supposing you get your way and Tom sends these people packing, then what?'

'You're beginning to sound like Tom. Am I being so unreasonable? This is the only chance for the rest of our lives to get away from him.'

'Sounds like he's a good businessman,' said Antonia.

'You need that more than ever these days,' said Elle.

'Cut it, you two!' said Carla. 'But yes, he's got all the qualities. Ruthlessness, all the bluster, bullshittingness, arrogance, greed ...'

'Everything Tom doesn't have,' said Elle.

'And you don't have, Carla,' added Antonia. 'But you're right, you do have to explore all your options...' Antonia thought for a moment. 'Can't he stay where he is?'

Carla laughed at the simplicity of it. Couldn't things stay how they were? Just a few weeks ago?

'Apart from already giving his notice in.'

'Muuuuuuum?'

'No. He was never bitter about the money Carliatti

105

made, that was the deal, but since the Speranza takeover ... his artistic integrity's under threat, that's the real problem. It's not something he can live with, therefore it's not something any of us can live with.'

'What's he calling the new range again – Supernatural?' said Elle.

'Paranormal.' said Carla quickly, ignoring Wilf's shouts.

'Oh, funny. He told me the other night Supernatural.'

'Paranormal's the range he's doing for Speranza – Supernatural is still on the drawing board.' Why had he told Elle about Supernatural? It was still supposed to be a secret.

'Supernatural will be very limited, no big manufacture base; he really wants to do these portrait chairs, that's the thing, and Danielle's saying "yes – Thomas – go ahead – have as much money as it costs, Thomas" ... *Thomas*!!'

'It's a pretty big carrot, Carl.'

'Don't I know it.'

'What's a portrait chair anyway?' said Antonia.

'Have you heard of the Margaret Thatcher chair? It's a famous chair which looks like Margaret Thatcher.'

'Has it got a handbag?' said Antonia.

'No – honestly, you take one look at it and you would say, that is Margaret Thatcher. The designer's taken the essence of the woman and put it into this chair. That's what Tom wants to do. He wants to start with someone famous. Morrissey's his favourite at the moment.'

'What does it look like then?'

'Like Thatcher, tweedy fabric, checks, stiff-backed. I've got a picture at home, I'll show you ... anyway that's what Tom'd love to do, to commission. Rather than all this mass production stuff.'

106

'Mass production, sounds scary.' Elle shivered. 'It must be so complicated.'

Carla sagged.

'What *you* need to do is get something new in *your* life, Carl,' said Antonia.

Elle brightened. 'Yes, something to take your mind off it.'

'We'd all be like you if we were involved in our husbands' business doings.'

'Thanks.'

'No, really, I haven't a clue who Otto works with and I wouldn't want to know. Sometimes I have to – I *used* to have to – go to boring parties, but so what really, the bores are for him to deal with. Let them get on with it and do what you want to do.'

'I have plenty of interests, thanks all the same.'

'Beside all the domestic and school stuff, you need to get right out of it . . .'

'Like what?'

'I don't know – a sport . . .?'

'*Elle!*'

'Muuuuum.'

'You could come rowing with me on the Thames,' said Antonia.

Elle laughed with Carla at that.

'It'd just be another thing to try and fit into my days. I'm busy enough, thank you, and besides I have my garden, my fabrics, I never get enough time for them and if I don't feel like it I read. There's never enough time to read. In a *minute*, Wilf.'

'It's got to be out of that house. Nothing to do with the home and what's in the home,' said Antonia.

'Get a job, maybe?' suggested Elle. 'Something part-time, something that would interest you.'

'I have plenty of jobs, thanks very much.'

'Something different – take you out of yourself, like my dancing lessons. . .'

'Oh and of course there's no ulterior motive there, is there, Elle.'

'I don't know. I might surprise you and be the most brilliant snappa of the castanetas you've ever come across.'

'Mum, come on, get ON!' shouted Wilf.

'I'm *talking*, Wilf!' she shouted back.

'You're *always* talking. Come on. Dad always does!'

'I hope you're not going to do anything you regret, Elle, that's all.'

'Are you kidding!'

'MUM!'

'She's a single woman anyway, isn't she . . .' said Antonia.

'That is so.'

'Well, stop being so bloody happy about it,' Carla snapped.

'Halloween party on Friday,' said Antonia. 'You and me, Elle.'

'And me. Tom's not going to be there till later.'

'Why?'

'He's got a meeting.'

'With Danielle?'

'With Danielle. A dinner. He'll be along, but late.'

'When everyone's drunk,' laughed Elle.

'Must be some dinner to miss Jo Salmon,' Antonia whistled.

'See what I mean?'

They went over to Dyl and Tallulah who were trying to clamber back into the swings.

'Is Otto going?'

'He wouldn't miss Jo Salmon's just because I'll be there.'

'I thought you were friends.'

'We are. D'you know, I'm quite enjoying being celibate.'

'Celeb rate, celeb rate,' yelled Dyl.

Carla turned her back on the children. 'Celibacy, Elle, means a life without sex, not a day or so.'

'How would you know . . .?'

Wilf called her again from the roundabout.

'All right, all right.'

Carla left her friends and positioned herself on a blue splintered wedge of roundabout, carefully smoothing her skirt under her bottom. It worried her, that skirt. For days now she'd been unable to wear anything else. Grey. Grey wasn't good. Jon ran off to the slide. Wilf grabbed one of the rails, leaned forwards and pushed. Slowly, feeling her weight. Faster, finding the rhythm in his steps. Antonia's red coat blurred sunset streaks into the low, grey sky and then Elle went all fuzzy. She knew they were still talking about her. She could tell by the way they were both looking away from her.

Try a sport, get a job, puh! How ridiculous. Maybe she *was* going off Elle a little bit. Friendship wasn't unconditional, was it. And Elle was quite a new friend. If there was such a thing as unconditional friendship, then it'd be Beth, her fossil friend, her one good boarding school friend, their lives full of shared histories. They didn't need to be in each other's lives all the time, even if they didn't see each other from one year to the next. Elle was a friend of circumstance, of the kids and husbands, but she did *like* her! She *did*. Did she trust her? Of course she did. Elle was as refreshing and clear as glass. There was nothing not to trust in Elle.

The graffiti-streaked yellow, blue, orange of the climbing frame and the dull silver slide and the half-bare trees and the slanting roofs and the black stick stick stick of the railings fused with Dyl – screaming his head off on the long, red horse 'Come here, mummy! *Mummy*, come here!' Colour melting into colour, dissolving into a blur of streaks till there was just Wilf in sharp foreground focus, his trainers thud thud thudding on the grit, trying to scare her into yelling.

STOP!

She gripped hard as the roundabout slowed, focusing on the dog-walkers circling the dog-shit green, waiting for her head to catch up with her eyes.

Out of the blur came the figure of Elle running over to her.

'I've got it.'

'Got what?'

'You must share my lessons.'

'What lessons?'

'My dance lessons.'

'Mum? Dancing! ha ha haaaa,' Wilf sniggered before running off to join Jon on the big swings, folding the chain links over, making the seat go higher and higher.

'My son knows me better than you, Elle.'

'Come on! Why not?'

Carla looked sideways at Elle. 'Because, apart from anything else, my presence isn't going to help you any, is it? Or have you got some mysterious role for me in your plan of seduction?'

'I'm trying to help you out. Go on, just give it a try, I'm sure he won't mind it being the two of us – I paid enough for it! Go on, just for once then. Next Tuesday, 10.30, at Hill Mansions.'

Chapter Eleven

The indicator clicked and blinked green as Carla slid into the slow lane. She kept her hands loosely on the cream leather steering wheel and kept her motorway stare calm, steady and straight ahead. The blue direction signs multiplied into complicated terminal directions as the sky widened around the airport ahead.

She could feel the puzzle that was coming at her from him ever since they'd left Richmond.

Why was she being so nice to him?

Why hadn't she let him get a taxi as usual, considering how much she hated going to airports when she wasn't getting on a plane?

'I'm only being the supportive wife you want me to be, Tom,' she said after another silence that'd lasted too long.

Another puzzled look.

'I wish I'd let you get a cab now!'

'No. I like it, I could get used to this.' He leaned back heavily, put his hand on her knee and looked happily out of the window. It was a big, ice-melting gesture. Her offer the crack that'd made it possible. For the first time in over a week, Carla breathed evenly, refusing to allow herself to wonder if there was an extra Danielle-sized layer to his excitement, just as she wouldn't allow herself to think of her own day ahead. Not with Tom still in the car, no, she'd let it hang there, glowing in the horizon of London behind them, waiting to happen.

'What I find weird,' he said as they drove round the Concorde roundabout and into the Heathrow tunnel, 'is as soon as we get here all the cars are full of smart people, slouching around. Because they're going on a plane! Why should they look more interesting?'

'You're imagining it.'

'It's because they feel more interesting . . . Like you do, when you're flying, like I do now . . .'

'Because they're going somewhere else?' said Carla softly to herself as she pulled up at the kerb.

'Hope it goes well.' She kept her eyes straight ahead. She really did hate airport goodbyes. No matter he was only going for a day.

'Do you?' Tom forced her to look at him.

'I do. Give my best to Danielle. Oh, and if you get a chance, try and grab some of those anchovies . . . they'll have them at the airport . . .'

'Will you pick me up then?'

She glared at him. He cuffed her cheek. 'Only joking, see you later. I'll be back by story time, *Simpsons* time if I can get that earlier flight. Love you.'

'Love you.'

She smiled to herself as she watched him walk away. His leather shoulder bag slung casually over his crumply beige jacket. The cheek cuff the final confirmation the row was now over, official.

She'd conceded, she'd endorsed the trip to Danielle HQ. Though she'd not told him yet, and wouldn't for as long as she could hold out, she'd had to change her objections to Bruno to ones of damage limitation. Ant had

112

helped her source a lawyer, poised to go over in minutest detail anything with any resemblance of a dotted line anywhere near it or its envelope.

Meantime, she had her own life to be getting on with.

'Strange, isn't it, the way you can live somewhere for so long and not know it at all,' she said to Elle. 'I must've passed this building a thousand times but have never noticed it.'

Waiting to cross the road, they were both looking up at the tall, skinny Edwardian block on top of the Hill. Splinters of wood showed through the bubbling cream paintwork of the matching, paired balconies. The window frames looked soft and unsafe and were painted a horrible brown that matched the dark red brickwork turning damp and dark at the edges.

'Odd for such a prime part of Richmond Hill left undeveloped.'

'Creepy. It must've fallen through a hole somewhere.'

'Invisible next to that thing.' Carla nodded towards its gleaming, 60s Mediterranean-style neighbour, with windswept palm trees and striped canopied terraces, uniformed porters and burgundy-red tennis courts.

They went up the short, broad, tiled drive and examined the list of fat white bells. There was a clattering behind the double doors. They jumped as one side opened. A little old lady peered up at them suspiciously as she carefully stepped down, closing the door firmly behind her.

'Can't see it here,' said Elle.

Carla watched the lady walking away, then looked out to the far horizon of the sea of trees opposite. Planes the size of fleas rose and fell into Heathrow. One of them, with an even tinier flea inside it that was Tom, clutching his even teenier V&T with its even teenier lumps of ice.

'What do we do? There's no number 2 here ...'

A flock of crows appeared from nowhere, flying left to right in the cold, sunny sky, calling noisily to each other. A cloud shadow moved across Petersham meadow towards the silver snake of river.

Carla turned back. Elle had disappeared around to the side of the building. Carla hunched her coat up close to her chin and followed.

She found her standing triumphantly next to a small, white door.

The bell made a rusty rumble.

No answer.

'That's that then,' said Elle disappointedly.

They stood in silence, listening to the Terrace fountain trickling on the other side of the road and the distant whoosh of traffic down in the town.

Carla pressed it again.

Drilling broke out on a distant building site.

Disappointed, but then, glad in some ways. They could go round to Cyn's and have a nice familiar cup of coffee in that warm, familiar post-drop-off atmosphere of bitchiness and gentle gossip.

There was a movement and then there he was, smiling and holding the door open.

She hung back a little, leaving it to Elle, who was apologetically checking they had the right time, and explaining that this was her friend she'd left a message for him about. Of course, yes it was the right time, yes, Carla was expected.

'Sorry I can't offer you a view,' he said, holding his arm up to usher them into the main room. Dark walls, dust swirls, whiffs of damp fusing with a musty joss-sticky smell. Not a squit of a hint of a child or children anywhere. No pee or powder; the dust felt like it had settled into the air undisturbed for decades by bursts of juvenile energy.

114

'Would you like a coffee before we start?'

'Oh – yes!' they said together.

Elle sat on the brown leather sofa against the wall opposite the tiny kitchenette. There was a lot of brown, and green. Ferns, plants, and crystals and dangly things in the window. Where were the family? Where were the two little boys?

Carla sat in an armchair. They watched him moving around. Everything about him was long: his legs, in faded black jeans; his ears, studded with silver stars; his Romanesque nose; his dark hair tucked neatly behind his ears. His movements, deliberate, like the way he'd walked that day she and Elle had followed him, the movements of someone who was sure of himself, of who he was, of where he was going.

She looked around the room. It was large, with chipped parquet floors disappearing up hallways and lots of tatty books on shelves everywhere. She went over and picked one out at random. She read without reading, turning the filmy pages, looking around. Balinese masks, Indian hookahs, Indian throws; her professional eye picked out a good one. She went over and touched it, felt the weight of it. Blue-tacked to the wall were large black and white photographs of landscapes which looked like women and of women who looked like landscapes. A dusty second-hand-looking TV. A CD player with untidy stacks of CDs. She resisted the urge to flick through them. She felt young again, studenty and different.

'Black or white?' he called from the kitchen.

'Black,' said Elle.

'Me too,' said Carla.

She never had it black.

Elle didn't notice.

He scraped the magazines and newspapers on the old

shipping trunk coffee table to one side and placed plates of
fruit cake, paw paw and melon.

'Where are the children?'

'They are my brother's. He has the penthouse here, the
whole of the top floor.' He sat down beside Elle, making
Elle's cushion go up.

'Oh, I see,' said Elle, cosily turning towards him.

'You didn't think they were mine!' he laughed.

'No – no . . .'

'I'm his manny.'

'Yes, we – know that.'

'Are you hungry?'

'*Star*ving.' Carla sat up straight, 'I had to drop my
husband off at the airport straight after school drop-off, so
I didn't have time for a proper breakfast.'

'How long is he away?'

'Oh, just for a day. A meeting, you know . . .'

'He's the designer, isn't he?'

'Yes. Yes, that's right.'

'So you saw the article then?' said Elle.

'Who didn't?'

'Mr Punjani, he, he put us out rather – prominently –
didn't he?'

He held his look at her as he handed her her coffee.

'You're a little nervous?'

'I've never done anything like this before.'

'Nor have I,' piped up Elle behind him.

'Nor have I,' he laughed, going back back into the
kitchen.

Carla sipped at her coffee. It was thick and strong. 'So
– how come you're here?' she called.

'It's like what you call gap year?'

'No, I meant how come – how come you get this place,
why aren't you up in the penthouse . . .?'

'It's better to be alone. Besides, my brother has the space, he owns the block.'

'The whole block?'

'Yes.'

Carla and Elle exchanged glances.

'So you're having a year off before starting work?' asked Elle.

He laughed. 'No. A few months only. To see London, help my brother a little bit. Then I do more studying.'

'Studying what?'

'Dance!'

'So – you're professional?

'I hope to be. Though I hope, of course, you will enjoy the lessons, you will be helping me. I have to learn to teach as well.'

He leaned across Elle and picked up a piece of cake.

'I've always wanted to meet one of those families you see in the magazines,' he said to Carla. 'There's something so strange about them, the husband, the wife, the children, everything worked out, even to the tea towels. I'll admit it, I didn't think you really existed, you people.'

Carla laughed politely.

'You live in beautiful houses in beautiful places ... You're married to successful men. . .'

'I'm successful in my own right,' said Elle indignantly, 'and I'm not married.'

'She's getting divorced.'

'I'm sorry.'

'You don't have to be,' said Elle.

'And what do you do?'

'I'm a photographer.'

'And you?'

Carla shrugged.

'You've seen the house,' said Elle.

'We're completely normal, really. Except it doesn't usually look that tidy.'

'It must have taken a lot of work.'

'We've both worked very hard.'

He turned to Elle. 'You know, I'm not so interested in what people do for work. I like to know what they do for play. What do you do for play?'

'We don't get time to play, do we, Carl?'

'My play's limited to Sneaky Sharks and the Yes No Game at the moment, I'm afraid,' said Carla.

'What do you like to do? No. What do you love to do?'

'Oh – Embroidery. Gardening. Cooking. The house, of course. My children, my family. The house, my husband's career needs looking after, I do the accounts, the bookings, all his appearances ... But I love embroidery, the detail of it, the rules, the structures. With something real to show for it at the end.'

'It is the same with dance! Flamenco has a lot of hidden structure. Through the structure it allows the emotion to fall out, tumble out, but first you get the structure. It's so hidden in your mind you forget it's there, only when it is in your soul... then you can let go!'

'Isn't it about time we did a bit of letting go?' said Elle, looking at her watch.

'OK, first lesson. What do you know about flamenco?'

'Er – lots of clapping, guitars, stamping ...'

'Gypsies,' added Carla helpfully.

'The first thing you must know is it is always an alive thing. What I mean is it is always adapting, changing. This is how it grew, from the gypsies, yes, but also the Phoenicians, the Moors, the Romans and the Jews, from all these places. And then new flamenco brings in the ballet, the contemporary dance ...'

118

'So what came first? The guitar or the singing or the dancing?' asked Carla.

'El cante! The song! Then behind it the guitar and the dance. Still, we are concerned with the dancing. The movements of the arms and hands, and the *zapateado*, the rhythms of the feet . . .'

'When did you start learning?'

'I began when I was five.'

He crouched down in front of the CD player, his back to them.

'The other thing you must know is the mixture. Of the song, the dance and the guitar, you cannot separate them. Then with this mixture you stir in the emotions: sadness, passion, joy. 'Now,' he clapped his hands together. 'Take your shoes off and stand up please.'

He reached behind the sofa and brought out three square metal mats.

'I'll keep mine on, if you don't mind,' said Carla.

'No, you must take them off.'

'But I never . . .'

'Look at them!'

She picked a foot up; they were only one-inch heels. 'No, really, I'll be fine.'

'Take them off, please.'

'We're not going to be leaping all over the place in our first lesson . . . Flamenco shoes have heels, don't they?'

'Short, thick heels. Apart from anything, the floor . . . please . . .'

Carla sighed, sat down and took her shoes off. She'd only ever worn flat shoes once on a one-off visit to a gym and didn't know which she'd detested more, the tracksuit which made her expand two sizes widthways or the trainers which shrunk her two inches lengthways.

She stood on tiptoe next to him.

'Put your feet flat on the ground, please.'

'I can't.'

'What do you mean?'

'My feet won't go flat, this is how I walk barefoot, honestly!'

'You have to use your heels, come on, try.'

'I'm telling you I *can't*!'

'You're talking to a woman whose flip-flops have got heels,' said Elle without irony. Carla made a face at her.

He looked flustered. 'Sit down please.'

Before she could stop him he'd knelt down and had his hands on her feet, gently massaging her instep.

Anxious to get back to base earth from where the sensations in her feet were taking her and away from the murder-her murder-her look on Elle's face, Carla hunted for something to say.

'That table there's an Erco.'

'What?'

'Your table, the varnish has peeled a bit, but you could get it done up.'

'It's not mine. Beside, it's an old table, what is interesting about it?'

'You're not interested in interiors, then?' said Elle.

'I hate design.'

Carla felt like she'd been slapped.

'Why call it interiors? All this fuss about this chair or that chair. What colour the wall is, what shape the tap is. This is all exteriors. Who cares?'

Sweat prickled at the back of her neck. 'It's a lot more than that,' she said defensively.

'What is a house?'

'Your home, the place you spend most of your time in.'

'A space enclosed by bricks.'

'But good space is interesting, isn't it?' said Elle.

'To make a nice place to live inside can be attractive – but to devote your life to it!' He shrugged.

'I can see you don't,' said Carla cattily, looking around.

'More interesting is what is outside.'

'We do go outside, you know, as well as having nice homes. What's wrong with that?' said Elle.

'But what do you see?'

'The same as you, I expect.'

'What?'

'Trees, the sky, the park, the view, friends, restaurants, shops . . .'

'Shops, shops, shops, to buy more things for the insides of your homes, for the insides of your stomachs. Everywhere is over-designed but all the same. The shops the same, the food the same . . .'

'But it's how you put it together. Every place is individual,' said Carla. 'It reflects your personality.'

'Your own space is without limit. Don't close it in behind walls. Better to go for a walk. I walk four hours every day.'

Both Elle and Carla laughed derisively.

'You're living in a fantasy world then. No one has time for . . .'

'Exactly what I am saying. Time and space, they are there to be taken.'

'Not when you have a family, they're not.'

'Except most people choose not to . . . You chose to have your children, but even with children you can work at it.'

'I don't think you understand,' said Carla.

'This is it!' said Elle. 'This is our time and space. Coming to your lessons. That's good, isn't it?'

'Yes, but it's not what I am talking about. It is the way you see.'

'Carla lives with a creative genius; I think she knows what you're on about.'

'Chairs. To sit on.' He laughed.

Carla pulled her feet out of his hands and stood up. 'Very special chairs!'

'Award-winning chairs,' added Elle.

'I'm sorry, I'm sorry,' he shrugged, still smiling, not looking sorry at all.

'I think I'll leave now.' Carla felt drained.

'You're bound to feel like that, you're a dancer,' said Elle, ignoring her. 'You have a different talent, that's all. You should respect other people's talents.'

'I do.'

'You have photographs on the wall. You should see Elle's photographs!' said Carla.

'So you judge people by their talent.'

'What rot!' Carla picked up her shoes and stockings.

'Good, I think we're ready to begin!' He took Carla firmly by the hand and led her to one of the squares.

'See!' he said to Elle. 'She's walking! That's good, very good! Now – stand.'

Carla stood simmering on her metal mat, glowering at Elle.

Though only an inch closer to the ground, Carla felt shorter, fatter, older and totally humiliated.

'Remember what I said, first you have the structure, then you can break out of it. We start with a very simple structure of course . . . think you are the bull in a bullfight. Think of the fury of the bull, the temper, the terrible terrible temper of him, like you now, Carla. Then the calmness of the fighter, the skill, the way a good lover is with a woman, in control, quiet, calm control. We are aiming for the space in between these two creatures where they meet in blood.'

122

'How the hell do you put that into a dance?' said Elle.

'You don't "put" it into the dance. It is not a cake you are making, Elle. It is a feeling, the feeling of deep, deep passion that your life depends on, like the bull's, but, most important, you are proud, you are ready to be taken but not yet.'

'I think we should have gone for the tap-dancing, Elle . . .' said Carla pointedly.

'I am sorry, I am getting a little too advanced for you, you are right. First we must learn the basics, but even with these steps it is up to you to interpret, keep to the discipline, the strict discipline, and then you can let yourself loose in it. Amazing things can happen. Let your heart speak, that is all.'

'It needs someone to pull the strings first,' said Elle.

'Are you comfortable with standing now?' He frowned at Carla.

'Now, you learn how to stand.' He moved about her, lifting her chin, loosening her shoulders.

'Good. Good. Now. What shall we do?' He looked at the ceiling in thought. 'OK, I know, we take this from embroidery, from Carla. This is the first lesson. Dance is a pattern, OK? You make a pattern with your feet, think of yourself as your thread.'

He picked up her hands and put them on her waist.

'Stand straight, Elle.'

Elle had gone into a slouch, hoping for a bit of the hands-on treatment, which she got. Though he was doing it half jokingly, like she was a bendy toy.

'Now, listen.'

'To dance you must be at one with the music.' He tapped his foot. 'With the beat. Not behind the beat. OK? Not in front of the beat. OK? Right on top of it, as it comes so you come.'

And he was off. His movements transformed.

'Don't think about the past. Don't think about the future. Stop all thoughts. Think only of each present moment as it comes. Be inside the moment. You are the thread, weaving yourself in and out, making a beautiful pattern.'

He began weaving in and out in front of Carla and around her and behind her, showing off for all he was worth.

'Don't be scared! Relax! Fall into it, fall in love with it, love it, love the beat. When you have so much love you can't fear anything, then you can dance.' He stopped abruptly. 'Now,' he clapped his hands together brusquely twice, 'your turn.'

'You. have. got. to. be. joking,' said Elle.

'Stillness is as important as the movements. Dignity. Control. First, always we begin with the simplest. Like this. OK. Clap your hands.'

'Count one, two, three, then stamp. That's OK. Good, now. One, two, three, stamp to the side. That's it. Now one two, three, stamp, one, two, three, stamp to the side. One, two, three, and turn around. Now, with your arm in the air, turn around. OK, now from the beginning, One, two, three, stamp, and turn around, and back, and good wrist work, that's right ...' Carla felt like her hair had been swept up into a bun, her lips as red as her dress. She'd gathered a clutch of skirt and was swirling it backwards and forwards as she turned ...

She wanted to yell out, to sing; instead she couldn't stop smiling.

The music stopped and they had to leave.

Cyn and Ant were waiting patiently up the road for the post-mortem.

'I think you needed to shake the air around your head a

124

little, maybe it was getting a little stale,' he had said to Carla as they left.

'Yes, maybe it was.'

'Told you,' said Elle as soon as the door was closed.

They tripped lightly down the path and along the road to Cynthia's. Carla felt her heels had grown six inches taller.

Elle was quiet.

'I really enjoyed that.'

'I could tell!' said Elle.

'He's an arrogant bugger though, isn't he? Do you still like him?'

'I'd be his bull any day.'

'Take a bit of advice from me for a change - don't be so up-front and flirty. Not all men like it.'

Chapter Twelve

'I thought you were going to invite him here for a coffee?'
'You didn't think, after one lesson, we would really do
that,' said Elle.

Feeling like an actor who'd forgotten her lines, Carla
kept her focus away from Elle and on Ant and Cyn.

'Did he dance with you?' Cyn asked.

'We don't want to know about the dancing,' said Ant.

Carla flinched.

Ant laughed. 'Look at her! She's gone all coy!

'You should have seen her!' said Elle.

'Shut it, you lot!' She couldn't help smiling. She wished
she'd gone straight home. She didn't want to share
anything. She sat quietly while Elle filled them in.

'So who is this brother?' said Cyn.

'You know, they were at the auction.'

'I'd like to get my hands on him, it's a disgrace that
building . . .' said Ant.

A young woman, still in her nightdress, padded past in
fluffy pink flip-flop slippers.

'Here's someone who gets up even later than me,' said
Elle.

'Leave her alone, she's been doing the Star and Garter

night shift,' said Cyn.

'How many relatives have you got stashed away here, Cyn?' said Ant.

Cyn shrugged. 'There's plenty of room, isn't there?'

'What does Rick say about it?' said Carla.

'He loves it. All the girls around, like being on tour, isn't it.'

'Come on Carla, give us a show!' said Cyn.

Carla bent down and unstrapped her shoes, kicking them off into the centre of the floor. She tapped her foot . . .

'Keen,' said Cyn. 'Did he dance with you?'

'He did more than dance with her,' said Elle.

They all looked at Carla.

'I got a bit of a massage, that's all.'

'Where?'

Carla pointed at her feet.

'I have to learn to put my feet on the floor, like this . . .' She stood up and gathered her skirt to one side.

'Here we go,' Cyn giggled.

Carla stopped, mid-tap and glared at Cyn. 'Do you want me to or not?'

'Shush up, Cyn, and let's see this,' said Ant.

Elle picked at her fingers.

'Come on Elle,' said Cyn.

'No, Carla will show you.'

'Weren't you paying attention?' said Ant.

'Cut it, and anyway, why aren't you at work?'

'Why aren't you at work?'

'I shall be in a moment.' Elle looked at her watch. 'Thanks for reminding me. I'm photographing toddler twins, can you imagine? I'd better get going.' She picked up her bag.

Carla swung her skirt, flicking it left and right as she tapped.

'This is how it goes, it's only the very basics but you can get quite a rhythm going can't you, Elle – tap tap, stamp, tap tap stamp.'

'What's Tom going to say?' said Cyn.

Carla looked up from her feet.

'I haven't thought.' She hadn't, she realised as she said it, she hadn't thought about Tom, or Bruno, or Danielle, or Tom and Bruno, or Tom and Danielle for the whole morning. 'Tom's not going to know,' she added, stamping herself around 360 degrees.

Knowing looks were exchanged.

'No. It's not what you think!'

More smirks.

'Stop it, you lot. He was far too arrogant for me. What I did enjoy, I don't mind saying, was the dancing.'

She gathered her skirt, stamped and began turning.

'It's as much about arms as feet.' She put one arm in the air, dropping her wrist and pointing her fingers.

'Look at those hands go,' said Cyn. 'Come on Elle.'

'I need a few more lessons first.'

Carla's fingers were moving, turning, twisting, spinning, pointing.

'O – lay ...' Cyn began clapping. Ant began double clapping.

She'd found her stage. Not Tom's. Not the boys'. Her own.

'Morning girls.' Everyone jumped out of their skins.

All movement and sound ceased.

A small, wiry man in black leather trousers and tiger-stripe shirt unbuttoned to the chest went to the sink, the chains chinking on his cowboy boots as he walked. A few moments later, a big man in a graffiti'd denim waistcoat and equally dangly, complicated-looking trousers came in and helped himself to a biscuit. Carla recognised him immediately by his red dreadlocks as Scud's drummer.

'Don't mind us, ladies, you all carry on!' said the small man, filling a kettle at the sink.

Cyn was the most shocked of all, her mouth opening and closing like a fish.

Rick clicked the kettle on. 'Got in at 4 this morning, love,' he said, twisting round to Cyn. 'Crashed on the sofa with the TV, didn't want to wake you. Don't let me stop you, ladies!'

They all moved to the table, changing the subject as they went to all things mundane – the Christmas fair, the recipe book.

Rick ruffled Cyntha's hair before lighting a cigarette and settling himself down with his coffee mug next to her.

'What's been going on then?'

'We're talking about the calendar for the school,' said Elle, still standing clutching her bag. 'We're looking for models.'

'It's a nudie one, Rick,' said Cyn.

Rick ran his tongue across his teeth. 'What, with blokes as well?'

'We – haven't actually decided that yet,' said Elle awkwardly.

Rick Sick might have a fan base of millions, but the Alexander household wasn't one of them. Whenever Carla looked at him she couldn't help having strange premonitionary feelings that Dyl could easily turn out to be part of whatever the 2020 version of Scud might be. Much as she would still love him, of course, she had nightmare visions of herself tiptoeing around his gangly friends, as they filled her house with their grungy size 8s. Not Wilf, though, she should be thankful for that. Wilf didn't have Dyl's hidden demons.

'If you find yourselves stuck, and I'm in the country . . .'

He smiled round at them like he was doing them the biggest favour ever.

'That's kind,' said Elle non-committally.

'See – Rocky,' he said, 'see what the wife gets up to when we're away.'

'Whassat?' Rocky dragged up a chair, his muscled, tattooed arms bulging out of the fringes of his waistcoat.

'Cyn's going in a naked calendar!' He leaned back and laughed.

Rocky and Cyn laughed with him.

The others sat in po-faced silence.

'I didn't say I was in it!'

'You are though, aren't you Cyn, you have to be.' He turned to Elle. 'She's in it, isn't she?'

'If she wants to be,' said Elle, shifting from one foot to the other.

'See?'

Rocky yawned and rubbed his eyes.

Cyn got him a mug and poured him a coffee.

'So, as I was saying,' Ant piped up out of the blue to Elle, 'if we could collect, say, thirty recipes, that'd do it. See how many you can manage. Out of 500 parents you're bound to . . .'

'And we must get the kids to illustrate it.'

Carla couldn't think about recipes. She resented this abrupt interruption. As much as she'd been reluctant at first to disclose any information about the lesson, having made the decision to tell all she was now missing talking about it. She got up to leave.

'I'll collect Dyl, if you like,' said Elle.

'Oh – OK, thanks.'

Glad she could be alone for a while, she stopped off at Hill Terrace and sat down on a bench by the fountain, trying to catch hold of her thoughts, her feelings. She

130

watched the squirrels, rushing around the grassy slopes in jerky film movements. Her mind, in the time she'd been there, had emptied. Emptied of other peoples' problems, other peoples' whereabouts. Even Tom's.

A cluster of mean-looking clouds was scudding in from the west.

The clouds reached the sun, putting out the sheen on the river below with a lightbulb-blowing ping. The passers-by began moving a lot faster, like the world had been dimmed and speeded up a notch all in the same moment.

By the time she reached the bottom of the Hill, she felt she'd sorted it out in her mind. Not telling Tom would give her a little part of her life to call her own, a little harmless secret. Then, when she was really good, she'd surprise him. She went into HMV. Bypassing the usual Easy Listening and Kids DVDs, she cruised the aisles looking for the World Music section.

Tom called to say he'd be late. She was glad for the time to herself after the children had gone to bed. Itching to get her fingers on some fabric, she wanted to make a start with the auction commission.

'You choose,' the woman had said. 'Nothing too twee, though!'

She went upstairs to her fabric cupboard, a large chest with drawers stuffed full of snippets of fabrics. Some she'd collected specifically to make clothes; other pieces just to touch, to feel, to stroke. She let her hands feel their way through, the way she always started. You want untwee? I'll give you untwee!

The mood of the piece always began with texture, the rough and smooth of her feelings which were, that night, bold, bright and flashing. She chose stiff, crunchy black poplin and grainy yellow silk she could already feel

131

descending from bold strips to the thinnest, finest threads barely there.

Her scissors met the black material with crunchy precision, slicing thread by thread through the fabric. She liked that sound. It had a richness, a no-going-back purposefulness. Once you'd cut, you'd cut. You couldn't change your mind.

She arranged the larger pieces of yellow and began tacking in big white stitches. As she sewed so her breathing slowed and her thoughts wandered. Familiar thoughts at first: Tom. On a plane somewhere, or stuck at an airport, or in Milanese traffic, or not stuck at all but enjoying some piss-elegant liquor bar with polished chrome and throaty gurgling espresso machines. Mundane thoughts: espresso machines made her think of hobs. Could she get a new hob in before all the uncertainty began? With a lava-stone barbeque they'd eat much more fish. Abstract thoughts: all the people she'd never meet and never see doing all different things right that minute whilst she was sitting there in Richmond. Mountaineers sheltering in their tiny tents; prisoners in sordid cells with hope their only option; lions prowling in Africa; lovers on warm coral beaches; big forests; fuggy nightlubs; the clatter and tinkle of elegant restaurants, their back-kitchens steaming and shouting; then back and round again, to the dance and to Elle, snapping the toddler twins. She pulled the thread through to the back and snipped it off. Otto. What had happened to Otto? He hadn't been around lately. Tom had been too busy to see him. She must get Tom out with Otto. See what was going on.

Before threading up again, she put on one of her new CDs. The guitars sounded soft and echoey. She pulled the needle through. People gathered on stools, old men in shabby suits smoking, women with flashing eyes and dark, serious beauty, shawls, fans, movement. She sketched with fine white chalk onto the black. Old Spain, with the Moors; the Alhambra. The bulls; blood-red Spain.

Her hand worked fast, tiny white stitch upon tiny white stitch, slashes, gashes, of the rain outside, streaking across the fabric. It was like nothing she'd ever sewn before.

Chapter Thirteen

Carla topped her glass of tonic water with crushed ice. The rich purr of Jo Salmon's sub-zero fridge turned to a deep rumble. With its Baumatic Freestanding Dual Fuel Cooking Theatre, interior-lit gliding drawers and runways of pale beech cupboards which opened in ingenious ways, Jo Salmon's low-lit Shaker kitchen was as American as Jo Salmon.

'I had to reserve the Gym for Toby's party back in July!'

Carla, momentarily struck that she'd been standing with Bryony Baxter without for once feeling intimidated, glanced down at her broomstick, wishing it could take her up and out of there. She was standing in an awkward early party group with Gandalf, two Dumbledores, three witches, a Frankenstein, a Goth, a ghost and a skeleton, gathered as if in homage around the double-doors of Jo's steel, almost walk-in-sized fridge.

'I had to! These parties are so – popular now, in fact I *might* set up a standing order ...!'

'It gets worse each year, doesn't it.' Hannah's dreamy voice floated from somewhere below layer upon layer of white sheeting.

'The shops are full of such *trash*, aren't they! And then there's Christmas! Now, whilst there's so many of us here I wonder if I could have a quick word about nits! YEOWCH!' Bryony thrust her hips forward.

'Muuu-m, can you open my Fruit Winder?'

All eyes went down to a slime-faced Toby Baxter, jangling with plastic masks, spiders, rats and brooms.

'No, Toby! And take that fork out of my bottom! Go *away*!'

Jo appeared, unable to look anything but gorgeous, even with her hair pulled into orange spikes and wearing an inflated bright orange pumpkin suit. With her pumpkin stomach, she butted her way through the gathering crowds reaching for their first drinks, clutching a large box of fireworks under her arm. 'Help. Help. Somebody, *help*, what do I *do* with these.'

'Here, let me.' The Frankenstein figure took them from her.

Jo shook her arms. 'Brrrrr. Thanks, Frank . . . Put them somewhere – *away*, will you?'

'What's the problem?'

'They're *fireworks!*'

'They're illegal in the States, aren't they?'

'Too right.'

'So it's OK to own a gun but not a sparkler,' said the skeleton.

'You got it, hey, come on, drink up.' Jo grabbed a bottle. 'Come on, you all look like a group of Richmond Hill Infant and Junior School parents at the beginning of a party, get it on . . .' She patted Frankenstein heftily on the back.

'We were just talking about nits!' said Bryony.

'You want a nit story? I got a nit story for you!' Jo put the bottle down and picked up her drink.

'. . . so, there I was having the most fantastic Korean head massage, and then the girl disappears, returning with my stylist.'

'Where was this?'

'This was at Reid's, where else?'

'Oh my worrrd,' Carla said, catching her American twang.

'Nnnnn huh. So there I was, one nit and kicked out by my butt onto the streets of Mayfair . . .'

'I'm surprised it didn't make the magazines.'

'That's why we pay their prices, honey. But it still could, so watch it you guys. If I'm reading about this in *Heat* next week – I KNOW IT'S ONE OF YOU. Oh Kay?'

'But you had wet hair! How did you get *home!*'

'Oh, I was put in an isolation area and blow-dried, without a comb of course, from a distance. Like the girl, the most junior of the juniors probably was employed for that purpose. I'm surprised they didn't put a screen around me!'

'Did you have to pay?' asked Frankenstein.

'No! That was the only good thing? They just wanted me out of there.'

'Good way to get a free wash and blow,' said Frankenstein.

Carla noticed his podgy fingers. Bryony's husband Phil, identified.

'You know something? In the States if a single nit is ever found on a child's head it gets sent home,' said Jo, looking over her shoulder. 'This place is filling up isn't it, the trouble is I don't know who anyone is . . . Hey HEY – how're you doing?'

There was a collective intake of breath as Jo departed.

Carla waited for it. And there it came.

'We should do the same!' said Bryony.

'Naah, they'd become currency,' said Frankenstein.

'They'd all be nicking each others' nits to get the day off,' said the skeleton dryly.

'Toby'd start breeding them and open a black market ...' said Frankenstein indulgently.

'A right flea market, that'd be,' said Hannah.

Carla's scalp prickled. A psychosomatic itching nagged at the back of her neck and she daredn't touch it.

There was a tugging at her dress. 'Mum, can you unwrap my Fruit Winder?'

Carla took the packet and handed it back to Wilf, who handed it back to Toby, standing right behind him, and handed her another one.

She unwrapped one of the small silver packages, looking around for Tom even though she knew it was far too early for him to appear.

'Toby isn't *allowed* those!' said Bryony.

'Take them off him, then!' said Carla crossly walking away, surreptitiously touching the back of her neck as she escaped through the utility room. The front room was almost empty. Sparse piano music with lots of spaces and silences was plinkety-plonking out of the speakers. At waist-level and below, phantom devil children raced and darted.

Through the clockwork bats whirring in the semi-darkness, peering through the eerie mist of dry ice shrouding the small groups of laughing, drinking ghosts and ghouls, she spotted Elle with Otto over by the grand piano, together but not together. Elle was wearing a black cat suit and a studded leather belt hanging loosely on her hips. They had their arms draped over each other, chattering, looking like the least separated couple she'd ever set eyes on. She felt her brow with the back of her hand. It was burning hot.

She imagined Tom and Danielle together at that moment,

137

talking intensively about the future. She shouldn't be here, she should be there, it was her future too. Wasn't it?

Tom always stuck close to her at school events, trusting her to beat away the Anne and Jonathan Frosts of the world with whips and forked tongues if necessary. On her way to Elle she was stopped by another sheet-covered person. Someone with a child with speech difficulties in year 1 who seemed to know her pretty well.

She was rescued from a forced conversation by Cyn and Rick.

'You look lovely, Cyn,' she said, looking down at her minuscule black fluffy mini-dress with over-the-knee black fur boots, 'but what are you supposed to be?'

'Spider's woman, man,' said Rick.

'What about Rick then? said Cyn.

For a second, Carla didn't know what to say. As far as she could tell, he was in his normal everyday black leather metal gear.

'Still in the country then Rick?'

'Shouldn't've been.'

'Berlin,' said Cynthia.

'We rescheduled.' He took a drag of his cigarette. 'Didn't fancy it anyway, to be honest.'

See? she nagged at the absent Tom; even Rick Sick managed to schedule a gap between stadium gigs.

'Who wants a beer then?' Rick's drummer joined them, cracking off gold cans of beer and handing them out.

'That's what I like to see, on the shorts already,' he said eyeing Carla's glass, a ferret-toothed grin appearing through his beard.

'No – no, it's tonic water, neat, thanks.'

'I'll get you another.' He took her glass.

She looked around. Looking for Tom through all the masks, skeletons, bats, ghosts and ghouls.

'G, B or V?'

She looked at her watch; it was nearly 9. She'd held off drinking long enough.

'A small V, thanks.'

The drone returned. For what seemed like an age, Carla listened politely, glad to have somewhere to stand which didn't take much effort.

More voices.

Rocky handed her her glass before joining Cyn and Rick, who'd been gently backing away from the drone, making two separate groups.

Oh dear, she hoped they didn't get Tom drunk and signing stuff. She should have gone with him, however uncool she might have made him look. She'd have to give herself a title, that was it. Something other than 'wife'. A name in the company, his manager, she'd have to start calling herself that, get involved before it was too late. If it hadn't been Jo's party she would have insisted on going.

There was a fluster of activity in Elle's corner of the room, where Jo and the celebutantes were hanging out. A gone-to-seed rock musician she'd once had pinned to the inside lid of her her desk at boarding school, and Marcus Dowe.

'OK, folks,' Jo called. 'Anybody who wants to see the show, upstairs one level and through the door straight ahead.'

Carla glanced at the front door as she passed.

Put together by Jo's 'friends', no one ever knew who might appear from the roster of the Hill's acting crowd. Anne Frost had been banging on for weeks about how she'd heard a rumour that Helen Baxendale was putting in a cameo role.

Elle joined her. 'Tom not here yet?' she said as they

went up the central staircase staircase together and into the drawing room above.

'No.'

'BLOODY hell!'

'What the FU...'

Smoking cauldrons lined the walls of the large, blackened-out room. Coming straight out of a mist of dry ice, dangling cobwebs and spiders, was a full-size mummy. Covered in white bandages with bits of blood around the mouth and eyes, walking towards them, its arms held in front of it.

Black, black, too much black. Carla felt dizzy, but other guests were now crowding in from behind, making it impossible to back out. Children squealed and darted hysterically. For a split second she wondered if the character beneath the bandages could be Tom, playing one of his tricks. She was pushed and shoved as the room exploded with shrieking, laughing children, leaping out from behind the drapes. Armed with twelve-packs of Sainsbury's economy loo rolls, they raced for the grown-ups and began wrapping them up.

'I'm going to get you little so and sos,' said Elle racing for them, grabbing a roll of tissue herself and twisting it round a squealing boy's midriff. The room turned into a battleground.

Carla fought them off with a successful gavotte of shrieks and growls till the room filled to capacity.

'Halt!' The mummy called. As one, all the children stopped what they were doing and turned to him.

He ripped off his bandages. Breathing heavily, Carla felt a tiny ripple of disappointment as she saw the slender, bouncing Tom-figure revealed as another stranger.

He ushered the children to the front of the makeshift stage, bubbling with more cauldrons.

'He's got them right where he wants them, hasn't he?'
Elle came and stood with her.

'Where does she find them?'

'RSC, probably.'

'Doing Hamlet every night at Stratford,' said Carla.
The image of Bruno poured out of the largest cauldron,
genie-like, laughing, boasting, in full smug preen.

The children froze in rapt attention as mummy man,
now in a white coat, with a pair of thick, black-rimmed
glasses, staggered onto the stage.

'Good evening, girls and boys.'

They all shouted back.

'My name is Professor Incompetence and I've come to
do a few *experiments* ... with you ...'

The room resounded with oohs and arrhs.

The children watched, frozen to attention as he poured
various steaming, fluorescent-coloured liquids from test
tube to test tube, spilling stuff everywhere and getting it
all wrong. Carla kept looking to the back of the room.
Tom would have loved this. She went to check her mobile.

'Don't worry.' Elle followed her into the cloaks
bedroom. 'Perhaps it's going well.'

Elle sat next to her on the bed.

'Elle – can I ask you something?' She didn't know
why, perhaps the vodka had emboldened her. 'What decided you and Otto, what was the thing that made you do
what you're doing? There must have been something,
something ...'

Elle sat down on the bed. 'Does there have to be a final
straw?' She thought for a moment. 'But yes, you are right.
I guess it was catching him ... Catching? I found him with
a friend of mine. A *friend*?'

'Where?'

'A dinner party. At the dinner table. There were ten of

us, so no one noticed for a while she'd disappeared. I mean, we were all quite drunk. The only clue was Otto's face . . .'

'What? You mean she was. . .?'

Not smiling now, Elle nodded.

'What did you do?'

'Pretended it was all a hysterical joke, of course. And kicked him in the balls from here to Sunday as soon as they'd gone.'

'That was the beginning of the end, I suppose. Except,' she said brightly, 'it's not an end, more a rearranging of loyalties. And I'm happy again.'

'I never knew you were unhappy.'

'No one thinks that. But now I am having plenty of fun. I have to say, that Professor Incompetence isn't bad, is he? Come on.' She held her hand out to Carla.

'Why is it, Elle, that wherever you look, more opportunities rise to greet you?'

'Because I'm always on the alert.'

When the professor asked for volunteers Elle was up there, shovelling herself through all the kids leaping for treats and chews and black-jacks, and making eyes at the professor all the while.

Carla felt a surge of tenderness towards her, up there, enjoying herself, enjoying her life to the full. It can't have been easy what she and Otto went through, I mean, imagine *that*. She felt ashamed of herself, of imagining she was having to endure anything worse than being alone at a party, surrounded by people she knew.

'Enjoying the show?' She felt a hand touching her waist. She jumped, then relaxed out of it and let the hand stay where it was.

'He's good, isn't he.' She smiled her best smile at Rocky.

'I prefer dancing myself.'

'Oh, so do I.'

'Want to?'

'What?'

He grabbed her hand and led her downstairs to the near-empty room, throbbing to the beat of House, Garage, Jungle; she wasn't sure which.

'Who's this?'

'I don't know, do I?'

'But you're a musician, you must know,' she said, jiggling from one leg to the other, twisting her wrists around.

'Hang on a minute.' She watched him go over to the stereo, fiddle with some CDs, then he was back. She stood awkwardly for a moment in the silence. Moments later four guitar riffs followed by a deep bass rhythm set her off . . .

'Who's this then?'

'This is us.'

'What – Scud?'

'Yeah.' He grinned.

'It's great!'

'Hear the music now?'

She heard the music.

'Hear the beat?'

She heard the beat.

'What?' he smiled.

She laughed and shrugged. 'I don't know.'

He might be big and weird-looking, but he moved well. He danced with his shoulders, moving one forwards then the other.

She felt the beat going into and through her. She kicked her shoes off. She could feel him looking at her. Looking her up. Looking her down. He danced closer. She could smell his beery breath. She danced backwards. He danced forwards. She waggled her finger at him. He took her waist. She unravelled his fingers.

The beat hardened.

The show upstairs over, the room was filling with people.

An audience!

She danced harder. She wanted Elle to see this.

He responded. He was lowering himself down to the floor now. She followed.

She wanted everyone to see this. That she was happy. She was an individual having a good time at a party. See? She didn't only dance with Gabriel. She'd dance with anyone who asked.

Other people began to join in; soon the whole room was a heaving mass of bodies. She'd stopped unwrapping his fingers from her waist and just went with it.

The music changed to a slow one. His hands went for her waist again; she could feel them sliding over her bottom and pressing into her. She put her arms around his neck and moved slowly to the music.

The song finished. In a brief waft of soberness, she realised that, though they didn't look like it at that particular moment in time, the spooks all around her were the entire parents of year 4, and that Tom, Tom could be there by now, dressed up as something, watching.

She hurried into the kitchen.

'No Tom. No Tom notom notom, nevermind notom-mmm . . . NeverneverNEVERyoumindnotom . . .'

She banged the end of the empty Smirnoff bottle over her glass. Never mind, there was plenty more to drink. She grabbed at the Bacardi: same colour, after all. She splashed some coke in and played with the ice machine. Weeeee. She liked ice machines. Maybe she should change their fridge. The bright yellow had seemed right at the time, but fridges had come on such a lot.

People were beginning to leave. Already! But the party'd only just begun, surely. It's not late, is it? No, no, it's the children. Cynthia's cousin, taking them home now, course, course. Nightnight darlings. No, daddy will be here soon. Tom's coming. Don't go yet? Yes, you better-gonow. Mummy home soon. Where's Elle? Whereshegone? Let's find Elle. Elle? Anyone seen Elle? And Ant? Where's Ant?

The music changed, ah, nice music. Nice drink. Nice, nice drink. Let go, that's what I'm doing. Let go let go. Gottoletgo. She couldn't believe it. The Gypsy Kings, how uncooly cool was that; she went berserk.

She welcomed him back on the floor like a long lost friend. His shoulder dancing had taken on another dimension. He was backing right down onto the floor! Wow, can he dance! So can I! She followed him down, lying back, before losing her balance and skidding down onto her bottom. Trying to make it look deliberate, she stayed down there, laughing. He lay down next to her. She began moving her hips up and down. 'Have you heard of this one?'

'Whassat?'

'Bouncing! Pelvic bouncing! Try it! It gives you *energy*, tantric energy ...'

He bounced next to her for a while, then he stood up, pulling her up.

'It's all a game, isn't it?' She laughed, staggering to her feet.

'You what?'

'Life! Treat life as serious it becomessirius, treat life as a game it's a game.' She wrapped her arms around him. 'It's a game ... a *short* game ... in my case, in my shoes,

145

not in my shoes.' Rubbing up against him, she flicked away, stamping and swirling and laughing. And laughing. And laughing.

Her headache woke her at dawn to the sound of even breathing behind her. The night a dream away, a nightmare away, what happened in all that black? No? No, oh no no no. She put her arm out. There was no one there. Her head was splitting like it was ready to crack apart. She opened her eyes to see Wilf and Dyl, at right angles, sprawled across Tom's side of the bed.

Wilf opened his eyes at her movement.

'Where's daddy, mummy?' he looked at her with his clear, grey eyes.

After a moment of disbelief as all the what ifs and A&E departments flashed through her mind, their policy always to be honest with their children kicked her into automatic response.

'I don't know, darling,' she said calmly and evenly.

'Has daddy gone for a sleepover?'

She tucked them both inside her arm and buried her head in the pillow.

'Yes, I expect that's it, Wilf. Daddy's gone for a sleepover.'

Chapter Fourteen

It was one big stomp. Exaggerated and full of ugly righteousness. From one end of the klounge to the other and out to the bottom of the garden and back.

'You didn't phone. You didn't text ... You didn't – *anything*!'

'It was a one-off.' Tom's voice trailed lazily down his Sheffield vowels. 'I couldn't not go, Carla. They took us to a bar, we had to ...'

'You don't *sleep* in bars, Tom.'

'All right, it was a bit of a celebration, I drank too much...'

'Celebration of *what*?' She stopped her pacing. 'You didn't sign anything, did you?'

'I didn't sign anything. It's a complicated thing, Carl, you've got to realise ...'

'Was Bruno there?' She set off again, not wanting to know the answer one way or the other.

'Yes.'

'So why didn't he put you in a cab if you were so drunk? Some friend! *I* got razzled last night, I was so worried when you didn't turn up, and Elle saw I got home safely.'

With the righteousness, it all came out crystal clear. She remembered the indignity of being dragged through the dead dregs of the party, her arms draped over Elle and Rocky's necks. Then him clambering into the cab next to her, his arm heavy around her shoulders. When Elle had hauled and pushed him out, he'd turned really snarly on her before planting his lips on Carla's like they were his own property and literally sucking her into a long kiss goodbye. She was too weak to pull out of.

'I had to get back to the office while the thoughts were still fresh . . .'

'I thought you were drunk?'

'I got inspired, Carl, I had to get it down on paper, quickly, and – I just fell asleep. Look, I've said I'm sorry, now leave it.'

'Why didn't you *call*?'

'I tried.'

'*When?*'

'There was no reply.'

'My phone was switched on.'

'If it were switched on I'd've got through, wouldn't I?'

'Voicemail, Tom. Text?'

'I'd like to see you sending a text message after two bottles of wine.'

'Is that how much you had?'

'I don't know, I wasn't counting.'

'You know how to *speak*!'

'I didn't think.'

'*There's no thinking to it*, the machine asks you. Why didn't you call Jo's to say you'd be late?'

'Jo's ex-directory.'

She sat down at the table, took a sip of coffee and was up again. Picking up toys, newspapers, towels, putting away cereal packets. Bubbling through her own guilt and

148

fury was a nasty cold chill of suspicion. She wished she could drop it but it wouldn't drop her; instead she felt driven on to more and more questioning, alert for clues, waiting to trip, to confirm.

'Carla, let's leave it be – *please*.'

'I'm sorry, Tom, but no, I can't – leave it be.'

'I'm under enough pressure.'

'. . . where – were – you – when – you – woke – up?'

'Sat at my desk, I told you.'

'And you didn't wake in the middle of the night?'

'No.'

'Your body didn't tell you it was bent in all the wrong places for sleeping purposes?'

'No!'

Deny, deny and deny again. Waiting for the questions to go away. Wasn't that what she was doing? But then, supposing he had just fallen asleep after working hard? She had to turn things around. Keep cool, calm, think a way out of it.

'Could we just go over this one more time?'

'Carl–aaaaaa.'

'Why didn't you leave a message here?'

'Because I thought I'd be *back*.'

'You were going to be late.'

'I thought I'd be here. Home. Before you.'

'So you'd no intention of going to Jo's party.'

'I didn't say that.'

'Yes, you did.'

'No, I didn't.'

'You said you'd be back here before me!'

'*When* I realised it'd be too late to turn up there. That you'd be back *here*.'

'So why. Didn't. You. Call. *Home*!!'

'Because I. Didn't. Know. I'd. Fall. Asleep!'

She watched him pouring himself another orange juice. Trying to pretend to herself that Rocky hadn't happened wasn't working. It was only making her go over the sordid events again and again, with – oh my God, No! Oh, no, no, NO it did happen, didn't it? The freshness of recollection was already becoming blurred through too many repeats, the memories fading into second-handedness, like they'd been played over too often.

'The good news is, if you want to hear it . . .' he turned to look at her, his face full of weary righteousness.

'Go on, then.'

'The reason we were celebrating is, the manufacture base for Supernatural has been approved by her accountants. I'll start in the new year; it'll mean a few more trips to Milan but basically, we're on our way, Carl. We can make plans.'

She should have said good, but she didn't. The dancing, that was what everyone had seen. That was what people did at parties, danced. Wasn't it? So, they'd disappeared upstairs. He'd led her upstairs, she distinctly remembered that. But she'd gone willingly enough. Who had seen that? Only the fullest set of parents of Richmond Hill Juniors and Infants year 4 which had ever gathered in one place on Earth outside the nativity play? Oh no oh no. They'd all seen that snog too, on the dance floor. At least she'd had the presence of mind to push him away after the spiral shock of the strangeness of his nipping and darting tongue and pincushion fingers everywhere. There were lots of other people dancing then; who were they? A horrible mesh of masks and fangs and bats in the blackness; and Rocky, coming at her, grinning like Catweazle through his pointy gingery beard.

Oh no, oh no, no, no. Should she come clean now, get it all out in one big row? She glanced up at him, with his sad, tired little boy eyes, hunched over coffee, called into detention. He wouldn't like it. He wouldn't like it one little bit. He wouldn't believe it. She couldn't believe it. Did it really happen? And so around her mind churned, bringing her back to the cold facts. She forced herself to remember it all.

He'd led her into the main bedroom and pushed her back onto the bed and landed himself on top of her, squashing the coats even more, muttering 'come on baby' as he ruffled her hair and kissed her neck over and over. She can't have been that drunk because she remembered being concerned about the squashed coats and had the presence of mind to struggle up and off the bed. Thank God she'd done that! She sweated at the memory. He'd kept a tight grip on her, and pushed her against the wall, kissing her again and rubbing his hand up her leg. Then there'd been the footsteps and she'd pushed him off with the mightiest force she could muster before he was back on her again like a magnet. She'd managed to lock them in the en-suite just in time to hear Hazel Macfernon and her creep of a hairy-voiced husband Brian coming in to get their coats.

There was a lot of pink, she remembered, pink and cream, very un-Jo she'd thought as she was gently guided to the wall between the marble double sinks. Something about being locked in somewhere they shouldn't be and the voices still going on on the other side of the door had made her giggle and that had been it, he'd taken it as a yes and before she knew it, his hands were everywhere all at once and he was whispering strange excruciating things Tom would never say in a million years like 'oh baby, yes, come on baby, you like to go, oh you like to go, oh yes baby ...' Then there were more voices, voices she didn't recognise and the handle just a couple of metres away from them wraggling up and down urgently. While

151

she froze, he appeared totally oblivious to it. If anything he got noisier. She could feel him between her legs, then, as the voices got fainter and faded away she could really feel him between her legs and before she knew it he'd slipped a condom on and was in her, rough, fast and hard.

'Can't you be even a little bit pleased?'

'I want everything gone over by an independent lawyer, Tom, that's all I'm asking.' She cleared away the coffee cups.

Tom shrugged. 'Sure.'

'So let's not do any celebrating yet, hmm?'

Tom put his feet up on a chair, took his phone out of his pocket and clicked a button with his thumb. He did *look* like he'd been up all night. She wanted to hug him and just be glad he was back and all was safe and well and all would be safe and well. But she couldn't, because it wouldn't.

'Otto, mate, all right? Yeah. Yeah . . .'

She quickly left the room. She picked up a pile of junk mail on the mat and tried to fill her mind with mini cabs and patio cleaning, Thai restaurant menus, wood flooring specialists and maintenance-free, leak-proof guttering. All our workmanship guaranteed. Shutting her ears she squashed it all in the bin and went into the garden.

The robin flew down immediately, like it knew something was wrong. She began raking leaves into damp mucky piles, snapping herself into forward planning mode. Not something she could write up on the wall calendar, but a new file to open all the same. When should she tell him? Before he went into sulk or after he went into sulk? Was one dirty, great, big, enormous row better than two medium-sized rows? He'd turned her anger around into his own now anyway. They were in for a few days of misery. If she didn't say anything now, all that would happen would be her guilt would build and build and then they'd have to go through all this misery again. She raked around the children's den, muddy and still, its ropes dangling, wet and cold. The robin's song sank into the low melancholy key of autumn, competing with a mistle thrush whistling in the trees above. Its merryness sounded hollow, lonely and empty. The robin had got it right. Only yesterday the garden was part of the normal world, but the normal world didn't exist any more.

Otto?

Otto!

No: Otto had gone home early, she clearly remembered that. In the kitchen. Had Elle told him? Call Elle, must speak to Elle about this. She rushed inside. As she expected, Tom, already into Sulk Part I, had left the house without a goodbye.

She looked at the clock. He'd gone to join the boys at football with Otto. They'd nearly be finished, he'd get there in time to go to the Marlborough. Sometimes she and Elle joined them with the younger ones. Sometimes they didn't.

'Hi, Elle, it's me.' She kept her voice chit-chat high and casual, but there was nothing she could do about the throaty wobble behind it.

'Carla! How are we feeling today, then?'

She cringed. Elle's comfortableness made her feel more wretched.

'Terrible.'

'A bit hungover?'

'What did I *do*?'

'Don't you remember?'

'Unfortunately yes, I do.'

'Don't worry about it.'

'He was so – ugh, Elle, I feel awful ...'

Elle laughed. 'It doesn't surprise me, Carla.'

Despite the laugh in her voice, the undercurrent of stiff primness was unnerving.

'Look, I have to make sure, Tom's just gone off to football and...did you ...'

'Did I tell Otto, do you mean?'

'I'm going to tell Tom myself, of course, but I've got to choose my moment so ...'

'Carla, you mustn't do that!'

'What?'

'Tell Tom!'

'I've got to.'

'You can't!'

'Why?'

'He'll go berserk.'

'I know that! But I have to, Elle, we've never had any secrets from each other, and, besides, too many people saw us.'

'They saw you dancing, Carla, that's all. That's what people do at parties.'

'It was a bit more than dancing.'

'Oh, a bit of snogging, that's all. Tom's a very jealous man, Carl.'

'I know that!'

'So don't tell him.'

'I have to!'

'Look, let's talk about this.'

'All right.'

'Come over.'

'Now?'

'No. Not now, I have a customer coming. On Monday, after drop-off, Dickens and Jones café.'

'What's wrong with the Bon Appetit? Oh, yes, I see all right, Elle, thanks.'

'But you have to promise you won't say anything to Tom. Promise me, Carla.'

'I promise, for now.'

But only for now. If she didn't get it out it'd stay there for ever, growing, festering, entangling. Living with this lie already lying like a stone in the centre of her soul wasn't an option. Surely, even Elle could see that.

Chapter Fifteen

'Hi!'

'Oh hi,' she joined in the morning chorus of Richmond B flat hi's.

Nod.

Smile.

'Hello!'

Oh hell, it's Paloma, look the other way.

Why they were called runs she didn't know.

School walk, she could understand.

School drive?

Perfectly logical.

'Hi–iii.' Even her own version of school stop, start, hurry-up-and-wait amble.

'Oh hell*ooo*.'

But where did *run* come from?

Who's this coming along? Do I know you? Do you know me?

No. Obviously not.

Another stranger.

Smile.

A wave.

A couple of mutual ignores with two half-knows.

Stranger. The fashion designer from year 1. But didn't Jo know her? Wasn't she there? Did she just look at her in a funny way then?

It felt like walking the street of shame. Elle's 4 x 4 was parking up in the one and only legitimate space clear of yellow zigzags, her blonde pony-tail swinging happily through the gap of her white Viking baseball cap.

'That's an 8 o'clock parking space you've got there.'

Elle threw Carla a breezy smile as she jumped down. 'Feeling better now?'

'No!'

'Oh, Carla.' Elle turned and gave her a sympathetic frown as she unclicked Tallulah from the back.

'I feel like I'm walking stark naked through a rugby pub on a Saturday afternoon.'

'It's not as bad as you think.'

'No, it's worse. I'll take Jon in with Wilf if you want.'

'What, and ruin my parking space?'

They both turned and looked at the crowded school gate.

'Looks like they've gone in already.'

'I'll see they're all right.'

'OK, thanks.' Elle clicked Tallulah back in her seat again. 'Oh – we're having coffee, aren't we? I have so much to get through this morning.' Carla's heart sank. 'Could we make it a bit later? Ten-thirty?

Her heart lifted again. 'Of course, fine.'

How did Elle always do that? Carla wondered, revving her pushchair up into battering ram mode, and aiming it squarely at the cluster of dog-walkers clogging up the pavement.

Did she drive round and round the one-way system until the space just happened for her?

Elle Olsson? Parked cars melting into the tarmac as soon as she drove into view, more like.

She was about to go into the cloakroom when the voice of Hazel Macfernon pulled her to a shuddering halt. She peered around the door. Hazel, her arm casually dangled across a row of coat-pegs was talking to Anne and Bryony. She crept away. She found Wilf already sitting reading *Horrid Henry* at his desk, pecked him quickly on the cheek and hurried away, 100 per cent convinced Hazel was giving Anne and Bryony a blow by blow account of the strange sounds coming out of Jo Salmon's en-suite.

Carla had never been to the caff at Dickens and Jones before. It took her a few wrong escalator turns and distractions in fashions before she found it tucked away behind home furnishings on the top floor.

Despite her dawdlings, she was still early.

She sat on a buffet seat and waited, listening to the claustrophobically quiet hum of the chiller cabinet, the random chinkings of cups against saucers and coins rattling into the till. She looked around at the scattering of old ladies, and pinnied waitresses behind the counter bustling about in an extinct kind of efficiency, the whole place trapped in the fug of a bygone department-store age.

'Sorry I'm late.' Elle raced up in a whirl of yellow and denim glitter, a sunflower amongst the weeds. 'I got caught up in handbags down below, I couldn't resist this ... what do you think? It would be good for Sicily, I thought ...' She pulled a candy-striped leather rucksack-type bag out of a large plastic carrier.

Sicily? All the Sicily they'd be getting would be a lost deposit, the way things were going.

'You should have waited for the sales.'

'Oh, you only get rubbish in the sales.'

'Not if you get there early.'

'I can't be bothered with all that. Hey, you look different, your eyes, what have you done?'

'I've changed my mascara.'

'Oh la la.'

'Shut it, Elle.' Carla smiled, she couldn't help it. 'To waterproof, if you must know.'

Elle laughed. 'You are funny, anticipating the tears before they've arrived.'

'That's not funny.'

'How do you get it off?'

'What?'

'The mascara – it's a pain to get off, isn't it?'

'Oh, sorry, I thought you said something else.'

'I forgot, it's self-service, isn't it, do you want anything more? No?'

Carla watched her at the counter, dreading the conversation ahead but at the same time desperate to talk about it. Elle would try and persuade her not to tell Tom and she'd try and persuade Elle why she must tell Tom. He'd turned it all around already anyway. That night he'd gone straight down to his den and put John Lee Hooker on, always the sign to stay away. The boys would go down and say goodnight. He'd talk to them normally, brightly, extra-brightly, as if nothing was wrong. Wilf might even pick up on the atmosphere and hang out with him for a while. She'd eat alone in front of the TV and take herself to bed with a book. He'd appear when she was asleep. That's what the next few days held in store. Yes, he'd be hopping mad, furious, hurt, cross, more cross than she'd ever seen him.

'It sounds like you have your rows as organised as the rest of your life, Carla.' Elle bit the cellophane corner off a packet of three custard creams.

'I feel – unclean.'

'Now, you want me to be honest with you, don't you?' Carla nodded.

'I think it did you some good.' She nibbled at her biscuit.

'*Good?* I'm in the biggest doggiest-do dog-do mess I've ever been in in my life and you say it's GOOD?'

'No one need ever know, Carla. You do have that option.'

'The whole of frigging year 4 knows!'

'All you did was dance – as far as *they* know.'

'And snog.'

'And snog. So what. It was a *party*, Carla.'

Carla put her head in her hands; if only that was all they had done. 'I didn't even fancy him!'

'So he wasn't a good lover?'

'Elle!'

'You seemed very happy when we left.' Elle smiled.

'Elle, you're supposed to be helping me here.'

'All I'm thinking is, maybe you've been caring about Tom a little bit too much, Carla.'

'He's my husband! He stopped out all night. Is that "caring" too much? And besides, *you* saw him with that woman.'

'I won't deny it, you are going through a . . . patch. All marriages do . . .'

'We haven't before.'

'Maybe it's time you did!'

'What and end up in a ridiculous muddle of *divorce-lite* . . . Sorry, I – I know it can't be as easy for you as you're making out . . .'

Elle shrugged. 'It's life, that's all.'

'Does Otto know?'

Elle left the pause for a little while as she buttered her scone.

'Elle!!'

'Of course not, what do you take me for? The first rule of any marriage is to never kiss and . . .'

'Is never to kiss, Elle. That's what marriage vows are for.'

160

'But if you do, as you do, as people do sometimes in this life – never tell. Never, never, never. Let it die down. You are feeling raw now, of course you are, but it will pass. I promise. In any case, I think you should go ahead, have a fling, get it out of your system!'

'What, see him *again*? Elle, you are bonkers. He was grotesque!'

'That's not what it looked like to me.'

'Elle – I was drunk.'

'Tom doesn't have to know.'

'But you'd know!'

'I already know!'

'That that is as far as it's going.'

'Or what about someone else, someone you really fancy, then . . .'

Elle made a castanet shape with her hands.

'Leave it out! He's yours anyway. I'd never do that.'

'It's you he fancies.'

'Stop being so childish. He's teaching us to dance, and I'm enjoying it, that's all. But as far as – I'm never going to get into that situation for the rest of my life, Elle; this has frightened me to bits.'

'I think you needed frightening, Carl.'

'Thanks for the sympathy. I took that wretched dance lesson too much to heart, that was my problem. If I'd never gone this would never have happened.'

'So it's my fault now?' Elle said in mock hurt. 'You are coming again, aren't you?'

'If you want me to.'

'I want you to. But, next time, could you do me a little favour, if you wouldn't mind?'

'What?'

'Could you ask him if he'd pose for the calendar?'

'Ask him yourself.'

161

'It'd be better coming from you.'

'Why?'

'Please. I'd feel stupid. All we do is this – I shall talk about it, set it up and all you have to do is jump in with the idea like you just thought of it.'

'I've got enough to think about at the moment, Elle.'

'Your problem is as big as you choose to make it, Carla. Let go, forget about it, move on.'

'Let go, let it go, I'm fed up with all this letting go stuff. I've given my life to Tom. All right, I'm old-fashioned, I live through him and he lives through me and the boys. We're a unit.'

'And so, if you want to stay a unit, which you do, and Tom does, then I suggest you listen to what I am saying. You are not controlling your life, Carla. You think you do with all your charts and calendars and homework tables and things, but what is really happening is your life is controlling you. What you did was to be a human being. You needed to break out of it. That's all. Now forget it. Move on.'

'Our marriage is based on truth, Elle,' said Carla quietly, 'not lies. It's not an option.'

'Love isn't as simple as truth, Carla. It is a lot more complicated, and it's about time you learned it.'

Carla didn't say anything.

'I'd go further. I'd say it has been a healthy thing for you, and for Tom. It's for your own sake. As for me, I promise, I swear I will never say a word.'

Elle chinked her coffee back into its saucer and began making getting-up-to-go movements. The light morning smells of coffee and pastries were already mingling with the heavier lunch-time cooking of fish and chips and chicken in wine.

'I must just go and look at the bed linen while I'm here . . . fancy it?'

'No.'

Elle looked suddenly serious; she grabbed Carla by both
shoulders. 'Carla – whatever you do – don't tell him.'

'I have to.'

'Not Tom – Tom of all people . . . He'd go ape. You've
said it enough times, he hates it if you say you fancy
somebody on the television. You've been big, you've put
up with his flirtations for years . . . now, be a bit bigger
and put up with your own, hey?'

'They're harmless. That's just Tom. They never go
anywhere . . . Well, hardly ever . . . as far as I know for
sure, never . . .'

'Call me later if you want to,' said Elle wearily.

They parted next to the racks of coloured towels.

'Thanks.'

'Oh, and don't forget to mention the calendar,'
Elle called after Carla as she slid out of sight down the
escalator.

Chapter Sixteen

Carla lay out her wooden spoons, mixing bowls, baking tray and cake cases in the order she'd need them, running up along the surface to the oven, warming to 180 degrees.

'Mum? How do you spell crown?'

'Curly c.' She measured and lined up 200 grams of everything, and two eggs as she spelled, humming quietly to herself, feeling the smidgen of warmth and contentment she always got opening her fridge for the baking butter. 'Rer oh weh nuh.'

She mashed the butter into the sugar with a fork. She preferred the feel of the butter, fluffing and crunching against the white glaze of the old beige mixing bowl, to the quick whiz, over in seconds, blender approach, reckoning all time saved was lost on the horrible spiky washing-up bit afterwards.

'Do you want a hot chocolate?'

'Mmm, thanks, mum.'

Allowed to stay up a little later than normal, warm currents of eldest-son-and-mum camaraderie were flowing between them. Despite the peculiarness of the 'to do' list going through her mind that day:

Make cakes for year 4 cake stall
Call Lion and Unicorn bookshop to order new *Horrid Henry*
Tax the car
Syon Park for yellow Silko
Test Wilf on all his lines for *Jason & the Argonauts* rehearsal tomorrow
Tell husband she shagged a hairy stranger in Jo Salmon's en-suite

She felt calm. A strange ultra-calm of acceptance. The most difficult thing, always, she mused as she mashed, was making the decision. Once that'd been done, all you had to do was carry it through. Like since she'd let the Bruno and Danielle thing drop, the agony had passed. Most of it had been in the resisting, like trying to push water backwards. As soon as she'd decided, she'd been moving forwards: meeting and briefing the lawyer and making sure Bruno knew about it. It was like clicking in one of Dyl's curving Brio rails. Trains on new tracks and away they'd go again.

Crack, the first egg broke neatly in half on the side of the bowl. She dropped it onto the fluff of sugared butter.

'Can we play something together?' Wilf crunched up his knee and poked the squashy bit.

'Wilf, don't do that. Have you learned your lines?'

'Yeeas.'

She picked up the photocopied sheet of A4.

'"What a magnificent fleece!" Is that really all you have to say?'

'Muum, I'm only Courtier 1.'

'So, who's playing Jason, then?'

'Toby.'

'Again!'

'Toby gets all the big parts.'

'Why don't they share them out a bit!'

'Muuuum. Can we play a game now? Pleease.'

'I'm busy.'

'Hangman? Just one game of hangman ...'

She quickly mixed in the flour, dolloped a spoonful into each casing before clattering it into the oven and setting the clock. Good choice Wilf, hangman was quick, ten minutes to bake, then bed.

'Have I forgotten something?' Tom stared blankly at the table set with candles and a bottle of rosé chilling in an ice bucket and then coldly at Carla, naked beneath bold folds of coloured crimson silk over rusty gold batik.

'No.' Carla wiped her hands on a towel.

'What have I done now?'

'Nothing.'

'It's not our anniversary is it?'

'I wanted to make up, that's all.'

'There's nothing to make up, and besides, I've had a bad day.' He turned to go down to the basement.

'Tom!'

'What?'

'Please.'

He still stood back suspiciously with a look that said their major-sulk rows, and this was most definitely a major-sulk row, were programmed to go on for anywhere between three and five days, not one and a half days, and what did she think she was playing at.

He looked tired. 'What's up, what have I done now? Or what haven't I done?'

'It's not you, it's me.'

She went over to him and put her arms around his neck. 'I'm just saying sorry, that's all.'

'What for?' He stood stiffly.

'I've been such a grump, we've both been. Let's drop it.'

'Have I?'

'It's my fault, I'm sorry.'

He leaned back his head and looked at her. 'Have you been drinking?'

'Not yet. Please. There's too much going on right now for these childish stand-offs.'

After what seemed an age, he returned the hug, 'I had a pain of a day.'

He took his jacket off and slung it over the back of a chair whilst Carla put the freshly cut chips in the fryer for Tom's favourite comfort meal.

'Elle called today.' He lit a cigarette and began smoking it like a cigar, knowing she wouldn't order him outside with it.

'Did she?'

'Odd, don't you think, calling me at work?'

Carla swallowed. 'What about?' She plonked an ashtray in front of him.

'Oh, some ideas for the calendar.'

'Oh, that.' She began breathing again. She felt a sudden burn in her cheeks, 'She wasn't asking you to be in it, was she?'

'No, actually she was wondering if I, well, also, if I could persuade you to . . .'

'Me?'

Tom smiled for the first time.

The chips fizzled in the fryer.

The damned cheek of her. 'Why didn't she ask me?'

'Because you'd say no.'

'And it's still no! What's she playing at?' What was she playing at? 'I'm seeing her in the morning; I'll tell her.'

'Have a think about it, she said.'

'So – you wouldn't mind, then?'

'Why should I? You have the figure for it.'

'I so don't, Tom!'

Tom looked down at her breasts.

'Topless! Are you out of your mind? She's got a cheek, calling you. She knows you're up to your eyes right now.'

'Oh, she just wants a few original ideas, that's all, it won't take any time really.'

'If it's sets and backgrounds . . .'

'No no, she wants to use natural light, outside locations, daytime . . .'

'Outside?'

'That's the point of it, isn't it. It's supposed to be Richmond Hill . . .'

'There'd be – *people* around!'

'It'll be early morning, won't it, before anyone's around, strip, click, click, and it's over.'

Carla shook the basket of chips before tipping them onto their plates. 'All right. I'll do it.'

'You what?'

'I'll do it.'

'Really!'

'What's the matter, did you expect more of a fight?'

She didn't tell him it'd never get past Mrs Armstrong so why not play along? Why should Elle have another lever on her, to tease her, to taunt her?

'So, what was so bad about your day then?'

'Oh Bruno . . .'

She might've guessed but kept her smug I told you so's to herself.

'His plans and mine for Supernatural aren't meeting.'

'What a surprise.'

Tom unscrewed the jar of mustard pickle.

'Sorry, go on.'

'He's saying the opposite of Danielle, that I'm to forget all thought of the sculpture chairs till the manufacture base is up and out there.'

'It's the business he knows, isn't it. He can poke more of a finger in there than he can in the art world.'

'It gets worse. He's got this fixation with *Big Brother*. Thinks we should put all our energies into getting the sofa and confession chair concession for next year. It's some daft competition between the big boys and I'm not interested. I've told him that and I've told him the Morrissey chair's what I do in parallel, not ahead of, but not behind the rest of it – at least Danielle's right behind the Morrissey chair, says she might even get me over to LA to meet him . . .'

Carla let him talk on, watching him tucking in with relish. She'd reckoned on mid-meal. He'd have to finish it then, he'd never left a spot of corned beef, chips and tomato in all his life. It'd give him something to do, something to chew whilst it sank in. All she had to do was get the words out. Maybe if he had become entangled with Danielle that night, he'd not go too ballistic. He couldn't, could he? Like she hadn't been able to on Saturday. Then they could get through their 'patch' as Elle called it, in one neat compromise.

'So, what about Elle?' Carla asked conversationally, playing for a bit more time, 'is she going to be in it?'

'She's the photographer.'

'Cameras have delay timers.'

Tom put his head sideways and nodded approvingly. 'Hmmm, maybe she would then. You should suggest it to her. She might be shy to put herself forward.'

'Elle! Shy!' Carla laughed. 'She'd be good, though, wouldn't she?'

She watched his chips disappearing one by one. 'I'll ask

her in the morning.'

The morning. Another dance lesson. A tiny, trivial secret now.

Go on – NOW ...

'Tom.'

'Mmmm?' He looked up at her, mid-chew.

'I've er, I've – arranged for us to go for a curry with Ant and her new man on Friday night.'

'You're going to have to start checking with me before you start booking me up for things, Carl. My spare time's not my own any more.'

'But enough to do the calendar.'

'Carla!'

'Sorry, but ...' She watched his knife and fork busily scrape up the final mouthful.

'I'm not going to be working twenty-four out of seven but I'll have to manage my time now. You can see that?'

'Yes, yes, all right.'

'Let's not argue any more, hey?' Tom gathered the plates and put them in the dishwasher.

Carla went up behind him and held his waist. 'No, Tom, let's not ...'

Oh, he'd had a tough day already and it felt so good for that chill to have gone, that horrible, horrible chill.

'It's going to be hard the next few months, Carl.' He turned and kissed her neck. She stood still, letting herself feel his touch. 'Come on, let's go up to bed.'

'Let's not.' She kissed him hard. All the kisses she'd known and ever known rushed back in an instant. The gentle but firm, familiar, smoky Weetabix smell of him.

She ran her hands down his back. Tom pulled away. 'Carla what's got into you?'

'Please, Tom, here.'

They kissed, more gently this time, before Tom pulled

away. 'Hold off, I'll close the blinds.'

'No!' She held onto him.

He gave her his what-the-hell-are-you-playing-at look.

'I kind of like it.' She smiled coyly.

'Mmm, turning into a little exhibitionist, are we?'

She felt the fabric of her dress gathering up behind her, the cold air on her legs. Memories of the strangeness of that man surfaced. Those prickly fingers. The fear. The spontaneity. The soft silk rubbing against her skin, keeping going, forwards till it reached her. Tom kept his hand there, moving it gently as their mouths met in a gentle, teasing kiss.

'Mmmm,' he said softly, moving his tongue round to her ear and back again.

'Breathe deep, deep breaths.' He kissed her.

'Faster, Tom, faster, please . . .'

'No, Carl, not yet, come on, slowly, slowly. Breathe, deep, deep, breaths, look at me, Carl.' He cupped her head and held her hair behind her in a pony-tail.

'No, Tom, now, please, fast.' She glanced at the black garden, the windows opposite ablaze with light behind the trees.

'What's got into you?'

'Please, quickly. Now. . .'

There was a clatter and smatter of knives and forks and spoons and dishes as he turned her around and pushed her down over the table. She felt him entering her from behind, coming almost at once. And so did she.

Chapter Seventeen

Carla stood erect and stern, wriggling her toes in anticipation, feeling the nakedness of her feet on her cold, steel mat. Out of the side of her eye she could see Elle next to her, studying him as he crouched over the CD player, his head cocked to one side as he found the track.

'OK.' He stood and turned and clapped in one swift movement.

The room filled with florid guitars, shouts and claps.

'We shall begin where we finished.' He marched across the room. 'Who can remember? Forward, side, turn. Forward, side, turn, like this.'

Carla followed his movements without hesitation.

Elle followed.

He took Elle's hand.

Good, Carla thought as she got into the flow. Good.

She'd blown off at Elle on their way there, telling her in no few words that if she had any questions for Carla she should address them to her and not to her husband at work. Spelling out how unbelievably busy and pressurised Tom was, and she'd have appreciated it if she might have asked Carla first if she could ask Tom for more help, rather than the other way round.

'Now we put a new step.'

He positioned himself on his mat in front of them.

'Like this: jump and stamp. Jump and stamp.'

'Jump and stamp. Jump and stamp,' Carla repeated, dead seriously.

'I can do this,' said Elle happily.

'Good. Now – together. Forward, side, turn, jump and stamp. Forward, side, turn, jump and stamp. No, no, Elle, like this ... Think about your arms, Carla ...'

Carla went with the music speeding inside her. Her arms moved up on their own, her hands began to twist and turn. Her nails, polished red for the occasion, spinning, twisting and forking into a fluid fence all around her.

'That's it, find the air, touch it.'

Elle stopped and put her hand on her hips. 'How can you touch air?'

'Find it and you'll know.'

Carla had found something. She felt lighter, like she was more in touch with movement than stillness. She wasn't in one place any more; she was everywhere.

'Right. We keep with these steps. I want you to explore inside the compass, the rhythm. Feel what is inside it. You can feel it, Carla, no?'

'Yes.'

'Feel. Feel. FEEL ... Elle.'

'I think I need someone to dance with.'

'For flamenco you can dance solo.'

'How can I feel when I can't get the sodding steps right!'

'Forget the jump, keep to the first steps, like this.' He went over and stood behind her, taking her arms in his hands and moving her like a puppet.

The beat hardened. Carla moved through the sounds.

Elle stopped again, flopping her arms down in frustration.

'Isn't it time for a coffee break yet?'

'You have only an hour.'

'I'd LOVE a coffee,' Carla lied, forcing herself to stop.

He looked at her, disappointed.

'OK.' he shrugged.

He stopped the music and went into the kitchen.

Every time his back was turned, Elle made funny signals at Carla with her hands and eyebrows. Carla felt embarrassed. Transparent.

'You look different, Carla,' he said, handing her a tiny white cup of espresso.

'Do I?' she said coyly.

'Do you see it?' he said to Elle.

'How?' asked Carla.

'Before, you smiled but there was nothing in your eyes but a question.' He turned to Elle. 'Now look at her.'

'It's the magic of the dance.'

'It is,' he said, not picking up on Elle's irony, and nodding in agreement.

Carla helped herself to a biscuit.

'Music is part of our bodies, you would be surprised how much.'

'It's obviously not part of mine, is it.' Elle sprawled herself across the leather armchair, leaving the sofa free for Carla. Stuff this damned calendar, Carla thought as she got another nod-and-wink eye signal from Elle.

'The core of the flame is always empty. If you practise enough, Elle, I promise, you will find it.' He sat down next to Carla. Her cup rattled on her knee.

'I don't think so.' Elle sighed. 'It's one of those things you've either got or you haven't got. And I haven't got it. Never mind! We can't all be Wayne Sleep, can we?'

'No, no. Come, Elle, please. You must help me to help you. Maybe I am going a little too fast for you ...'

'I wish, Gabriel . . .'

'Please, we will work together, by the end of the lessons I promise you will be dancing.'

'I hope so.'

'No really, I think so. Everything is in motion, everything changes, you can't stop that. And so everyone can dance. Even if from the inside they don't know it. It is a release we all have. But come, we don't learn by sitting drinking coffee, come, come . . .' He stood up and clapped his hands.

Carla went keenly over to her mat. Elle reluctantly joined her.

'I'm sorry, Elle,' she said as soon as the door closed behind them, 'there just wasn't the right moment.

'All you had to do was lead him in.'

'Why didn't *you* just come out with it, then!'

'I feel shy.'

'You?'

'Yes me!!!'

'Oh come on . . .'

They waited to cross the road.

Elle turned on her. 'Is it so long ago, Carla? Have you been with Tom so long you've forgotten what it's like to have a crush on somebody?' Her voice hardened into crisp cold sentences. 'No! Come to think of it, I expect you have forgotten, haven't you. I'm trying to help you out, here, I introduce you to the lessons, I listen to your – your *banging* on about your one-night stand, I do all I can to help you, I ask for a little help from you and you don't think it's important! You think it is trivial. You think it is Elle being daft nonsense again. Then I ask your husband one small favour and you question me like you don't know me as a friend. It hurts, Carla. Believe me, it hurts.'

'Elle, Elle, ELLE!'

175

'You think it's funny I can't dance. That you find it so *easy* . . .'

'*Elle!*'

The exhilaration inside her sank into a puddle of despair. She stood watching her friend dodging dangerously through the traffic as she ran across the road and off down the hill.

Chapter Eighteen

Carla arrived at the playground at a very early five past three. She'd been fretting all day, mooching around the house, picking up the odd bit of clutter and listening to Elle's answerphone over and over.

She didn't like being early. She stood outside Wilf's classroom, all lights ablaze in the semi-darkness, watching the trickle of other early-birds sauntering by. She chose a spot beside the privet hedge. She pulled her navy fun-fur ankle-length coat tight around her but still felt horribly exposed. As if big arrows were pointing down at her from the sky with 'adulterous bad mother' written on them.

A plastic carrier dangled from her pushchair with the finished cover in it. She'd worked furiously at it all day, the rhythm of the sewing helping her mind order itself, determined to finish it, to get it and all of its strange patterns out of the house.

Other year 4 parents began to arrive. A sensible, vague half-smile on her lips, she watched them gathering in groups all around her, excluding her, talking about her. It was her over-sensitivity making her mind work overtime again, but the fear was real enough. Whispering and turning their backs, 'How could she!' and 'Did you *see* the state of him'. She went over to the notice board outside the classroom and pretended to read it. She could hear the conversations nearest to her now.

'I don't think we can do better, it's only 500 yards from the beach and there's a child-friendly restaurant right next door . . .'

'We've got a beach cottage now. It took us *years* to get it, Rushy Bay is comp*lete*ly dead man's shoes these days!'

As it was already November, summer holidays were a hot topic.

Hazel jogged in, Orlando reclining regally in his pushchair, tucking into a large Granny Smith.

'Ah, Carla.' Hazel peered down her clipboard. 'Where are we? Pint pots, bottle tombola, tea towels . . . festive cushions – that must be you, no? No – I don't see your name . . .'

She relaxed a little. Halloween was history. Christmas fair plans had brought Hazel and Bryony out in rashes of toxic volunteerisis. There were no peculiar looks, not even a glimmer of a 'you're such lipstick trash' glint in either of those ginger eyes. She really can't have known they were in there.

'I'm on the raffle.'

'Oh? Oh yes, I have you here, early shift. Can you make sure you're ready well before opening? Grabbing them as they go in is always a good idea . . .'

Elle and Cyn arrived together, followed by the banker's wife. The first time she'd seen Cyn since. It was just a snog, that's all it was. Only Elle knew the whole of it. Didn't she?

Carla quickly untangled the Marks and Spencer carrier from her pushchair. 'Here's your cushion, I hope you like it.' She gave it to the woman as she passed. Not that it had turned out badly, it was just a different style, that's all.

'How are you, Carla, are you all right?' Didn't Cyn's

smile look even wider than normal?

'Yes, of course, I'm fine . . .'

Carla studied her face. That naughty glint in her eye was always there, wasn't it?

A swarm of chest-high activity of bags, guitars and lunchboxes being thrust into faces took Cynthia away. Elle had her back to Carla. Carla put her hand on her shoulder. Elle turned to look at her, blankly.

'Elle, I'm sorry about this morning. Can I walk back with you?'

Elle shrugged.

'Jon can come and play if he wants.'

'He's got chess club.'

Within minutes the playground began to empty as quickly as it had filled.

'You can come and have tea if you want, Tallulah and Dyl can hook into the *Fimbles*. I'm really sorry, Elle, I'm feeling pretty raw and exposed at the moment.'

'So am I.'

'I should have realised. I mean, I knew your – separation – had to be affecting you more than you were letting on but . . .'

'I wish you weren't so damned protective . . .'

'I'm sorry, I am sometimes, I know . . . but it's a difficult time. And Tom didn't mind at all, you calling, I mean. He was rather chuffed, I think. Having another woman calling him at work. It lightened his day. He needs that right now.'

'You didn't – tell – him, did you?'

'No – no, of course not. Elle, I've decided not to go to any more of the lessons.'

Elle looked up at her sharply.

'I'm too much of a distraction. It's not fair, you bid for them.'

179

'But you're loving it!'

And look what trouble it's got me into.

'I think I've learned enough for the time being. It was kind of you to offer to share, I really do appreciate it, Elle.'

All risks had to be minimalised. Any making Elle feeling inadequate wasn't good. It was bad. Could be very bad.

'Don't be daft, Carla. I'm mad that you're much better than me but...'

'No. I've made up my mind. I've got so much on at the moment. Sorting out Tom's new job, Christmas...'

'Christmas! Don't mention it.'

'I might find a class, next year, when things are more settled. Or tap dancing, I've always had a hankering after tap dancing.'

'You'd be good.'

'Good – that's settled then.'

Elle puffed her cheeks and blew out through her mouth, 'He'll wonder where you've gone.'

Carla laughed. 'Not for long! Hey, you're not *shy* of going on your own, are you!'

'Of course not!'

'How's Otto?'

'Otto's fine.'

'Around – much ...?'

'Yes yes, if anything he's around more than ever now he has the freedom to be out.'

'That's always the way,' Carla said as if she knew what she was talking about.

'Seems to be.'

'Is he seeing anyone then?'

'Not that I know.'

'So – things are – normal then?'

'If there is such a thing.'

'So – do you *want* him to be seeing someone?'

'I want *me* to be seeing someone.'

'Well, get working on it, girl. Without me there to cramp your style you'll be much better off.

Elle laughed. 'We hope!'

Chapter Nineteen

Lost behind a sea of cellophane-wrapped hampers of beauty treatments and champagne, Christmas cakes and wine, teddy bears and guitars, Carla sat poised for opening time. Handy for last-minute stocking fillers, preserves and decorations, the Christmas fair was usually fun, but this year she could barely be bothered. Though on schedule with all her presents wrapped and well hidden, she was experiencing for the first time what people who hated Christmas felt like. She was dreading everything, from Tom's dad's flimsy, scribbled, glitter card, always the first to arrive (what would *he* say?) to their annual outing to Wisley to buy the tree. All that tinkly, sparkly cheeriness in the main hall only reminded her how much Tom and the boys adored all the nonsense.

In the hall behind the swing doors, the breathy sounds of the B recorder group striking up 'Good King Wenceslas' triggered an avalanche of children through the main entrance, racing in and out of the hall with urgent looks on their faces. She sat ready with the tickets as a queue of people, still cold from the wind, formed at her table, unhunching themselves in the powerful blast of central heating.

Tom, Wilf and Dyl, still all in their red and white football strips, were amongst the first.

'Don't forget you're on skittles at 12,' she called to him as they disappeared behind the swing doors.

Carla worked quickly and efficiently, handing out different coloured tickets, writing down names and phone numbers, clattering the cash into the empty ice-cream carton.

She was about to pass her shift over to Kathy Thexborough when a hand she recognised put a £5 note in hers. She never forgot hands. Especially these needly ones with two, tiny tattooed skulls below the middle joints of the first fingers.

She tried to smile. 'I didn't expect to see you here. How many would you like?'

'One strip.' He stared, not a flicker.

'Just the one strip? Name?'

'Rocky, just put Rocky.'

She looked up and quickly down again. Her fingers wouldn't grip, she couldn't write the name.

The woman behind him jangled her money.

'I'm sorry, could you write your phone number, just here.'

Looking straight through her again, he took the pen, scribbled a number and turned away to join Cyn and Rick and a whole crowd of their family, friends and hangers-on.

Carla was scared to leave the safety of the table.

'Go on, off you go, it's quietened down a bit now, you've had the busiest shift.' Kathy eventually shooed her away.

She crept gingerly into the heaving main hall. Christmas? The whole place had taken on all the charms and characteristics of a Bosnian minefield.

The smell of Noel incense on Hannah Hargreaves' card stall, mingling with the tinselled, sugar-stranded spice of cinnamon and mulled wine, made her feel sick.

'He wants to see Santa,' said Tom, dumping Dyl, before racing off again.

'Where will you be?'

'Giant Scalextric, year 1 classroom.'

'Shall we go and see Santa, Dyl?'

'Yes yes yes – let's see Santa, NOW, where's Santa ...'

'Don't WANT to,' said Dyl half an hour later as they reached the end of the queue for the sports equipment cupboard.

'What?'

'Don't want to go in.'

'We've just waited for half an hour for this and *you're going in* ...'

'No.'

'Yes.'

'Waaaahhhhhh.'

Mrs Teasdale the nursery nurse, a tangle of tinsel and reindeer antlers, crouched down and spoke gently.

Carla waited.

'WaaaAAAAH,' Dyl shrieked in her face at double velocity.

'Oh come oooon,' said a small voice from behind.

'If you turned the music off he might go in,' said Carla, nodding to the dark depths of the grotto beyond the flashing lights.

'Err ...'

'No, no, it's all right, don't bother.' She hauled Dyl away from the Early Learning Centre Christmas tape, quietly praising his taste.

After dropping Dyl in Nativity Puppets she stopped to

talk to Anne, manning the ice-rink campaign.

Wilf and Toby skidded to a breathless halt in front of Festive Foliage next door.

'Where's dad?'

'Don't know. Muum – muum, can Toby come for a sleepover?'

'Not tonight.'

'Please, please, pleeeease.' Both boys jumped up and down.

Bryony Baxter appeared from behind a sheaf of wreaths.

'He'll have to be back by 10, he has judo on Sunday mornings!'

'Wheeeeyyy.' The boys hugged each other, jumping up and down before racing off into the crowds.

'You don't *mind*, do you?' she asked, seeing Carla's face.

Yes, actually. Yes, she did mind. If Wilf had got over not being invited to Toby's birthday party, she certainly hadn't. And why the hell should she now host this inhospitable, two-faced, house-wrecking monster child?

'I'll drop his toothbrush and pyjamas off later!' Bryony nudged Carla with her elbow. 'Oh, Carla! Have you seen who's here?' Bryony nodded over at the school dinners hatch, the one place she'd been carefully avoiding looking at. Carla turned casually to see Rocky and Rick perched, knees up in the air, on child-sized stools, sipping beer.

'Should have taken the job of Father Christmas! Wouldn't have needed to dress up would he, with that beard!'

'Have you seen Tom?' Carla said, not knowing whether to defend what had been, after all, her one-night stand, or agree with her. As agreeing with Bryony Baxter went against all her principals she felt ignoring was the safest option.

185

'I saw him just now! Yes! He's through there, look, on the skittles with Elle!'

She went through to the junior hall.

There was no sign of Tom.

Marcus Dowe was rolling the balls down the alleyway.

'Where's Tom?' she asked Elle.

'Oh, he was here just now. Marcus was late arriving so I sent Tom off to the bar. Yes, four balls for a pound, thank you ...' Elle even made a zipper purse belt look sexy, drooping from her waist to her hips.

'What's the matter with you? Go on, go and have a drink with him.'

'I can't.'

'Why?'

'Haven't you seen who's here?'

'Gabriel! – where?'

'No.'

'Oh – who then?'

'You know – HIM.'

'WHO?'

'Rocky,' she hissed, hating saying his name.

'Oh *no!*' Elle's seriousness made Carla feel even more wheezy.

'Oh no, yes.'

'What's *he* doing here?'

'Keeping Rick company whilst he performs his parental duties, I suppose.'

'You haven't said anything, have you?'

'Does it matter? Just about everyone else knows ...'

'Come now, don't get paranoid,' said Elle, looking utterly panicked. 'They're not all there thinking about *that*, are they. They'll have forgotten by now. It's good he's here. Look, this is what you do. You go up, you talk politely ...' Carla let Elle talk over her; she hadn't mentioned he'd not recognised her, or was deliberately ignoring her, she didn't know which.

'. . . pretending it never happened.'

'It *did* happen.'

This was unbearable. Even a punch-up between Tom and Rocky would be preferable to the ghastly subterfuge she was feeling right now. Why not bring it all up here and now, get it sorted. Of course, the mother of all rows would ensue, a record sulk, five – six days – a week – with any luck it'd be all done and dusted before Wisley. She felt desperate to get it in a box marked 'murky past' before Christmas got under way.

'You know, I really am beginning to hope Tom did have a fling that night.'

'It would be so neat. So tidy for you, Carla.' Elle turned to a group of small boys crowding at her waist, holding out their coins.

Marcus joined them.

'I'm off to the bar, darlings.'

'Marcus?' said Elle.

'Mmm?'

'I wanted to ask you something. Have you heard about the calendar?'

'Who hasn't.' Marcus' face cracked into two strips of even veneers.

'We were wondering if you . . .'

'Moi!' Marcus roared with delighted laughter.

'It would be good publicity . . .'

'Indeed it would, darling.'

'It's for charity, Marcus!'

'Listen, darling, I don't floss without asking my agent. And you're suggesting I take my clothes off . . .' He stopped in mid-sentence, his face dropping into a brief frown before suddenly lighting up again like a Terry

Thomas beacon. 'Well, helloooo.'

Carla turned to see a buxom blonde woman in Marks & Spencer vintage striding towards them. Mrs Yvonne Armstrong, the headteacher, was in their midst.

Elle turned and smiled easily at her. 'I was just asking Marcus if he'd appear in our calendar.'

'What a delightful idea!' she said, frowning, looking preoccupied as always.

'That's what I said,' said Elle, doling out money and ferrying small children along.

'YESSSSS!' Yells of excitement behind them as a year six girl got a strike.

'Well done!' Elle yelled at her. 'Come and get your prize from Mrs Armstrong.' She grabbed a packet of love hearts and shoved them in Mrs Armstrong's hands.

Carla looked on in wordless amazement.

Watching Mrs Armstrong stride away, she whispered, 'So it's all happening then?'

'Of course.'

'I half thought for a moment you were going to ask her.'

'There's an idea, I hadn't thought of that! Now, where's that husband of yours? This is all getting out of control. Come on, give me a hand Carl.'

Tom arrived from the opposite direction to the bar. 'What have you been up to?' she said lightly.

'On the Scalextric. Go on, off you go, your turn, I'll keep Dyl here.'

She made a wide circuit of the hall, avoiding even glancing at the bar area. She spent ages at the bookstall, sorted through all the books, trying to get interested in what she was looking at, reading without reading, buying more than she intended, for everyone but herself, from a big hardback biography of John Lennon for Tom to a

188

Where's Wally for Wilf and Tom to argue over. Every few minutes she wondered. Wondered where Rocky was. What Tom and Elle were talking about.

The Singalong Singers group chorusing 'Oh Little Town of Bethlehem' in all their innocence didn't help. Elle knew something he didn't, it didn't feel right. It was intruding on their marriage. It was a farce. And the *nonchalance* of that guy over there, at the bar. Having an easy Saturday afternoon drink. Having a casual fuck at a party. Something that hadn't even registered with him could trigger so much damage to, potentially, to the rest of her life.

The raffle over, the hall emptied fast. Tom, Toby and Wilf went for a last go on the Scalextric in year 1. She stole a look. He was still there, with Rick, drinking steadily. They were standing now, elbows on the dinner hatch bar.

Cyn, sitting at a crowded table, had turned, as if she'd known she was being looked at. Damn. Damn, damn. She was waving at her now.

'Hi–iiiiiiii!' She went for the bold, unmistakable entry approach.

'Carl, have a drink!' said Cyn pulling up a stool for her. 'Riiiick,' she called to the bar.

Rick and Rocky turned around.

'Another mulled wine here for Carla.'

Did he know her name? Had she told him her name? Still no recognition.

Good. Was it good?

She perched awkwardly on the stool, feeling she was there but not there. She'd got herself there and now she must get through it.

'You know Rocky, don't you, Carl.' She heard Cyn's voice bubbling through a distant gurgle of nerves as they returned.

'Yes, we met.' Carla smiled cheerily at Rocky, who was still looking at her blankly.

Oh dear, she wasn't *that* unmemorable was she?

'At Jo Salmon's party.'

His face looked like it had been turned on at a switch. His beard flickered, his cheeks chubbed up into a half-twisted smile of recognition. 'Ahhh, the dancing lady!'

Why had she said that? Why? Why?

'All right then?'

'Yes. Fine.'

'Gor, we had a few, didn't we?' He drew his stool closer to her. The smell of petrolly fabric and fags was bringing it all back.·

'Did you get home all right?'

'Yes, did you?'

'Somehow. Who was that silly bitch who was pushing me out the cab? I was only going to take you home.'

'Oh, she ...' she flinched visibly; Tom was coming over.

'Where are the boys?' she said loudly and pointedly at him.

'Playing footie in the playground.'

'Best place for 'em, isn't it.' Rick grinned at Tom.

'Is Toby with them, Tom?'

'I didn't notice.'

'I'll just go and check!'

She got up and walked smartly but quickly outside.

See, Elle. This was why she had to get it all out and over with. It wasn't fair on Tom, it was horrible, weird. Like she was outside herself, watching herself. He barely remembered her. It had been just that, some stupid flirtation at a party. See? The boys were all there, of course. Now what would she do?

No. She'd go back and join them. She'd not run away. Running away would only raise more questions. She needed answers right now, not questions.

Cynthia whispered in her ear as she sat down. 'Don't worry, Carl. They're rock 'n' roll, you're very safe.'

So, what did she know? Had they said something when she was away?

Rocky was smiling genially at her.

Tom was talking to Rick now. Only one away and he'd be talking to – him. They were looking at their watches. Oh no! They're talking about the match. Please don't invite them back, Tom, please no, no, no.

'What team does Rick support, Cyn?'

'What team? Football, you mean?' Cyn laughed. 'Oh, nothing. He hates football.'

'We're at home against Wolverhampton Wonderers,' Tom took a serious sip of his beer.

'Aren't they the ones who stopped you getting through to the Premiership last year?' said Rick.

'Yeah.'

Cyn shrugged and raised her eyebrows at Carla.

'What're you up to now, then, Carla?'

'We've got Toby for the night.'

'Oh, poor you.'

'If the Blades lose, I'm in for double misery. I am anyway with Toby. Last time he stayed I had to get Zita in on an extra shift to clear up and she's refused to do it again. When I get home I'm going to hide any game with small parts in it, all the pick-up sticks, all the toothpicks . . .'

'That boy, when he grows up, what will he be?'

'A shit spreader like his mother.'

'Carla!'

'Look out, here she comes.'

191

'Carla, I need to remind you about Toby's teeth! He has to brush for three minutes or he can't watch a video on Friday!'

'Sure,' Carla nodded.

'And he's not allowed more than an hour a day on the Playstation!' She looked at Cynthia. 'And only at the weekends!'

Bryony looked from Carla to Rocky. 'Have fun!' she said with a knowing smile on her face

'She's so cheeky,' said Cyn in a low voice.

'What really grates is she makes out she's doing *me* a favour...!'

'Let him go on it as long as he wants.'

'Don't worry, I will. I'm going to give myself some time out this afternoon.'

'You need it.'

Carla patted the carrier bag full of books on the floor beside her. 'I'm bunkering down in my nice warm bedroom with a large mug of tea and this little lot. Thanks for the drink, Cyn. Tom, come on darling, time we were going.' She stood up, took a firm grip on Tom's arm and physically pulled him away from the bar.

Chapter Twenty

Needing to be alone but scared to be left with her thoughts, Carla was glad of the books. One of the few blessings of having a football-mad family were these patches of time she'd have with no interruption. She wiped each book with a cloth as she piled them next to the bed in size order. Big children's books at the bottom, chunky hardbacks in the middle and paperbacks at the top.

It kept coming back; Rocky's horrible nonchalance, Tom's unsettling innocence as he chattered away to Rick; Bryony's smarmy elbowing; Cyn's reassurances and Elle's undisguised horror. Not telling him wasn't even an option any more. Even Elle must see that now.

Ten minutes into the game, she heard a shout and then a collective moan from down the stairs. Sheffield United were one nil down.

She put aside the Lennon book to wrap as a stocking filler. Lennon was one of Tom's only heroes outside the design world. They had a lot in common, the same easy daft humour, the same loving but difficult childhood. Pillows propped behind her, knees up, book resting in front of her, she flicked through the pages, looking at the photos. Of John as a boy. As a teenager. With Cynthia in her funny 60s haircut. Of his house in Liverpool. Of Aunt Mimi. Of John and Sean. John and Paul. John and Yoko. See, he loved her, didn't he? And how short and older-looking than him she was. There they are in bed. In their Amsterdam sleep-in.

At least she was only short and dark and didn't look as strange as Yoko. Not yet. And she wasn't weird. Not yet. She'd only get weird if she let these stupid thoughts start taking her over. She turned a page and sat a little straighter. John wasn't with Yoko any more. He was with a Chinese-looking girl with long plaits and a big smile. She thumbed through quickly, looking for the relevant text: John's 'lost weekend' with May Pang. She read quickly, of how Yoko arranged for John to leave New York and go off with his assistant to Los Angeles. She studied the photo of May Pang. Much younger-looking than Yoko - she would be. And pretty, in an intelligent kind of a way – looking like the cat that's got the cream.

On the next page, Yoko was back at John's side and May Pang had vanished. How did May Pang feel about that? Hang on, how did Yoko *do* that? And who for? For John? For her? Could she see something coming? Did she think he was going to have an affair so she went ahead and arranged it? Is that really what happened? Did she love him so much she'd do that for him? Arrange for him to have a lost weekend? Get it out of his system?

She slowly put the book down, went into the hall and slid downstairs. No one looked up. Even Dyl, who was building a complicated Brio track at their feet. She crept behind the weeping fig in the garden corner and switched on the computer.

Are you feeling lucky? asked Google. She wished. Ignoring the wider search she clicked on the luck, sitting up straight as the insides of the computer juddered and whirred.

'Yess,' she said to herself, as the thin, grey rectangle at the bottom of the screen filled with blue. After a concentration of urgent, deep clicks, flowers began popping up on the screen and a big sign surrounded by yet more flowers, asking what was happening.

She moved the arrow around the screen till it changed into a hand on the words 'Read My Bio.'

May Pang, she read, had been John and Yoko's assistant. She'd written a book about her relationship with John – Carla scrabbled in the drawer for a pen and wrote down the title. She'd been happily married to a record producer for a long time. Oh well, that's all right then, everyone ended up happily. She scrolled down.

Till John got shot, of course. She frowned, remembering her history teacher Mr Lacy turning up all in black. Black suit, black tie. She clicked through to the photos. There'd been a lot of sniggering and he'd got uncharacteristically, foot-stampingly furious with them, rubber-stamping John's death day in all their memories.

She studied a close-up of May and John. He was wearing Elton John's silly glasses with big spirals circling way out of his face. She had silly glasses on too, with concentrated clusters of jewels; she looked very sultry with her big lips and sad-looking oriental eyes. Then a slightly sinister, blurry shot of backs in sunloungers and John walking across from left to right behind them, on what looked like a very un-Californian day indeed.

She looked up. Tom was at the fridge, unclicking a beer. She clicked on Back, Back, Back.

He was behind her, touching her shoulders, looking at May Pang's opening page, asking what was happening.

'How's it going?' she asked, not looking up from the screen.

'Terrible ...'

'I hate my bum, I hate my mum.' Wilf and Toby tore past into the play room.

'It's only half time, isn't it!' she said brightly.

'It's only a matter of time the way they're playing.'

She could feel the utter, dejected sadness seeping out of every pore of his body. She sat and stared at the screen and waited. In situations like this, no consoling was worth the energy.

He slumped away to Dyl and the Brio.

Forward, Forward, Forward, she quickly clicked, then held her finger down, scrolling to May's final chapter. She left May and went back to Google and found a different website. This one said John had gone to live with May in Los Angeles. So, what was all this about a lost weekend she'd been reading about, then? This was no weekend mini-break after all.

Disappointed, she pulled herself up. What was she thinking?

That she could cope if Tom had a short fling?

Providing she set it up and knew where and with whom?

Mad Carla, you really are going bonkers, woman. As if such an insane idea would solve the surge of insecurities wasping round her mind. But then, why? Why had you wanted all of that which happened to those strangers so long ago, why did you want it to be just a weekend? What did it matter to you? Didn't it make it even more amazing how Yoko had done that over a longer period of time?

She'd forget about it now. Forget. Forget. Click, click, click.

Do you want to disconnect now? asked the computer.

She clicked on YES.

Chapter Twenty-One

One small ball landing in the wrong bit of netting 176 miles north of 22 Richmond Hill Grove succeeded in blanketing the whole house in gloom for the rest of the weekend. How a man could get so passionately miserable over one game of football was one of life's deeper mysteries Carla would never solve. He was so miserable, she'd even leapt at the chance to take the boys to Wilf's Sunday practice, leaving him to drink his sorrows away in the Marlborough.

Hunched up against the cold in her heaviest coat and one of Wilf's bobble hats, Carla stood on the touchline of the damp, winter field, her arms full of coat, sweatshirts and refreshments.

'Leave your hat on, please, otherwise mummy will be cross!' said a voice behind her.

'No – you can't have that.'

'Lottie, come *here*.'

Not feeling like joining the touchline gossip all around her, she kept a steady, level gaze on the muddy thuds, kicks and shouts, hard-nosing Dyl every few minutes if he dared even think of running out on the pitch again.

'Dyl, stop that please. Now. Right now.'

'No, you can't.'

'No.'

'Go ON, Wilf!' she shouted as he finally got hold of the ball, high-kicking it, even she could see, far too soon towards the goal. He did look cute though, in his new, almost knee-length Blades strip.

The boy in the red anorak in goal caught the ball with ease and high kicked it back. Then a burst of frenzy right under her nose made her grip hold of Dyl as high-flying clods of earth flew everywhere, till a boy lay sprawled in the mud, right by her feet. The whistle went. Wilf lifted the front of his T-shirt, flapping it to get rid of the heat.

The sky was dimming to dusk. Carla looked hopefully at her watch. It was only 3.30.

An angled kick towards goal.

The goalie stopped it with his chest and threw the ball back into the pitch.

'Leave it alone ...!'

'Hey, have you heard what Hazel said – the siblings are oversubscribed this year!'

She didn't rise to it till she dropped Jon at Elle's.

'Oh, not to worry.' Elle spun around her steel and white kitchen in a steam of herbal tea.

Elle's kitchen was a vision of cool modernity. Otto's slick, hard-steel practicality rubbing up against the fresh organic naturalness which was all Elle. The wood and steel units, like almost everything in Elle's house, were mounted on castors. Outside her neatly stacked cupboards, her shelves were sparse and her surfaces flawless. Every bowl was artfully displayed, with the odd piece of white crockery here, a Venetian glass jug there, adding just enough interest. Enormous panels of acrylic dyed photographs of Jon and Tallulah in fields of daisies covered the white-brick walls.

'Elle, you've got to be worried! Where else will they go?'

'I bet you're already working out who lives closer to the school than us, aren't you.'

'It wouldn't be hard to work out.'

'You'll be out like Mrs Armstrong next, with your measuring tape, seeing who lives the closer.'

'Don't you think it's slightly worth doing that?'

'What difference will it make?'

'If Dyl isn't going to get in, I'd rather like to know about it a little more than a few months before he's due to start.'

Elle opened a cupboard. Carla turned her face away. Elle's fridges and larders were like a sub-branch of Holland & Barrett. The sweet, grainy smell of health always made Carla feel ill, bringing on instant cravings for chocolate and cream, jugs of milk and thick, buttery wheat-filled toast.

'All you do,' Elle said, sitting down with her at last and spreading some disgusting brown paste on the oatcakes, 'Is if you don't get a place, find out who has got one and write a letter to the school, pretending to be them, politely declining your place ...'

'Elle!'

'It's been done ...'

'I bet it has ...'

'Here, have you seen this?'

Elle flung an *OK!* magazine on the table.

'What?'

'Have a look.'

Carla flipped through the pages. 'Oh, my ...'

'You see her in the magazines and on the screen and

199

she's so beautiful, then you see her in real life and I think
– I could look better than that!'

'Speak for yourself!' said Carla, feeling a cosy ripple of
companionship at Elle's indiscretion. 'That's why she's a
star and you're not.'

'You know what I mean. Her legs aren't that long, are
they, and they're not that colour either. And as for the
wrinkles, they paint them all out these days. All right, I'm
a bitch, I know, I know.'

She poured tea.

Carla turned the pages of *OK!* slowly. There was Jo,
'Happy to be single and free again', in her kitchen. In
her lounge. Was this taken before the party or after the
party?

'How many pages has she *got*?'

'How many rooms has she got.'

Sprawled on her bed. Her bed – the bathroom . . . in a
fresh surge of self-disgust, Carla flung the magazine
down.

'I can't get away from it!'

'What? – Oh – that!'

'Yes, oh that.'

'Oh, forget it, Carla. You know,' she said, pointedly
changing the subject, 'sometimes I think we're so lucky
. . .'

'What?'

'Having all those women in the playground to bitch
about.'

Carla flushed inside. 'And don't they have something
on me.'

'Doesn't it make you feel a bit better now you've seen
him?'

'Faced my demon? No! It brought it all back . . .'

She could have gone on but thought it wiser not to. Otto

and Tom were at the pub; that still scared her. Better, though, not to let on how scared she was.

'You know what those rock 'n' rollers are like. Now you should get yourself a real love, Carla.'

'I've got a real love, thanks very much.'

'All right, something to be properly guilty about. I tell you I wish I could find someone to have a fling with; Gabriel's just not biting.'

'He will.'

'I don't think so. I think he finds my useless dancing a real turn-off.'

'Sorry I haven't asked you, how did it go?'

'He wondered where you were.'

'And you explained . . .'

'I said you'd learned more than enough . . .'

'And how did you get on, with his – undivided attention?'

'You are not making fun, are you?'

'No, I want to know!'

'He insists I can get better, but I don't think so. And the chances of turning the sessions into a different kind of session: I've given all the signals.' She shrugged. 'It makes me feel – so *old* . . .'

'Are you sure?'

'I'm sure.' Elle shrugged.

'Maybe he's playing a game with you.'

'What kind of a game?'

'Hard to get?'

Elle pouted. 'I doubt it.'

Not knowing quite what to say, Carla said nothing.

'What's the time? Oh, come on, it's close enough to cocktail hour.' Elle poured them some white wine and they went through to the lounge.

A wall of textured breezeblocks arranged in zigzags

separated the kitchen space from a series of open-plan rooms. The soft, springy kitchen floor tiles gave way to sisal floors, huge abstract paintings and baskets. Elle was mad about baskets. They were scattered everywhere, filled with toys, CDs, towels, magazines, making even her clutter look elegant. The whole house looked virtually empty. A blue and white painted corner cupboard and one shelf of books in the living area; a papyrus plant and an iMAC G4 on the glass table in the office; a hand-thrown stoneware pot by the front door.

'I'm so bored with black and white, I thought I'd shoot the calendar colour.'

'That'd make a change for you.'

'I want to bring Tom with me for the recce, do you mind?' Elle flung herself down on one of a pair of cream sofas, the only comfortable-looking furniture in the place.

'No, of course not. Why should you ask me?'

Elle turned to look at her in astonishment.

'Why, she says! Who was it who got so mad the last time I asked Tom to help me?'

'No – I think it would be a good idea, a very good idea. It'll take his mind off all his problems, and that stupid football match.'

Carla lifted back the wall of Venetian blinds at the double-height windows and looked outside. Elle's garden left her cold. Overextending to create all the cool space inside had shrunk the mossy lawn to a tiny rectangle, out of all proportion with the house. She watched the raindrops flashing through the lit, brick flower borders, too scared to acknowledge that the plan seemed to be coming together all by itself, but at the same time finding a mad kind of comfort in it. At least she knew where she was with plans. Plans had patterns. They had beginnings, and

202

middles and ends. There was a template to set up. A schedule to be kept to. An action to be set in motion until the end was achieved – goal!

Chapter Twenty-Two

The sound of BB King drifting up from the basement later that week was the first real sign Tom was over the worst of his gloom.

Carla sat in front of the TV, sewing and wondering about the *Sex and the City* women. Worrying about them, that she might become one of them. With all plans, there had to be contingencies, preparations for the worst. Marrying so young, she'd missed out on the single girl buddy thing. Which one would she have turned out to be if she'd never met Tom? Miranda, her favourite? Or Charlotte? Not Carrie. Certainly not Samantha. Would she still be out there, like them? Looking for her soulmate?

Was she really stuck in some kind of time warp? Was supporting her husband and family all these years something so out of date as to be laughed at? Marriage had taken some of her individuality away, it couldn't not if it was any kind of a partnership, yet at the same time it was Tom who'd given her her first real sense of herself. Who'd made her feel she didn't have to apologise for being.

Like with her sewing. On their early dates, they'd discussed art and craft endlessly. Never running out of things to say. They'd talked about sewing's bad image. He laid it squarely at the door of the Renaissance. In mediaeval times embroidery had been just as important as painting. The idea of an artist being a unique person rather than just another person who worked at something didn't exist then. Painting was a job, like any other. So long as it paid, painting a shop sign, a picture, it was all the same to them. It was when everyone became obsessed with perspective, of making things appear to be there that weren't there. That's when all the fuss began.

It didn't work for embroidery: apart from anything else, the light was all wrong and the big works were all communal when the buzzword was the individual. That's when the artist became someone different to be set apart. As all the necessary craft-like skills like clothes and furniture and jewellery-making went to the lower classes, embroidery became a job to be done at home with love as the reward. Amateur, to be done for love; why was that a derisory word when the exact opposite was true, he'd asked. Wasn't love the greatest reward? Wasn't it more fulfilling than going out and making a public display of yourself and being patted on the back by strangers? Wasn't that what everyone was looking for?

It wasn't till long after the Renaissance that embroidery became associated with all the feminine graces – to be humble, to be chaste, to obey. She had been those things in Tom's eyes, she had, but it had been totally natural. She *liked* reflected glory. She liked being the moon to Tom's sun. She'd never wanted to be a Wimbledon champion; she'd always hankered after being the girlfriend sitting there in the shades, looking cool. Maybe it was time she changed. Maybe she'd have to change. Or was time changing around back to her? There were more women artists, some using embroidery now; it was an important statement, more than was on the surface, for women. And look at those *Sex and the City* women. They weren't happy, were they? If they were happy, there wouldn't be a show.

Telling Tom would be so much easier if she knew if anything had gone on with Danielle. She wished, she wished so hard it had now. She'd started thinking positively about Danielle, and talking positively about her to Tom. This had pleased him. She pushed the big, new thought from her mind but it kept returning.

Just the once, a quick seduction. If Elle and Tom were going to get it together, it would have happened by now after six shared years and three shared holidays. Elle wasn't after Tom, she was after Gabriel. She was always joking about the tantric sex thing; why not let her find out? Could Carla really go through with it? After all, she and Tom always shared everything. If she'd had a fling, it was only right that he had one too. Her fingers moved fast over the fabric.

At 11.30, she stopped sewing and set to darning each end in. She finished the lot before creeping silently up to bed.

She didn't have to decide just yet. She had one more opportunity coming up to see Danielle in action. Perhaps she'd give something away. After that, she'd make her decision.

She slept better that night than she had for many weeks.

Chapter Twenty-Three

In the party pause between taking the first drink and wondering where to go next, Carla looked idly around at the expanse of Brazilian slate floor, wondering if Bruno's decluttering stretched to furniturelessness or if he'd just not got around to buying any yet.

Bruno's kitchen was more of a wall than a room. A shiny metallic job with an alarming-looking system of built-in gadgets curling round to a state-of-the-art juice bar. The row of fixed mesh high-stools had already been grabbed by clusters of groovy young things, all talking extremely loudly and energetically, their voices echoing and rattling off the brick walls in the cavernous gallery-like space that was Bruno's new penthouse.

She decided to stay put for a while, positioning herself by a conveniently placed bit of steel wall jutting out into the room. Carla was no softie, but a designeratti-filled do like this was enough to freeze molten lava in its tracks. She gauged the scene. The usual mixture of strangers and half-knows. She preferred strangers. The half-knows would talk to her if she was standing next to Tom, otherwise they'd look right through her.

No one had been brave enough to sit in the only two

chairs in the main living area and she wasn't going to be a mould-breaker. A low-lit 50s classic Bertoia Diamond chair stood, sculpture-like, in the far corner. In another, facing away from the room, looking like it was enjoying the view of the river and the dome of St Paul's all by itself, was a low-slung wooden chair painted blue and red with broad arms and an eccentrically exaggerated slope of seat which almost hit the floor.

And there was Tom standing next to it, happily hijacked by a couple of admirers. Even from that distance she knew what he was saying word for word, waving his arms around, happily absorbed in design-speak. It was funny to see it again. The thing that started it all. The chair Bruno had snapped up along with Tom's life – and her own – at his degree show all those years ago. Apart from a minuscule state-of-the-art sound system, there was no other furniture in the place. The walls were still bare apart from a couple of industrial-sized Warhol copies – they were copies, weren't they? – and a cinema-sized plasma TV screen. There was no music; there'd have been no point in competing with the calls of recognition, nervous girlie shrieks of laughter and refined chatter filling the spaces between the intensive little groups.

There was something different though, from Bruno's normal parties. The seriously intense black polo-necked brigade she'd grown to love to hate over the years had been infiltrated by a new, flamboyant-looking crowd. They couldn't all be friends of Chlorine. Too young for a start, she thought, eyeing a violent clash of red hair and searing scarlet blanket dress talking to a strange-looking Japanese woman. Everything about the Japanese woman was tiny: her pointed nose – her little round glasses – down to her child-like bodice dress and pixie hat perched on her head. A surge of dowdy-wifeness wafted over her, though she was far from it in a buzzingly vibrant orange, bold enough to take any shocks. She'd gone for a simple Miyake-like elegance with baggy trousers over her highest heels, covered by an even baggier knee-length smock, slit open at the neck, its folds hanging elegantly beneath a sharply tailored jacket.

She looked at the chair again. It was only an object. But there it was. An object that had settled their futures so solidly for all the years since, looking for all the world like a living creature that'd snootily decided to turn its back on the invasions of the unknown art crowd.

If she was to avoid being mistaken for a sad, lonely soul or part of the furniture, she'd have to move along. She couldn't stand there for ever, half an eye on the lift disgorging crowds by the minute, half an eye on Tom, hoping to capture Danielle's hello kiss. Fixing her face with a pleasant, relaxed half-smile, she drifted purposefully. At a safe distance from Tom, she joined the chair in its study of the view outside. Perhaps it was lonely; there was much more furniture activity happening on the terrace than in there. Maze-like paths of turquoise floor-lit tiles, walkways and bridges over rectangular ponds glistening like glass; they might well be glass. She went to have a look at the Balinese outdoor bed, surrounded by big tubs of tall grasses and out-of-season blue poppies swaying in the breeze. There was no one, no one at all in that room she had any desire to strike up a conversation with whatsoever, and she wasn't going to waste her breath or her energy even trying.

She knocked back her drink and went for a refill before making her way to the food end of things. Bruno not being one to waste a minimalist opportunity when it presented itself, she wasn't surprised to see the table laid with nothing but bread and butter. But every kind of bread and every kind of butter imaginable. She went for a wodge of black rye with creamy white, resisting the temptations of the packet of Mother's Pride sliced and Utterly Butterly tub present and correct in the ironic corner next to a big retro steel toaster. She piled her napkin with some honey and walnut loaf for the journey and launched herself into the centre of the room.

Holding his Badoit Evian cocktail high above the crowds, Bruno was in full flow. From his Desperate Dan chin to his bulging brown eyes, everything about Bruno was big. If it wasn't for the campness in the way he stood, knees too tightly together, his upper torso bending to one side, he could be mistaken for a boxer. His 80s stubble, like the black polo neck, was a fixture in any design gathering. Except Bruno's stubble extended all over his head, and probably all over his body from the look of him, apart from his forehead, which was completely bald and at that moment glistening like a beacon under the halogen.

'... Well of course, you know what it is, don't you ...' he was saying as Carla neared the great orbit, '... what they have in common is their differences. By the way, is Dom here? Federica,' he called across the room to his long-suffering assistant, 'Feders dear, has Dom – Dom *Ballard* arrived yet? Let me know when you see him, will you, darling, I've got someone here I want him to meet.'

Ghad, he doesn't change, the name-dropping old poser! But then – Dom Ballard! One of Tom's heroes. Ballard was an independent, doing what Tom wanted to do. What Tom would have done if he hadn't been snapped up by Bruno. But then it would have taken years and they wouldn't have had the house, the ... she backtracked for another vodka, smothering her house fears with full-flow fantasy thoughts. Of Dom and Tom hitting it off, of cheery, mutual, respectful high-fives. The polite but firm snubbing of Danielle and her sidekicks before an effortless sailing into partnerships – Dom & Tom, she could see it now! She took a big gulp, looking around for the great man, before she realised she hadn't a clue what he looked like. No, hang on, he always wore a hat, didn't he, that was it, his trademark, a blue Chinese-style Mao hat. She filled her glass again and made her way through, keeping her eyes open for that hat, doing a little detour away from the honoured circle, even though Bruno was smiling broadly at her, in his full-on kind and friendly mode. If you didn't know him, you could almost be fooled by it. Bruno unnerved her in the same way Bryony did in the playground. Over-the-top friendly or completely blank; you never knew which was coming.

Bursting with the Ballard news, she set off towards Tom, holding back a little way away.

'No – don't tell me,' adorer no. 1 was saying. She had one of those annoying sharp, unignorable voices, her words hitting the air like shards of glass.

'De Stijl,' she said triumphantly, 'after Mondrian. Made in 1918, abstracted pure form, geometric shapes and primary colours . . .'

'He never forgot his roots though, did he?' said Tom grinning like a child getting the prize in assembly.

'But this is what you've done so brilliantly! You've married the intimate connections between form, function and beauty.'

'What I'm really interested in doing now is mixing the old craft techniques with new technology. You know, there'll be a lot of . . .'

Oh dear, oh dear, he's no idea he's been sucked into a design-speak wank. I'd better rescue him.

Before she could move, she saw Tom's expression change and then Danielle was in front of him, kissing him, cheek, cheek, cheek, three times, a little way behind Gilbert and George, as ever in attendance. She turned to another man she was with, a man who had to be her man. She summed him up quickly. Good-looking in a swarthy after-shavy European sort of way but *grim* – and tiny. She should go over now. Be friendly, warm, businesslike. Smooth, smooth, smooth, Carla, she breathed under her breath as she prepared to move. By the time she got there the two women had gone and Danielle was introducing Thomas like he was her latest acquisition, won at a closed-bid auction. Which, in some ways, Carla supposed, she had.

'Danielle!' Carla went for the kiss, kiss, kiss, bold approach. 'How lovely to see you.'

This Danielle was no fool when she picked her men, Carla thought, as she shook hands all round. Danielle's man, Serge, had the slenderest hands, beautifully mani-cured and the softest, sexiest touch; his eyes, however, were as cold as cod.

'So these are the people you're wasting all my money on,' they seemed to be saying. She had to work now, work hard to reassure whoever he was that they had chosen well. There were only two more pay cheques to come from Carliatti and that'd be it.

Tom greeted Serge with an enthusiasm he couldn't but respond to. They had three sets of factory premises to look at in Camberwell, Stockwell and Feltham; two were vacant but the best wasn't going to be free until February, could they wait that long? She felt foolish for her churlish thoughts and began to feel anxious about the lawyer, waiting to go over the paperwork in his office on Richmond Green. It seemed mean and ungenerous but no, this was the game. One to enthuse, one to peruse, that was business. She had a role.

'Dom Ballard.' Carla nudged Tom with her elbow as a Chinese hat passed by.

'What? Oh – yeah.' Tom barely registered and turned back to his conversation.

Emboldened by the vodka, she decided to follow him, perhaps make contact, who knows, this was business ... She pushed on forwards through the meaningless conversations,

'... sustainability ...',

'... industrial chic...'

'... innovators ...'

'... the *beauty* in anger ...'

Heads thrown back in laughter.

'... it has to be interwoven with human identity ...'

'... Paris is *so* much more directional than Milan these days ...'

A giggling girl in white lamé was taking pictures with her mobile phone.

Oh no. She'd put herself on a course running straight into Chlorene. She made a last-ditch attempt at fixing her eyes at a distant point in space. Too late.

'Carla, darling, how's Tom?'

'Fine. He's over there if you want him.' She made to walk purposefully on but ...

'Lazslo, this is Carla, Carla *Alexander*, wife of Tom Alexander. Lazslo's over from Extremadura.'

'Really,' said Carla dryly.

'Someone told me Margeila was coming?' Chlorene said. For such a willowy strange-looking person, she had an incongruously deep voice which came out from somewhere between the back of her nose and the top of her throat.

The dreadlocked Lazslo squealed like a pig, which Carla took to be some form of laughter. 'We'd never know, would we!'

She tried outside. It was much mellower here; she

breathed in the fresh air. People were lounging around, smoking, chattering quietly, sprawled across the Balinese bed, taking in the view. Music with lots of vibraphones and tinkly bits was coming out of speakers on the glass-tiled blue-lit wall.

There was Tasmania Cunningham from *Household Harmony* magazine. Standing in the breeze, talking to a woman in a silver lamé turban and black chiffon dress with very unusual arm arrangements.

She thought about going over, but no. No. Why did she even bother coming? This wasn't a place for her. She wished she was at home, like it used to be. The children upstairs in bed. Tom downstairs, clearing up his clutter ready for supper and a cuddle on the sofa in front of Graham Norton, or some mindless reality show.

Chapter Twenty-Four

'Here, Carla, here.' Anne Frost took her coat off the seat next to her.

Carla hunched herself, ready to clamber through a formidable row of knees,

'Carla! You're not free this afternoon, are you?' She smelt minty breath and a hand hovering over her shoulder.

'What for?' Carla asked suspiciously.

'The swimming rota, that's all right! Good! I'll tell Miss Cresswell you'll do it!'

Annoyed and guilty for forgetting to put herself on the list, Carla sat herself down in the Richmond Hill Juniors and Infants equivalent of a front stalls aisle seat.

'You must've got here early,' she said to Anne, glancing over her shoulder. The back of the packed hall was a concentrated crush of dads dangling off the climbing ladders and perched on gym equipment and plastic chairs with more cameras than Dixon's strapped to their hands.

'Melissa's the Virgin Mary,' said Anne proudly, 'we'll do you a copy if you like.' She nodded at her husband hovering behind a studio-sized camera, snarling away any amateur who dared stand too close.

'Thanks, Anne!'

At least Tom would get to see a video, even if it would be mostly of Melissa.

'Where is Tom?'

'Working.'

'That's a shame.'

'I've been through the worst bit.'

'Telling Wilf.'

Carla nodded. 'Most dads were away much, much more, I told him; still, it's a shame he'll miss Wilf's first ever speaking part.'

'Poor Tom,' said Anne.

Poor Tom.

Murmurs of anticipation thickened as Mrs Armstrong took the 'reserved' cards off the few remaining empty seats in the front row. As if on cue, Elle arrived, with Otto. As soon as they'd settled next to the MP, the year 3 recorders started on their breathy opening notes of 'Once In Royal David's City' like they'd been waiting for Elle and Otto to arrive.

The side and central aisles filled with a procession of five-year-old tinselled angels and tea-towelled shepherds. A panic of clicking erupted. Carla felt a welling in her throat. The girls were pretty but the boys as angels were something else, such clear-faced beauty, so fleeting, so short. She snapped herself out of her elegiac thoughts, glancing around quickly to see if anyone else was gagging. Not even Anne, when Melissa appeared, showed anything more than a proud smile. She felt her face filling as soon as Wilf trundled down the aisle, his crown pulled down to his eyes. She lifted her tiny instamatic and clicked as he approached. He stopped and posed.

'Go on, get on,' she hissed, pushing him forwards, his velvet robe trailing out behind him like Snoopy from the Seven Dwarfs.

Swallowing hard, she took her eyes off the back of Elle's head to the stage. On the crowns, the sequences, as Dyl called them, glistened red and gold in the spotlights.

Carla settled in her seat to watch the best-known play in the world with no one following the plot.

Her eyes, though, kept drifing to the backs of Elle's and Otto's heads a few rows in front. The more she looked at them, sitting there together, the more she became certain that Elle could quite possibly have said something to Otto. The more she told herself this, the more convinced she became that Otto could possibly have told Tom. Either that or he'd kept the secret and had been boozing with him but holding back, as she was doing.

'There's no room,' said the innkeeper, and that was it. She rummaged in her bag for a tissue. She felt Anne's concerned glance. A deep well followed, uncontrollable and from somewhere else. These were no silent tears and they couldn't be held back. She touched Anne on the knee, before slipping out of the door.

She kept her hand on the swing door, making it close quietly behind her, before reaching forward like she was being sick and running into the playground. She leaned against the railings, putting her hand to her burning forehead. She scrabbled for her mirror, her body still doing little involuntary heaves. When the tears finally stopped, she checked her eyes carefully, not sure whether to go back inside or go home. She had no choice: if she disappeared, Wilf would be distraught.

She crept back in, just in time for Wilf's big moment.

After endless speeches and applause and lots of 'Didn't the children do well,'s from Mrs Armstrong, the audience finally began to shift.

Elle and Otto left arm in arm, the only couple in the whole room making such a show of coupledom. There was nothing but Otto's normal, crispy friendliness to give her a clue as to whether he knew.

Though she hated swimming pools, she was glad of the swimming rota to take her mind off itself for a few hours.

Tom got home late and, too tired to go downstairs, passed out almost immediately.

Unable to sleep, she lay staring at the ceiling. Even the sound of his steady sleep breaths next to her were a fraud. All their habits had been moulded out of plain and simple truth and honesty. He'd been the first person ever to believe in her as she believed in him and she'd thrown it all away. They knew what to expect of each other and what not to expect of each other. Their well-defined roles were the foundations of their success. To do nothing wasn't an option. Someone like Elle or Otto only had to say the word and he'd hit the roof and the roof would fall on top of all of them. She couldn't have that. She simply couldn't have it.

Chapter Twenty-Five

'Since when has Jon been on silver stars?' Carla flipped through the pages of the tiny writing in Jon's reading book, feeling a proxy pang of inadequacy for Wilf's large print yellow circles.

'He did one of those leaps,' Elle said, filling the percolator. 'Wilf'll do the same any time.'

'I doubt it. If he had his way he'd stay on *Horrid Henry* for the rest of his life.'

'Did you hear what Toby Baxter's on?'

'*Harry Potter*?' Carla flipped through the pages of close-up writing.

'*Lord of the Rings* – Book 2!'

'What about Keira Thexborough then?'

'What?'

'She's writing her own version of *Lord of the Rings*.' Elle put out the mugs. 'Now, come on, tell me what's happening. You do look a bit pale, come to think of it.' A shadowy frown fell across her face. 'You haven't told him!'

'No.'

'Good.'

'I keep meaning to but it never seems the right time.'

'Because it never will be, Carla. I thought you were over all of that.'

'On the surface.'

'I know it has affected you but – you just have to move *on*, Carla, everybody does. And besides! Who's to know what he was up to that night? He's probably as hopeful as you that you forget about it all.'

'If only I knew.'

'Don't *think* about it!'

'I've tried that.'

'Think of the pluses – at least you got a fuck out of it. Now you must put it behind you. Tom's a great guy; he's fantastic with the boys. You're lucky to have him. And he's lucky to have you,' she added quickly, 'everybody knows that.'

'Thanks.' Carla took her cup.

She did know that. But those thoughts about what would have happened if she hadn't met him. If she'd chosen a different course at a different college . . .

'So, why all this end-of-the-world stuff?'

'It's not Tom. I mean, so what if Danielle seduced him? All it was is the modern equivalent of the casting couch.'

'That's right.' Elle nodded enthusiastically.

'I'm never going to be seeing her, am I, except at Bruno's stupid parties, which I have every intention of avoiding from now on.'

'You're talking sense at last.'

'What really niggles me is not *knowing*.'

'No one knows everything, Carla.'

'If only I *knew* if he, if they, had been together that night.'

If she knew she wouldn't be about to suggest the unthinkable to Elle . . .

'You'll never know.'

'I know.'

Like she'd never known before. He'd never stopped out all night, but there had been a few heavy attractions over the years. Danielle hadn't been the first.

'No, it's not what he got up to – or not.' She shrugged casually. 'Who's to know? It's what I got up to. It's me I can't live with.'

'Not much you can do about that, is there, except what I've been saying over and over. And at least your—'

'Don't say it, please. There's nothing "mine" about him.'

'At least he wasn't gorgeous!'

'Thanks for reminding me.'

'It's not as if you've fallen for him or anything, is it? Supposing you'd enjoyed it!'

'Well – I did a bit ...'

'Carlaaaa!'

Carla smiled. 'In a – physical kind of way of course ...'

'Are you telling me all that tantric stuff you get up to isn't what's written on the packet?' Elle sat down opposite her. 'Maybe you need another book.'

Carla laughed. '*Tantric Sex – The Sequel* ... No, we're still on the first one anyway.'

'What chapter?'

Carla chose her words carefully. 'I think it's all a bit of a con, if you really want to know.'

'Why?'

'I realised that was what was missing. After – Rocky ...'

'What?'

'Spontaneity. All this tantric stuff, it's all too – like designer sex really, it doesn't press my buttons any more.'

'You're disappointing me here!'

'You know how it's supposed to be all to do with the soul, not the body. But we have that anyway. Tom and I have always breathed in and out at the same time, naturally, we don't need some manual to explain it all.'

'There's more to it than breathing from what I've heard.'

'You're supposed to get rid of all those sex is dirty thoughts. All those lustful, naughty and not soulful-enough thoughts and for me, it doesn't go! That was what was so – liberating about the other night . . .'

'You like dirty sex.'

'In a way, it was an experience, yes! It was weird, but the wrongness of it was such a turn-on. Only at the time though, I'm paying for it now, aren't I.'

'And tantric sex isn't a turn-on?'

'Oh, the first time you try it, it's, well – like everything for the first time, a novelty, isn't it. But really, it's all a bit too – you know, macrobiotic for me.'

'Hmmm.'

She could see Elle thinking.

'It's too much – mind and not enough body . . .'

'Not from what I've read.'

'Why haven't you tried it, Elle? I would have thought Otto would have – even just for you. I mean when you were . . . I'm sorry . . .'

Elle sighed. 'No, no, it's all right, you know what Otto's like about anything alternative.'

'And you're free to explore now, aren't you,' said Carla cheerfully.

'You have to hunt before you explore, and hunting's not fun for a woman. All I've been getting is rejection, rejection. Otto finally having enough of me. Gabriel . . .'

Carla banged the table so hard Elle jumped. 'Elle!'

'What is it?'

'I have an idea!'

'What?'

She poured herself another coffee, she had to get the words out. Dangerous words which had to come out all in a tumble, and once they were out there they wouldn't be going anywhere but would linger and hang about her life for some time, her marriage, her friendship with Elle, everything. The plan in her head was one thing . . .

'I think, I'm thinking you could maybe do me a big favour here.'

'If you've made up your mind to tell him, there's not much I can do except carry on telling you it's a bad idea.' She looked at Carla suddenly. 'Oh no – *I'm* not telling him! I suppose at a stretch I could get Otto to—'

'No, no, NO! Listen.' She kept her voice level. 'You – you've always liked Tom, haven't you.'

'Everybody likes Tom,' said Elle flatly before a cloud of recognition swept over her face.

'I *know* Tom really *really* likes you and . . .'

Elle sat stiff with disbelief. 'Carla – what are you saying?'

'Don't you see?'

Elle lowered her voice and hunched over the table, her pale blue eyes showing the whites all around. 'You mean you want me in on a *threesome*?'

Carla nearly fell off her chair. 'NO! No, no, no.'

Elle visibly started breathing again. 'What then?'

'I was thinking if you . . .'

Elle was smiling now.

'If you could perhaps er . . .'

They both looked up sharply as Bridget the nanny strolled in.

'Sorry,' she said and walked out again twice as fast.

'What I mean is, most people, er women, find Tom very attractive and . . .'

223

'And . . .'

'In a little boy kind of a way.'

'He has charm, Carla.'

'The thing is, what he needs is . . . It'd only be fair. I was thinking, if, if you're, I mean you're so curious, it would, you could . . . without me knowing, of course. . . I'd get out of the way, you know, and then . . .'

'Then *what*?'

'Well, then, we'd be quits. I could stop feeling so damned guilty. As far as I know he's never actually – well, *done* it with anyone else. So, if he *did*, when I tell him, he can tell me and we can put it behind us and carry on as if . . .'

'What – aaahhh, I seeeee, you want him to. . . !!!! You want us to – me to *what*?'

'What we BOTH need to do, me and Tom, I mean Tom and I, I mean. Is to go forward out of this together and so I thought – just the once, of course, I'm not, just so's . . .'

'You want me to seduce your husband?'

'And then, when you've done er – it . . . I can tell him what happened to me, and then he can't be too angry, can he? He might even be relieved. What do you think?'

'Carla, you scheming bitch! Can I have it in writing?'

Elle threw back her head and roared with laughter.

Chapter Twenty-Six

The sound of glasses chinking, shiny heels on shiny wood and the low murmur of muted, clever conversations made Carla want to turn and run home. Instead she stood stock-still, studying the upside-down figures in wire mesh and see-through Perspex hovering dangerously low from the ceiling above mutilated musical instruments and a smattering of early guests. She couldn't remember the last time she'd been out on her own like this, but it seemed appropriate somehow. If the worst came to the worst, she could test out how it felt. This being alone business.

Her silk printed dress clung to her in a cold sweat. She'd forgotten how harsh yellow could be in the wrong light. She looked down to the group of cellos, bobbing with big, coloured plastic balls instead of scrolls. Tom would like those, she thought. Next to them were two big kettledrums with barbed wire instead of skins, and on the wall behind, a flute with keys but no holes. She found the oddness of it comforting. The familiar become strange, like everything else happening around her.

She imagined Tom was with her. Wondered what he'd make of the exhibit. He'd probably say they looked like characters, chattering over the canapés. And he'd sip at his beer bottle, looking around at the people.

And she'd agree and run with it. 'The dodgy neighbours, asked in for a drink and then staying too long.'

She looked around, startled. She hadn't said that out loud, had she? No, good; no one was giving her peculiar looks. She inspected the guests. Tom would be making quiet jokes about them. He'd like that girl there, though, the one with the loosely woven blonde plait draping over her bare shoulder.

'We must be in the right place tonight,' she'd say, taking his eyes away from the girl, pointing out a TV art critic hovering at the entrance with a bored-looking film crew.

'Carla!' Chlorene floated into her orbit like a butterfly. 'Where's Tom?'

'Working'

'But – everybody's here! I've just seen Danielle – and Bwruno's arrived, and Barton and Char . . .'

'He doesn't always work with Danielle, Chlorene.'

Chlorene gave her a strange, perturbed frown. 'No, of cwourse . . .'

'He's working on other projects.'

'Other pwrojects!!'

Oh no, she'd better not stir it. 'A charity thing, for the kids' school.'

If Elle could be called that.

'Oh!' She smiled at her strangely again and wafted off.

Oh dear, I should have said something about her work. I haven't seen it yet, where can it be? Where is Danielle?

She moved cautiously through the galleries, catching her thoughts and turning them back on themselves. Danielle, why couldn't she could just go up now and ask her? Ask her blank outright, what happened that night? Put in a quick call to Elle, tell her not to go through with it.

It was too late now. Thinking was dangerous for a missing person, standing outside her marriage, outside her way of doing things. A horrible feeling of betrayal swept over her. She was a festering, suspicious wife, hiring a private detective. She suppressed it. This wasn't like that. This was all planned. Nothing was amiss. She was moving forward. Letting go, that's all. Doing what everyone kept telling her she should be doing.

She stopped at a wall of postcard-sized pen and ink drawings and began reading the blurb next to them. She imagined Tom's frown over her shoulder.

'Don't read it,' he'd be nagging, 'If the work can't tell you, it's not working.'

Well, stuff you! You're not here, are you. She took her time.

Celia Acciene places her poems and etchings on postcards and displays them in post office windows across the country. Each work is unique, being reproduced in no more than a limited edition of eight. Book compilations of her work are also issued in limited editions usually only obtainable at auction. If you see one of her works displayed in a post office, which could be anywhere from Penzance to Uisk, you are entitled to go in and claim the work for yourself. Celia's work is fusion. It merges the concepts of the found object, poetry, sculpture, fine and performance art.

She'd learned something from that. She learned all about the artist and what she was about. See, Tom? she said smugly, they're not just postcards on a wall. How else would I have known that? I should do this more often. Maybe I need this as much as he needed – as he needed his bluff to be called.

She found Chlorene's display.

She stood in front of a small, glass-fronted box mounted on the wall. Inside was a white cross, smeared with blood at its tips.

She heard Tom's stifled giggle. 'Bloody Norah, what have we here?'

'Bloody's the word, Tom.'

She challenged him, hiding the blurb, insisting he tell her what it was about. 'Er, the feminine, obviously. Erm, blood on the cross, sacrifice, female sacrifice . . .'

'*Flesh and Blood*,' she read out, twisting her lips in disgust.

A couple came and stood behind her. The imaginary Tom's elbow dug into her side and they stood stock-still in a conspiracy of earwigging.

'Is that blood or paint?' asked a droopy, drawly American voice.

'Don't know.'

'If that's real blood I'm going to be sick.'

'Is body part art *still* all the rage?'

'I don't believe it.'

'Tampon art's *so* passé these days.'

She moved on to a little transparent box mounted on the wall. It was half filled with earth with the tampons sticking out of it, their strings visible.

Tom would be sniggering away at this. 'Looks like Wilf's worm box,' he'd probably say.

'Roots? Boots, more like.' Her laugh mingled with his as they moved confidently into the crowd.

A tray of white and red paused in front of her. She went to take a glass, then changed her mind. Then changed her mind again just as the waitress moved on, nearly knocking the tray over. She could hear Bruno's voice nearby. What should her take be with Danielle?

228

Friendly and sweet? Cool as ice? Distant? Distant. Distant and mysterious. Stay as far away from her as possible. She wouldn't want more than a hello without Tom there anyway.

Taking a small sip, she turned away from the wall for a moment. Feeling instantly lonely, she turned back to the wall again. Happy to be away from Chlorene now and onto a different wall, a different artist. What have we here, then? She looked at the vast areas of black with white rectangles looking like babies' bottles.

She could hear her mother's derisive laughter now. 'Babies' bottles, Carla, is that all you can think of? You are such a phillie sometimes.'

'What's a phillie, mum?'

What would her mother have to say about her little plan? Like Yoko, Japanese women accepted little liaisons here and there. For the wives to arrange them wasn't unheard of. Part of their culture, like for Swedish women to divorce-lite. Like for English women to be married and dumped by year 4? Except they did the dumping these days, a lot of them, didn't they? Not that that made them any happier. She stood straight and serene. Thinking of others who'd been there before made her plan seem more reasonable, like a part of her piecemeal culture was slotting into place. Like bringing the fragments of her past together, like this was as much her destiny as meeting Tom had been.

She stared at the Rothko-like expanses of black canvas. More of a thing than a colour, a thing which absorbed everything in its path, taking everything around it into its one darkness.

Through the black her own picture formed. She could resist it no longer; she had to picture what was happening between Tom and Elle, right at that moment. They'd have

229

started off at Elle's studio, as was the plan. He'd be there by now. Talking all legitimately about layouts and locations and things. They wouldn't be staying there long, though. She'd suggest they go for a drink. Not to the pub. Otto might be there. Otto, what would Otto think? Where, then? A hotel? What hotel? Oh, I know! But surely she wouldn't use that Richmond Hill Hotel voucher she'd bought at the auction? Would she?

A woman came up to them and handed her a card. People were turning around, looking at her. A woman next to Carla momentarily lost her gallery cool and dug her elbow into Carla's side.

'What is it?' whispered Carla.

'Celia Acciene!'

Carla looked at her blankly.

'The cards, the *cards*! Keep it safe. She rarely gives out in performance these days.'

'Oh.'

'It's worth a fortune.'

How much? Tom would want to know, his voice so sharp in her mind she turned around, half expecting to see him standing there.

'The Tate's already bought,' said the woman, peering over her shoulder.

She looked at the card in her hand. A pen and ink drawing of a parcel. Newspaper. String. Badly made, falling apart. Beautifully drawn, the newsprint all crumpled, every miniature word and photograph pixel reproduced. Below it a message: 'Pass it on.' Carla looked around like a startled cat, suddenly aware she had a huge audience, the documentary film camera, lights and all eyes all pointed at her. She looked around for the artist, who'd disappeared. She looked down at the card.

Bewildered, she looked up again, directly at the

camera, hunting for her. Bryony's playground smile. She spotted Bruno.

'Hello, Bruno!!' Cheerful as hell, she was.

'Hello, Carla!! Where's Tom?'

Bruno took the card greedily. He read it and looked around sheepishly before pocketing it. A collective intake of breath went around the room.

'Hey, you're not supposed to do that!'

'It doesn't say *when* you have to pass it on,' he said smugly.

The little theatre over, the cameras stopped rolling and the murmur of collective talk struck up again.

Bruno looked at her. She hated the way he looked at her.

'Look, good to see you, but I have to see that chap over there before he leaves ...'

Bruno left, leaving an embarrassing gap filled by Danielle, Gilbert and George. Carla smiled at George, who evidently hadn't a clue who she was. She looked quickly to Gilbert, to Danielle.

A cloud of recognition crossed over Danielle's face. 'Ah ... er Mrs ...'

'Carla.'

'Carrrla, yess of course ...'

It felt strange to be staring at the person who'd started it all off. The person who had triggered her drunkenness and all that had followed, that was following right now ... Right now maybe ...

'Where's Thomas?'

'Tom. He's busy tonight, erm, excuse me, I have to see that chap over there before he leaves.' She hurried off to the next room. Instinctively heading for the bonkers cellos.

The girl with the blonde plait was there. Circling the cellos, her wine glass aloft.

She knew Tom would have liked these.

'There's something so sad about them, don't you think?'

Tom twanged one of the bobbles.

'Don't *do* that! But yes.' Carla nodded. 'Terribly sad.'

This would be the time she and Tom would look at each other and decide it was time to go.

'Yes. Yes, let's leave now,' his look would say.

She looked up at one of the angels from hell, dangling above her head, wishing it would fly away.

'Let's go home.'

Chapter Twenty-Seven

When she got home, Tom was sprawled with his legs up on the sofa watching *Monkey Dust*.

'I'd thought you'd be later,' she said.

'I thought you'd be later,' he said. 'How was it?'

'They all wondered where you were.'

'Who?'

'Bruno, Chlorene – Danielle was there!'

'Was she.'

'How about you?'

'What?'

'The meeting. With Elle.'

'Oh. Fine.'

'Sort the locations out?'

'Yup.'

'How was Elle, then?'

'Fine. Chlorene all right?'

'Mmmm.'

She unstrapped her shoes and sat down next to him, tucking her feet under her knees and leaning against him.

He put his arm loosely round her. She wriggled into their normal TV-watching position. There was no sign in the movement.

No change. He was calmness personified.

'How did you get on then?'

'All right.'

'I missed you.'

He patted her shoulder.

Either he was a much better actor than she'd ever given him credit for or Elle had bottled out. If she'd tried it on and he'd resisted, he'd say something, she knew he would.

At the commercial break, she went to the kitchen and lifted the rubbish bag out of the bin. It was half empty.

She slipped her bag over her shoulder and went outside. Oblivious to the cold, she dumped the rubbish and clicked off the night lights. She leaned behind the fattest tree-trunk, looking up at the cold, moonless sky. The garden felt dark and strange without the light, and smelt of muddy air. Her heart thumped, her breathing quickened.

Otto answered.

No, Elle was out, did she want to leave her a message?

He spoke slowly and clearly. She could hear the bafflement in his voice.

She went back inside, thinking of Elle, lying amongst the ruffled sheets in the Richmond Hill Hotel, pouring the last of the wine from the ice bucket. *Monkey Dust* would be on her TV as well.

'Get yourself a glass, there's a movie coming up after this.'

'I think I'll turn in.'

Tom's definition of a good movie was rarely hers. Feeling the need for solidarity, she read a bit more of John and Yoko, drawing strength from their undeniable togetherness, enabling her to eventually fall into a dreamless, twitchy sleep.

There was no sign of Elle in the playground the next morning. She hung around the slide, keeping Antonia talking, feeling foolish when Otto turned up with Jon, quickly getting away from Ant so she could call the house before Otto returned.

No answer. Her mobile was switched off.

She went through the morning routine like a robot. Picking up, picking up, clearing up, clearing up, bin laundry in the machine, new laundry in the bin, uneaten breakfasts scraped and stacked, all that was upstairs that should be downstairs chucked downstairs, all that was downstairs that should be upstairs piled at bottom of stairs. Floors swept, bathroom wiped, loos squirted, sheets changed.

First the beds. Always first the beds. She couldn't be in a house with an unmade bed in it. She could hear Elle's teasing, the first time they'd gone to Sicily, laughing at her suitcase full of Peter Reed sheets. It wasn't much effort. Zita did them with the boys' beds on her Wednesday day, leaving Carla the Fridays and Sundays to do their own. The machine washed them; one of Cyn's girls ironed them.

She found Elle when she wasn't expecting it, while she was busy squashing as many olives into her pot as possible at the Waitrose self-service deli counter. Dyl came back from the bananas with Tallulah by his side. Not sure if she was seeing things or not, Carla ducked, peering through the Perspex of the olive and salad bar. Elle's back was towards her, her blonde hair falling over her black leather coat. She hadn't noticed Dyl.

Not on a major trolley-job then, she thought, eyeing the hand basket dangling from the crook of her arm like a fancy Fendi. If you stay in hotels with other people's husbands what need is there? Stop it, Carla, stop it. This is all your doing, now *deal* . . .

With trembling hands, she clicked the lid over the

235

squirting crush of olives and made for the bananas.

Elle physically jumped as she turned around.

'Carla!'

With none of her smiles working, Carla's frown stayed. 'I've been calling you all last night, all today; what's with the hiding?'

'Hiding?' Her smile evaporated.

'You're not in the playground, you're not at the nursery . . .'

'That's because it's Otto's day.'

'I didn't know he had a day.'

'Should you?'

'Well – I – so—'

'If I were hiding from you, I'd hardly be *here* on a Friday afternoon, would I?'

Carla looked down at Elle's basket. Shopping trolleys were like hands, she had to look. The contents scared her – smoked salmon, stargazer lilies, rosé wine.

'Those bananas will clash,' she said feebly.

'How was the opening?'

'OK. So – what happened?'

The telling in the twinkle of her eyes said it all.

Too late for lunch and too early for afternoon tea, the Dickens and Jones caff was deserted enough to let Dyl and Tallulah loose.

Carla toyed with her teaspoon, not knowing which question to put first.

'Stop looking so glum, Carla, you're making me feel guilty.'

Where? How long? – *How*? Did he resist at all? Or was he butter in her hands? Did she have a right to ask? All the time, the image of Tom last night, relaxing on the sofa, being so – *normal* . . . In retrospect, had he been *too* normal?

'All that you wanted happened. Carla, are you all right? It's what you wanted, isn't it? Isn't it!'

That's what she'd said. That's what she'd heard. Hadn't she?

'It's a bit of a shock, that's all. He was so *calm* last night when I got back.'

She thought of herself, in the gallery, whilst it was going on. Alone. Feeling alone.

'Did he ...?'

'Resist?'

Carla swallowed.

'He was a bit surprised!'

A bit?

'Where – did you go?'

'Do you really want to know?'

'I really want to know.'

'To the hotel – you remember, the one I bid for ...'

'I guessed that ...'

She remembered Tom in full-on flirt, mucking about with his paddle. How would he be with her now?

'How did you get there? What did you – did you – *do*?'

'You want to know all my seduction techniques!' Elle laughed, a funny little laugh.

She looked like she was pleased with herself whilst trying hard not to.

'At least tell me if he was a walk-over or not; if he for a moment paused to think of his family ...'

'Did you?'

'Elle! I was drunk!'

'So were we.'

'He didn't seem drunk.'

Elle laughed again. 'I think he sobered up pretty fast.'

Carla didn't like the tinkle in her laugh.

'What did you drink?'

237

'Do you really want me to tell you what happened?'

Carla nodded.

'From beginning to end?'

Carla nodded.

'All right. But then I suggest we never talk about it again, is that a deal?'

'It's a deal.'

'Stop looking at me like that. It *is* what you wanted, isn't it?'

Carla nodded. 'It is.'

'And if you want my serious advice, the best thing for you now is to forget all about it. You are quits, you have what you wanted, now forget it!'

'You mean, not tell him at all?'

'Why not? All lovers have little secrets from each other about their pasts; all you are doing is joining the real world. It's not worth the risk, Carla. You still have a loving, a very good, loving husband. You haven't lost him and you won't lose him. Believe me.'

'So you're not – planning to do it again?'

'Carla! Of course not!'

'Wasn't he good enough?'

'Carlaaaaaa!'

'Sorry, sorry, sorry – it'll take a bit of getting used to, that's all. So, you were going to ...'

'OK. He came to my studio, as arranged at 6.30 ...'

'Was Otto there?'

'No.'

'I wore a sexy little dress with no underwear. You know, it's very strange the way men know when you've got no knickers on; even if you are covered from head to toe with layers of fabrics you can sense them honing right in, can't you ... and then ...'

*

238

'Here we are, what about this one?' Tom held the spiky top of the tree and banged it on the ground a couple of times to shake out the branches.

Carla stood back, her head to one side. 'I don't like it.'

'Why?'

'Muummm.'

'It'll never fit in the car.'

'That's not a reason.'

'Mummmm.'

'I'm not driving in this weather with a tree tied to the roof, it's bad enough as it is.'

'MUUUM!'

'WHAT?'

'Can we go and play now?'

'Go on, off you go,' said Tom. The two boys raced off into the snowy grounds of Wisley.

'Look after Dyl!' she called after Wilf.

'I think it's the one.'

'Come on, let's have a look round.' Carla set off through the forest of Christmas trees. 'We haven't come all this way to pick up the first one we see.'

Tom kept his hold on the tree. 'This is the one, Carl,' he said stubbornly.

'Come *on*, Tom.'

Tom stood his ground.

'There's thousands to choose from, that's why we've come all this way.'

Carla walked on. When she finally turned back after Tom hadn't caught up with her, she stopped and sighed. 'Oh, no.'

The tree wasn't in his hands any more but being clutched defensively by a smart looking man in a long, black cashmere coat.

She went back.

'You'd put it down!' the man was insisting.

'I was just going to get my wife back. I'd been holding onto that tree for a full five, no – ten minutes!'

'Had you paid for it?'

'No! I was just persuading my ... here she is, Carla, come here and tell him to give me my tree back.'

'We don't want that tree, Tom.'

'Yes we do!'

The man and his wife looked smugly in cahoots with Carla. She glared back at them.

'Just come over here and look at it from this angle. It's scrawny, and the top branch is too long, much too long, *look* at it ... it's the most miserable sample of a Christmas tree I've ever set eyes on in my entire life ... if we wanted one like that we could have gone to Kingston market ...'

Tom was the one smiling apologetically at the man now as Carla led him away. When they were a safe distance they turned back to see the man, still clutching the tree, arguing with his wife.

They giggled. Tom put his arm around her. 'Right as always, Carl, talk about a tree with bad vibes ...'

'I'm beginning to feel sorry for the tree now.'

It took them another good hour of picking up and shaking and standing back from the thousands of non-drip, non-drop, ready-potted, ready-rooted trees before they found the one they both agreed on. Tall enough but not scrawny, thick and bushy, the branches tapering evenly into a fine point at the top.

'Come on, let's go and find them and show it off.'

'Don't be childish.'

'I bet they haven't got *Homes to Die For* coming to film *their* tree.'

'Where are the boys? Which ones are ours?'

They looked across the grounds at all the Gore-Texed, bobble-hatted children, like little Lowry-figures against the white of the snow.

Carla felt the peppermint air in her nostrils. 'I hope it sticks till Monday. They'll be up and ready for school in a flash.'

'Here we are then; come on, tree; let's go and make you ours before some smart arse comes along and grabs you for himself.'

'I'll get the boys.'

'You can leave them there, they'll be all right.'

'Will they?'

'We could have a cup of coffee? A nice quiet sit-down. I'll go and pay for this first before you change your mind.'

Carla chose an outside edge table by the pond so Tom could smoke. Wishing she felt her usual snug in their annual tree ritual. She looked at the mish-mash of cracks, like marble terrine jelly below the smooth, ice surface of the pond.

This day would be the hardest. That was to be expected. She had to practise being in the present, trusting the future, to know it was hers.

Her guilt had been totally replaced by utter disbelief at Tom's completely normal behaviour. Should she believe Elle? But, whatever she'd said, that look on her face, in the supermarket, and all the avoidings. And what she'd said! She couldn't have made all that up, could she? How she'd given him a drink and they'd started talking through the calendar concepts month by month and then she'd suggested as the hotel was one of the locations, perhaps they should go and find the manager, and stop off at the bar there for a drink. As soon as they'd sat down she'd produced her free B&B pass she'd bought at the auction and reminded him of his teasing, and began teasing him.

241

Not for a night of course, just a few hours, she was missing physical companionship. Otto had a new girl, which, it turns out, Tom knew about and didn't know she knew about. Fancy that, too! Tom was better at keeping things from her than she could ever have guessed. Then Elle had told him she'd just made that up and Tom had given the game away, which made them both laugh. She assured him it was OK, it was fine, she was a free woman now. The first move?

'It had to be a bold one, I didn't want him to take fright, I didn't want him, as you said, to think of his family. He had to get beyond that quickly to a point of no return.' She'd picked his hand up and moved it to her leg and round to her inner thigh, 'you know, that really soft bit.' His mouth had dropped open and she'd planted a little teasing kiss on it, muttering, chirruping him on, 'just for an hour'; she'd let his hand find her. She was, she confessed, totally turned on by this, the situation, and he'd felt her ready for him. She'd picked up the token on the table. 'I had to make sure we went together; there was every possibility he'd run away back home if I let him go, so I held him very tight, and we went to the reception and checked in. Once we were in the lift I felt him; I had to keep him aroused. We kissed properly for the first time, missing our floor. Going up and down, up and down in the lift until someone got in and we straightened up.' Carla had wanted to know the floor number, the room number, but she kept quiet, afraid Elle'd stop; she wanted every detail, every tiny detail. 'As soon as we got into the room we were on the bed. I pulled down the covers, lay him down and sat astride him.' He'd have liked that, Carla thought. She'd stopped going on top ever since reading a magazine article about how unflattering it was for anyone over thirty-five to go on top. Elle would have been all right, she didn't have any secret chins lurking . . .

Each day would become a little easier. She'd slept on the story now and woken up with the story. Even the day had started like a new slate with the children waking early, hysterical with excitement, barging into the bedroom, putting paid to the question about whether there'd be any lovemaking that morning or not. As soon as she'd opened her eyes, the house felt different. The snow light touching every corner of the house, making it feel still and mysterious, in the one light, connected to all the other light. It was like the snow had brought her out of her darkness into another state where everything was cold and still and strange.

She left Tom to sleep in. The boys refused to settle till they'd got their boots on and were out in it, stamping their footprints all over the garden. Scraping the thin coating off the ground, London snow, never thick enough for snowmen or snowballs. He'd been quiet at breakfast, as well you might, she'd thought; she knew what he was going through, the horrible guilt, the feeling of being in a danger zone.

She nearly told him, right there and then that she knew, and not to worry, the same thing had happened to her. But stopped herself. No, she'd leave it a few days.

As they'd left Richmond, the boys' squeals changed to roars as the snow thickened with every field that they passed. But only the boys, she'd noticed. Not Tom. He'd driven steadily and seriously, his eyes ahead on the road.

Tom arrived back with the tray. Carla took the cups and plates and propped the tray up against the wall behind her. He rummaged for a cigarette. Was he about to tell her now?

The woman at the next table fanned his smoke away exaggeratedly almost before he'd lit up.

Tom turned to go for her.

'No, Tom.' Carla shook her head grimly at him.

Tom's mobile rang.

He stood up and set off on his mobile phone pace, walking slowly away, hunched over his hand, taking quick drags of his cigarette.

She hated herself for it, but she couldn't help listening intently. No. She could hear him talking about square meterage, buildings, sawmills. But had he? Had he last night? Had he ever? Despite all the flirtations she doubted it. He might have liked the idea of it, but – no. He would have been too scared to go through with it. That's what she'd always thought, and that hadn't changed. She couldn't believe Elle was telling the truth, either. He wouldn't be so relaxed if they had. Or was she just wishing that, pretending to herself? Why would he be so quiet in the car otherwise? Questions, questions. There were more questions than ever. That was the only difference now.

He sat down again. Talking about work seemed to relax him a bit.

'You know she's right on our side. All your worries about Bruno, he's putty in her hands, Carl, she deals with him.'

'That's because she's richer than him.'

Tom laughed. 'The only people Bruno looks up to, you mean? You're probably right. She's talked him out of his daft *Big Brother* ideas anyway. We'll have a minimum manufacture base, just enough to keep a steady income, leaving me to get on with the Morrisey chair ... Then she's getting me into Belsay Hall in the spring. That'll be my first solo exhibition ...'

'Why didn't you tell me?'

'I am telling you.'

'Before. That's big news ...'

'You haven't wanted to talk about it.'

'I have.'

'Whenever I mention Da ... Danielle, you go over all queer. Don't say you don't because I know you do, and frankly I've enough on my plate at the minute ...'

'I just thought you'd tell me, that's all.'

'Well, I have, all right?'

'What's Belsay, anyway?'

'It's a big, old house near Newcastle... everyone's showing there, Linley, Silvestrin ...'

'Can I come?'

'Of course you'll come!'

'Don't say it like that. I'm feeling a little left out of it all, that's all. Like, you not telling me things. I don't like it.'

'If I talk about her you object, if I don't talk about her you object; what am I supposed to do? Hold up ...' Tom put his hand out to the Christmas tree leaning against the spare chair.

Carla looked over her shoulder then turned back quickly. The black cashmere couple, dragging their tree behind them, settling themselves down at a table underneath a heater by the pond.

'Look at that, it's a different tree,' said Tom happily, squashing his cigarette stub firmly into the ashtray.

'They're still arguing though,' said Carla, noting their black faces.

They left the café and walked through the gardens. She tucked her hand into the crook of Tom's arm. He gave her a little squeeze.

Neither of them said anything.

Her boots made funny little snowy squeaks as she walked.

Be in the snow, she told herself. Feel the footsteps on the soft ground.

They stopped when they got back to the lawn. Tom went to call the children. She turned to look back at her footprints. Gazing fondly at the imprints of her spiky heels of her boots, the neat little round sole, heel, sole, heel, sole, and Tom's big snow boots next to them, before turning back to the pure virgin snow up ahead, waiting to be trodden in.

Chapter Twenty-Eight

Carla unpacked the end of another year, carefully sorting the soft tinsel strands from the shiny shell-thin balls, Winnie the Pooh candlesticks and old pine cones in a whiff of deadwood attic dust.

'I want the balloons.' Wilf dug anxiously through all the boxes.

'Hang *on*, Wilf, we need to get rid of a few things first.'

'You can't throw that!' Tom snatched the rubbish bag. 'That's Dyl's first angel.' He proudly held up a soggy mass of cotton wool and bits of dried-out thickened glue perched on top of a graffiti'd toilet roll.

'I don't think he's bothered.' She untangled a string of badly wrapped spiky lights, cracking together in their crumpled plastic bag as she took them out.

Dyl, sitting cross-legged on the floor, was staring at himself in a large purple glass ball, his head to one side, his mouth fixed in concentration.

'I do!'

'We've got this year's angels, *two* of them, plus all these snake spirals and wizards.'

'Don't chuck them, all right? Keep them in the boxes at

least. Where are the chocolates?'

'They're not going to be in the old boxes, are they.'

'BALLOOOONS! Where are the balloons?'

'Not to be eaten until Christmas!' she said sternly, reaching for a new, smooth M&S bag from under the table and pulling out a flat cardboard package

The beginning of the chocolate subterfuge, with everyone sneaking the odd one when no one was looking. She had boxes of spares seriously hidden away for when they thinned out. One of the nicer Christmas chores – replacing the chocolates on the tree.

Tom checked the balance of the bare tree on its curly metal stand in the centre of the front bay. Adjusting it and standing back, over and over.

Outside, the snow had already turned to slush.

Finally satisfied with the tree, he busied on. 'Right, drinks.'

'CD first, Tom.'

'Where is it?'

'It's here somewhere.' She rummaged through the boxes. She found it beneath the pile of last year's cards, stacked in shape order and tied with an elastic band.

As King's College Choir filled the room, Tom poured the drinks.

Wilf sat himself on Carla's lap and leaned into her.

'Muum?'

'Mmmm.'

'You know you said I couldn't have a James Bond electric car.'

'Mmm.'

'Because it was too expensive ...'

'Mmmm.'

'Does that mean Father Christmas goes to the shops, then?'

'I don't know, Wilf, I've never asked him.'

'So – could I put it on my list then?'

'You could try.'

She smiled at Tom as she took her sherry. Wilf had decided that a continuing belief in Father Christmas was a potentially far more profitable state of affairs than any brutal denial of his existence, in the same way it made no economical sense to blow the gaff on that other out-and-out-lie, the tooth fairy.

Tom dangled and untangled the lights. 'Shall we get some new lights this year?'

'Why?'

'These are getting a bit ropy, aren't they. We've had them a while ...'

'They work perfectly well.'

'I was wondering about a change of colour ...'

'We've got every colour in the spectrum there ...' She paused to take in the way Tom was looking at her. She threw her head back and hooted. 'Tom, you're not suggesting we go all designer on our TREE, are you!'

'I just thought what with the show coming up ...'

'Tom Alexander, I'm ashamed of you ...'

'Your tree is a statement, isn't it ...'

'Tom, you're not seriously suggesting we go down the white lights and fluff road!'

'I didn't say that! There's all sorts of new tree designs these days.'

'No.'

'Everything else in our lives gets a makeover every now and then so why should the tree be any different?'

'That's exactly why it's different. We're keeping with our flashing colours and bits of what the children have made ... We're decorating this tree for ourselves not for *Homes to Die For*!'

249

She pulled out a decoration she had made six Christmases ago and put the small rectangle of fabric to her nose, sniffing the stale cinnamon.

She held it up. 'Chuck or revamp?'

She fingered the glittery fabric: John Lewis, Oxford Street, when she still used to go shopping in the West End. She remembered sewing it. She looked down at Dyl. He didn't exist then.

She took a packet of balloons out of the new, uncrumpled supermarket bag. Tom and Wilf and Dyl pounced on them. Balloons!

Tom and Wilf began blowing. 'Hey, Wilf, you're doing it!'

Dyl screamed with frustration and began eating his.

Carla pulled it out of his mouth.

She picked up another one to blow for him.

'No that one, I want that one.'

He handed her the soggy, chewed piece of yellow plastic.

'No, Dyl.' The phone rang.

Carla looked at Tom, his face covered by a silver, rubbery, puffing orb.

She began puffing too, but he didn't make a move, so she rushed to grab it.

'Hi, Carla, it's Elle, what's that noise?'

Carla continued blowing.

'It sounds like you just had a curry.'

'Balloons, dratted things.' She let it go and it wheezed in a squiggle all over the room. Dyl chased it, shrieking at the top of his head.

'How's it going?'

'Fine. Er, is Tom there?'

'We're decorating the tree,' she said coldly.

'How cute.'

'What do you mean – cute.'

'You all doing it together.'

'Don't you? No, sorry . . .'

Elle laughed. 'It's OK, we never did anyway.'

There was a silence.

'So.'

'So. Could I have a quick word with him?'

'Tom, it's for you.' She took a big gulp of sherry, looking hard at his expression as he took the receiver.

'Elle, how's it going?'

No cracks in his voice, no wavers as he nodded, muttering agreements.

'No, I can't do the twelfth, I'll be away that day. Yes, mmm, no . . . OK, the fourteenth, I'll give you a bell. No. All right. OK, Elle, tell Otto I'll catch him later, see you soon.'

Carla kept on looking after he put the phone down.

'What?' said Tom.

'What was that about?'

'What do you think?'

'The calendar?'

'Another meeting, that's all.'

'But you're busy! Why didn't you tell her how busy you were?'

'A couple of hours of an evening, that'll do it.'

Of an *evening*?

'Where?'

'At her place, of course.'

'She could have come here.'

'What's the big deal? Look, you come too if you want.'

'No, no no no . . .'

So this was it, then.

'What day? I'll put it on the calendar.'

'Wednesday, 8 o'clock.'

Carla marked it up.

'Right, who's going to put the fairy on the top?' said Tom.

'I'll do it!'

'No, me, me, me, you did it last year!'

'No, I didn't.'

'Yes, you did.'

'I know, I know,' said Wilf. 'Ip dip dip, mummy's on the loo, I do not choose *you*.'

'I won, I won!' Dyl grabbed the angel.

'No – I said do *not* choose you ...' Wilf snatched it back.

'That's not fair, you cheated!'

'I didn't!'

'You knew, you counted it.'

'Wilf, let him, please ...'

Dyl sank into hysterical sobs. 'That's Wilf's angel. Where's my angel? I want my angel ...'

Wilf threw his angel on the floor. 'That's not *fair*!'

Carla watched him stomping off, all stiff and shoulders hunched, to the play room.

The King's College Choir sang on ...

'No–elle, noelle, No oh Elle, no Elle...'

Chapter Twenty-Nine

'I'm sorry, Carla, I didn't stop to think it would bother you.' Elle's voice at the other end of the phone was sweetness and light itself. 'I was only being natural after all. Which is best, you have to agree.'

'Is that what you're saying to Tom, too?'

'Why don't you come over, too, if you don't trust me.'

'That's what Tom said.'

'Did he! Why don't you then?'

'Because I'll look a prat, Elle. Can't you come over to us?'

And so with a few puffs and sighs she had. Lugging her big leather portfolio up the steps, spreading her work across the refectory table, chattering on as easy as anything to Tom, pencil in ear, relaxed as Larry in Laredo, pointing out positives and negatives to each location. Even when they reached November, and the Richmond Hill Hotel, Carla felt hers was the only heart a-leaping.

'I thought we'd have Gabriel for this . . .'

'You've asked him?'

'I finally did, yes.'

'And he agreed?'

'Oh yes.' Elle looked up at her matter-of-factly. 'But it has to be soon, he's going back soon after Christmas.'

'That's a shame.'

Tom picked up on it as soon as Elle had gone.

'Why's it a *shame*, then ...'

His jealousy pleased her so much she fell about laughing hysterically and hugged him hugely.

He wriggled away angrily. It was all she could do to stop herself blurting it all out there and then. Let it trickle out in an Elle-like tinkle and get all the blame and guilt and shame behind them in a few easy words.

'Oh, and Tom, I'm out tomorrow.'

'But I've got the BB Italia party.'

'I know, I've got Zita booked.'

'Where are you going?'

'The mums' Christmas outing.'

'Why'd you want to go to that?'

'Elle's arranging it, it might be quite fun this year. Jo Salmon's coming; Elle's arranged limousines.'

'Limousines to where?'

'It's a surprise.'

'I'd rather know where I was going myself.'

So would I, Carla thought. So would I.

The limos did give an aura of success to the evening from the off, though there were a few dissentful, dubious mutterings as they found themselves being driven away from London along the Petersham Road towards Kingston.

'And I thought we were going to Sketch,' said Ant sarcastically as they cruised around the Kingston one-way system before pulling up outside a black door in a wall with the words 'Sundance Club' picked out in twinkling fairy lights above.

'They will let us in, won't they?' Anne peered dubiously out of the window.

'I should hope so.'

'Nice idea, Elle,' said Jo. 'I haven't danced round my handbag since I was at college.'

A man with beefy lidded eyes in a black bow-tie suit stepped forward to open the car door.

'Doesn't this mean it's not very good?' said Bryony loudly as she clambered out of the car.

After a flurry of coat-checking at a tiny cloakroom inside the door, they walked timidly in one big lump behind Elle down a narrow, dark corridor. The distant beat of 'Isn't She Lovely' grew louder. A left turn brought them into a surprisingly large space. Low, padded, deep red velvet sofas lined the walls and filled the room in intimate little circles. But nobody was looking at the sofas. At the far end of the room, broader than it was long, a stage ran the whole length with a catwalk jutting out into the centre.

'I don't believe this!'

'Elle, why did you ...'

'Look at ...'

'Where are we supposed to look?' said a jaw-dropped Anne.

'What's the idea?' said Bryony.

'Let's go,' said Hazel.

'Aw, come on, at least have one drink.' said Jo. 'Look on it as an implants recce if nothing else.' She hooked her arm in Bryony's and hurried on after Elle, who was already halfway across the room.

'The chairs are comfy, aren't they,' Carla said, for something to say.

Anne smiled nervously.

Carla looked around. 'It's kind of fascinating, though, isn't it.'

'They're students, most of them, paying their way through college and some,' said Elle.

The waiter brought a black and gold menu; bottles of wine and water were ordered.

'This'll be all over the school by Monday, I can guarantee it.'

'Look at the knockers on her!'

'What about that one, she's straight out of *Vogue*.'

'They wear clothes in *Vogue*.'

'I wish I had an arse like that.'

'Ant! You so still do, you could be so up there!'

'And you, Jo,' said Elle. 'I saw you on Channel 4 the other night. What was it?'

'The Fortune Hunters.'

'You were brilliant. And you still look, I mean . . .'

Jo laughed. 'I might have to pick up a job description on the way out, the way my career's going.'

'Jo! You're always on TV.'

'Exactly, the movies aren't happening for me any more. But hey, not to worry. I really want to stay at home more . . . hmmm, at least this'd be regular hours.'

'You're not worried someone might see you in a place like this?' said Anne.

'Old news, honey, everyone goes these days.'

Jo's unconcern made them feel more relaxed; they began looking around more.

Carla focused on a group of businessmen at the next table but one, sitting talking to a giraffe-necked girl in a sparkly dress. She had pale skin and short, dark hair. Suddenly, the girl stood up and took her dress off. She was stark naked underneath.

'How can they *do* that?'

'They make more money than my hourly rate per *second,* that might help,' said Jo without irony.

'If only I were ten years younger,' said Cyn wistfully. 'I'd be down here like a shot.'

They watched the girl thrust her breasts forward millimetres from the man's nose.

'I mean,' said Anne, 'if you saw that man in the street, you'd have no idea, would you, he'd be coming to a place like this ...'

'They get a choice,' said Elle. 'They can have them naked or in g-strings.'

'How do you know about this, Elle?'

Elle grinned. 'You'll see!'

There was a kind of interval when everyone went and sat down and the stage went dark and three girls appeared and put on a staged strip-tease with stocks, whips and lots of peacock feathers.

'It's not exactly the old Top Shop changing rooms, is it ...' said Ant.

Soon the surroundings had taken on the normality of a night at the Orange Tree pub and the familiar old subjects began to surface again. Tutors, music lessons, skiing resorts and who had played who in the Nativity play, till the giraffe-necked girl came over and squeezed herself in between Elle and Anne, shutting them all up into silence.

She beamed round at them all.

'Hi, ladies, my name's Juju, how're you all doing tonight?'

Anne, looking like a rabbit caught in headlights, sat as far back into her chair as she could go.

'We're fine – you?' said Ant.

'Oh, I'm great, thank you. So – where are you all from?'

'Richmond. You?'

'Morden.'

'Are you a student!' asked Bryony.

'You got it.'

'What are you studying!'

'Philosophy with law, at the LSE, do you know it?'

'She's a lawyer,' said Anne, helpfully, pointing at Ant.

'Is that so?' She turned to Anne and fiddled seductively with the zip of her sparkly dress. 'So who here is getting hitched?'

'Nobody, we're a school outing,' said Cyn.

'That's interesting. Would you ladies like me to dance for you?'

An involved discussion on swimming-pool regattas immediately broke out between Bryony and Hazel.

'Yeah, come on, babe, show us how it's done,' said Jo, handing over a fiver, 'Come on guys, pitch in!' There were a lot of cross glances followed by a flurry of polite, hesitant bag-fumbling.

For the next five minutes, Carla was torn between watching Juju, and nervously siding with Hazel, Anne and Bryony, who all looked like she felt. She was also aware that the activity in the rest of the club had gone very still and everyone was watching them. The men at the table but one had turned round in their chairs and were staring full on. Juju started her strip in front of Anne, but the fear and loathing on Anne's sheet-white face made her wisely turn towards Elle, who sat there leaning back, appreciating it all, letting her bend over her, dangling her body over her. When Elle at one point broke all the rules and touched Juju's waist, Carla fully expected Bryony to go into netball foul mode. She nearly did it herself.

When the music stopped Juju bent over Elle, whispered something in her ear and was gone.

'Look, there's more women arriving,' said Ant.

The chilled-out leery hum of the club had grown overtones of female chatter and laughter. At a table on the far side of the room, a group of smartly dressed city-types were ordering drinks and another group of 20-something women were positioning themselves along the catwalk chairs.

'Look at a girl like that, what man could resist her?' said Hannah.

'It's like having a bar of chocolate for them, isn't it,' said Cyn.

'But why are they doing this?' said Carla. 'Why aren't they modelling for magazines?'

'They probably are.'

The music faded. The girls disappeared. The chatter got louder.

'Here we go, another show.' Jo turned her chair towards the stage.

'Gentlemen and, *ladies*, we are proud to present for you this evening, the one and only...'

Sparklers and strobe lights flashed to the high trumpets of spaghetti Western-like music, 'Medallion Stallions!'

Three figures in black cloaks and fedoras marched onto the stage and stood stock still with their backs to the audience.

There were whoops and shrieks from the audience as the first one turned, and in a series of elaborate manoeuvres of tanned and baby-oiled muscle, removed his cloak to reveal his jock strap beneath.

'Look at the size of that lunchbox!' said Cyn, grinning widely.

'That has to be a cucumber,' said Hazel flatly.

'It's ghastly,' said Hannah, her eyes glued to the stage.

The first set off up the catwalk as the second turned; he was slimmer, a bit scrawny, Carla thought, but no less endowed. At the turn of the third, Carla slapped her hand to her mouth. All of them looked at each other but only for a moment before their eyes collectively slid back to the stage amidst mutterings of:

259

'So this is why you ...'

'Elle, how did you?'

He was moving now in that lank, lean way he walked across the playground, his head proud, his hat held firmly over his credentials.

Even Hazel, Anne and Bryony were lost for words as he cajoled and teased the audience, working them up into a frenzy.

Carla realised only moments before it happened what was going to happen, by which time it was far too late. That a large part of male stripper shows relied on audience participation wasn't something that'd immediately come to mind, so surprised had she been; but by the time cucumber muscle man and chicken-gizzard jock strap man had hit on the other two groups of women, it became obvious which way Gabriel would be heading, and it wouldn't be for the group of businessmen sat one table but one away.

The music had changed its beat, the spotlights turned to their table and she found herself pulled up, staring up at him. A familiar series of guitar chords brought it back: one, two, three, stamp; she moved her feet. Stop all thoughts. Think only of each present moment as it comes. Be inside the moment. You are the thread, weaving yourself in and out.

She began to weave, turn, fly, she could feel his movement around her, touching her waist, spinning her. She is big. She is beautiful. Everyone began clapping, whooping, calling.

Everyone except Elle.

Chapter Thirty

By the time they were purring home along the deserted Petersham Road, Elle was all life and soul again, chattering away brightly with Ant, and Carla was the one staying quiet.

'It doesn't work like that for women,' Ant was arguing.

'Why not? Why shouldn't we be turned on by beautiful bodies?'

'Because it's not with the bodies, is it,' said Ant. 'I don't go "phwoooar" like when a man sees a woman. For a man, like all those men in there . . .'

'What about all those women in there?'

'That was just playing on the hysterical stereotype . . .'

'They were having a good time, what was wrong with that?'

'They were ugly, gross. . .'

'Ant, you surprise me. They were sophisticated women of the noughties, lusting after a bit of male flesh,' said Elle.

'That's why it was ugly. Women are selective, men are non-selective, men need to spread themselves about. It's basic stuff, Elle.'

'That's what I'm saying. We have evolved, as women,

we can do this now, if we want.'

'Men have switches that say "off" and "on"; if a man sees an attractive woman, bam, he wants to sleep with her.'

'And if I see an attractive man . . .?'

'If you see an attractive man what you're thinking is wow there's a good-looking guy, sexy guy even, but you're not thinking about doing it with him . . .'

'How do you know what I'm thinking?'

'What you're thinking is yes, maybe, yes he's attractive.'

'A big yes.'

'You're giving yourself that permission for him to get closer to you, if the situation happens; you might catch his eye even, go up and chat even, but you're not in the sack with him in your mind . . .'

'Listen to her, telling me what I'm thinking!'

Carla and Elle were dropped last. They sat opposite each other in silence for the few minutes it took to reach Carla's door.

She held back from apologising. Besides. What for? If it led to an argument, she didn't think she'd be able to hold herself back. Elle's unreasonableness was frightening her. She'd given up the lessons, loaned her her husband, what more could she do? She didn't even fancy Gabriel, she could tell her, but it would probably come out all wrong. And even if she did fancy him, she wasn't going to make another stupid mistake, was she? Like hell. What she couldn't do was let Elle's feelings hold her own to ransom like this. She had to tell Tom and if it did all come out, so be it. She could explain her way out of it. At least there'd *be* a way out of it.

She went inside to find a very happy Zita, already pulling her coat on. Carla unfolded her purse. She'd already glanced at her watch outside – ten minutes over the midnight deadline which meant extra double time, plus a full extra hour. She'd long ago switched off the worry-button on that one, otherwise evenings out were eclipsed by a bright neon meter chinking away in her brain. What was the odd tenner here or there when you had Zita to rely on? With Tom's last pay cheque already in the bank, it had started to seem a dangerous way of thinking.

She switched on the TV and settled back on the sofa to wait for Tom to come home and get it all out and over, once and for all, before Elle did it for her.

She woke, seven hours later, with Wilf and Dyl snuggling into an armpit each side with their juice-boxes and mini-cereals and someone on the television called Dick, who was being sick.

'Please stay and watch it with us a while, please, mum,' said Wilf snuggling in tighter.

Wearily, she reached out for her glasses.

The winner of *Make Dick Sick* was being presented with a plastic vomit kit, and a signed sick bag.

'This is fun,' said Dyl, clutching hold of her other side 'Oh, this is great, mum, watch this, this is good.'

She lay back, closed her eyes and sighed.

A photo of a viewer's bogey wall was next, and then a clip with Dick and Dom creeping around the National Steam Museum seeing who could shout 'bogey' the loudest, scoring decibel levels on a bogeyometer.

'I think this is more your dad's kind of a show.'

Wilf and Dyl were apoplectic with laughter. Realising her own disgust only doubled their glee, she extricated herself from their tangle of arms and went upstairs, taking a quick peek around the bedroom door before going for a long, hot shower.

She snuggled back into bed and Tom's big cosy armpit for her much-needed lie-in.

Chapter Thirty-One

With Christmas truly under way, the *Homes to Die For* TV crew filling their home and Tom going through his last days at Carliatti whilst trying to get his factory deal sorted, Carla had little time to fret about Elle's moods, and the tiny window of opportunity she'd had to tell Tom all shrank to nothing.

Elle left for Sweden on the first day of the holidays, cool but friendly as she dropped their presents round on the way to the airport, both of them making noises about all getting together sooner rather than later in the new year.

By then, Elle was back to her old self, Gabriel was no longer to be seen loping across the playground, and Carla had started to feel a lot less jumpy and more hopeful she could carry on into their new life without having to make any potentially life-threatening statements.

'Hello, Wilf.' Christine Baker, the prettiest girl in year 4, came up to him at the playground gates a few weeks into the new spring term.

Carla nearly collapsed.

Had her son scored?

'Pinch punch.' Christine pinched and punched. 'The

first of the month, and no return.' She ran off across the playground, laughing.

Knowing any hint of a tiniest clue of witnessing his humiliation would be a mistake, Carla quickly kissed his burning red cheeks and turned to walk home. Poor Wilf, having to deal with all that playground stuff for all those years to come.

She'd stopped taking him all the way to the classroom, which meant less hanging around the slide and less chance of getting into conversations. In a few terms' time, he'd be walking to school on his own and she'd be free of her playground torments for a while. She couldn't imagine it, Wilf going out on his own, but by the end of year 5 they all did and she guessed somehow she'd know when the time was right. The escort service would start up all over again with Dyl, of course, assuming he'd get a place, but there were real possibilities she'd need never be standing in the same section of playground as Bryony Baxter ever again.

Carla slammed the front door double-hard, prompting the desired snuffing out of TalkSPORT radio blasting from the kitchen. After parking the pushchair, she stiffened before walking purposefully through to the klounge.

'Glorylory.' She looked around.

A dark, whiskery man in a blue skull hat and denims, ripped at the knees in a genuine but unfashionably dirty way, sat at the table, feet up, one hand held droopily to his ear. Without missing a beat, he moved his legs casually sideways until his tan boots dangled off the edge.

'Oh. Is it?' His round bird eyes looked up at Carla without engaging.

'Give me Mick on the line, then. All right, Mick, how you doing?' He held his what-do-you-think-you're-doing-here stare for a moment before slowly turning away, taking his shins off the table as he stretched forward to check his radio switch with an exaggeratedly pointed finger.

Without changing her expression, Carla made a mental note. She'd been out of the loop so long, these were fourth-choice builders she hadn't quite sussed yet, suspiciously free at short notice, but if feet on table and radio strops were all she'd have to deal with she'd be laughing.

She unplugged the kettle, went over and held it up to his face in mock question.

'All right, Dan, how you're doing?' said Rod to his limp, dangly wrist.

'No worries, mate. It's gone, mate. Yeah, it's all been sorted.'

Rod gave her a thumbs up and nod. 'That's an outside, isn't it? Naaa, can't do it, mate. 8 o'clock? Yeah. Allrightmate. 8 o'clockish. Take it easy, bye mate. All right love.'

'All right – ISH. Where's Ron?'

'Upstairs. No, I tell a lie. You must've heard the kettle going on, mate.'

Ron landed from the slide making a wee Teletubby voice. Everyone did the Teletubby sound. From distinguished interiors journalists to the snooty TV researcher from *Homes to Die For*. After all the fuss and bother, the *Homes to Die For* show had never been aired, something about plugs pulled and schedules changed. Tom was furious but Carla was secretly pleased. All she wanted was for everything to be normal for a while. Nice and quiet and normal. Like this. Choosing which hob to fit with a grumpy builder whilst pretending to be cheerful felt quite like old times again.

The fear which had seeped in and around them, right through her bones to the very bricks, that had all gone. They wouldn't be going anywhere. It had been the fear of

266

change rather than the change itself. Now that Tom had left Carliatti and ploughed through all the leaving parties and speeches and weeping secretaries and calls from the press, and since her lawyer had approved his new contract with barely a change, she felt a real sense of continuum and new beginnings. Even Danielle had faded from the scene a bit, content to be there to do the deals when deals needed to be done. Bruno was still around, if anything more than before, but then, that was nothing new to deal with, and she'd been encouraged by the fairness of Tom's contract.

'Made yer mind up, then?'

Carla looked across the floor at the different hobs.

'We'd only do this for you, y'know, other customers have to go round all the showrooms. Have a look.'

'Yes, yes, I know, thank you.' She'd insisted on this. Partly because she needed to see everything *in situ* before she could make a decision and partly to see how far she could push them. If you started off making them do more than was expected, it made them back off a bit. She looked around at the different hobs, combinations of double and one big single, two big doubles, griddles in the middle, steamers in the middle. It was, she thought, truly amazing how far hobs had advanced in a few years.

'We, er, we do need to get on...'

'What – yes ... The steamer, that was what I was wanting ...'

'They've all got them.'

'That one hasn't.'

'Don't pick it, then.'

'I think that one ... no – no, hold on ...' she loved their exasperated sighs and tuts. She picked up an empty Kit-Kat wrapper, scrunched it up and threw it in the bin; she left the lid open for a moment, staring inside the silvery surface to the chaos of the rubbish inside, holding her gaze on it before dropping it in and flipping it shut.

'Leviosa Wingardium . . .'

'You what?'

'Never mind. All right, now, let me see . . .'

'Hurry up, love, we haven't got all day.'

'Nor have I, loves,' she said.

After making her choice she strolled down into Richmond to do a bit of holiday shopping before collecting Dyl.

Chapter Thirty-Two

Carla ran her hand over the calendar on her lap, chewing at the tip of her pen, the days ahead looking as smooth and unruffled as the sea glistening in the sun in front of her. She sighed happily, taking a sip of her drink. However many times they returned to Sicily, the clarity and intensity of the blues all around her were always a surprise. It was the same with the first lick of their first ice-cream breakfast, the forgotten delight of cold buttery almond ice and hot fresh espresso.

She wrote against **Monday**:

Tom and Otto – fishing all day
Elle – shopping
Carla – babysit and planning

She always wrote her bit in even though she was sitting there doing it.

Evening – Grilled fish, Otto cooks

After so many visits to the Villa Solorono, Carla's weekly plan was part of the routine.

She'd never been so glad to chuck that old, cruddy, cartoon calendar away, along with all its angst and clutter and fear. All of Tom's energy was still going into Supernatural but it was going well. He hadn't been able to get back for *The Simpsons* every night at six, as he'd hoped, and had even made alarming noises about having to miss the holiday, but after a lot of argument with Tom calmly pointing out that small businesses didn't know the meaning of the words 'leave' and 'holiday' and Carla insisting there was no way she was going to gooseberry Elle and Otto, together or not, or stay at home in Richmond over Easter come to that, and besides, he needed the break even more than she, he'd made it.

She would never have interfered in the old set-up, but a few discreet calls to Bruno had been her only option, forcing him to make Tom see he could leave his baby behind in safe hands for a week.

Day one was going to plan, with everyone doing what they most wanted to do. Tom and Otto were lounging in a lagoon somewhere on the speedboat, with Tom's mobile phone deftly nicked, switched off and well hidden away in her bag. The insides of her cheeks tingled at the thought of Elle in the thick of Palermo, scouring the markets for the choicest pastries and lemon-baked breads. As for herself, she could quite happily sit there in the breeze on that broad, old stone terrace for the rest of the week, surrounded by the light of sky and sea, the children splashing in and out of the crystal clear pool in front of her with not a whisper of an argument between them.

She had come to accept the new secret corners of herself, a self she felt she could live with at last. A self, she had to admit, on sunny, positive days like this, she was quite proud of. She'd steered her husband through their first marital crisis without him having much awareness it was happening at all. The longer she learned to live with it, the less important it seemed to bring it all out, especially with Tom's shed-load of new worries and responsibilities. She began writing again:

Tuesday
Carla and Tom – Monreale
Elle and Otto – babysit
Dinner – Enrico's Porticello

For the first few days there was no point in trying to get the children away from the pool until well after sundown. They'd refuse all attempts at getting them even as far as the rocky steps down to the tiny private beach until Wednesday, possibly Thursday. They loved Enrico's though. He'd welcome them like long-lost friends, and the children like they were the most delightful creatures ever to be born into the world. Which was enough, along with the fresh tomato pasta even Dyl loved, to stun them into shocked silence for the rest of the meal.

Wednesday
Carla and Tom – stay at villa all day with children
Elle and Otto – out
Dinner – Enrico's Porticello

She heard the distant thud of the front door slamming, a floor above. Elle was back with her two big Sicilian baskets full of goodies. Minutes later, already stripped to her bikini briefs, she came onto the terrace and placed a plate of pastries on the table.

'Oh, you know how to please a woman.' Carla smiled. 'You've arrived at the right moment. I'm down to yours and Otto's day out on Wednesday. Do you know where you're going yet?'

'Who's saying we'll go out together?'

'Oh – well – but have you any ideas yet?'

'Does it matter?'

'I'd like to get it down. Maybe Otto wants to know. . .'

'You mean he might not want to go bird-watching – yaaawwwwn – on his own?'

'What about Zingaro? There's a national park and the book says there are good beaches . . .'

'Mummy, mummy!' The children ran up to Elle.

'Hang on, hang on.' She left them dripping all over Carla whilst she fetched their ice creams.

'Careful!'

'Sorry.'

'Get some towels will you?' She wiped the drips off the calendar.

'Here we go, here we go.' Elle handed out the ice creams. One by one the children disappeared into the Wendy house till all was peace and quiet and still.

Elle poured some wine and stretched herself out on the baroque sofa in the full heat of the sun. 'You know, Carla, I think we deserve this!'

Carla took a roll of cannoli, letting the thin, Marsala-fried pastry melt slowly in her mouth. She flipped idly through the school calendar, pausing at June.

'You happy with it?'

'You know I am.'

Cinnamony chocolate and ricotta, pistachio and candied fruits blended pleasingly in her mouth.

For her picture, Carla had half-turned towards the camera, the ancient arch of Richmond Bridge behind her. She was half-smiling, though she hadn't intended to. Perhaps Elle had. All that was visible of her breasts were voluptuous curves.

'You know, I think Mrs Armstrong's ban on nipples and bits brought out your artistic side to the full, Elle.'

'What could I do? Lots of over the shoulder shots and carefully arranged profiles and shawls.'

'It works well. I'm sorry Tom couldn't help you more, but you can see how it is.'

'You should hide that mobile.'

'I have.'

'Anyway, you turned out to be the better help, Carla; I should have realised that before.'

'I enjoyed it.'

She had. Having her own meetings at printing companies, choosing layouts, nagging models, designing the monthly page-spreads.

'You were born for the job, Carla.'

'I didn't realise how many different ways there were . . .'

She looked at the chart of days, running the whole width of the photograph.

'You see, this way it leaves enough room to make any combination of adult and child activities, or two families like us, or husband and wife or work and social or . . .'

'Carla, you've told me this a thousand times already.' Elle stared out to sea.

Carla flipped back. 'And as for March. What a pleasant picture for our holiday here.'

'People don't realise the subtleties of calendar design, do they.' Elle covered the cream silk-striped sofa with a towel and began rubbing cream into her legs. 'Like we have Marcus Dowe for August when everyone's away.'

'Maybe they take their calendars with them.'

'I think only you do that, Carla.'

'And Bryony.'

'Oh yes, and Bryony.'

Carla looked at the picture of Gabriel, on top of the Hill, the view opening behind him. Crouched down in a carefully arranged profile, laughing like she'd never seen him laugh before.

'I am pleased with that one,' said Elle.

So am I, Carla thought. She'd never asked what had happened on that day, but felt enough time had passed.

Carla looked up at Elle.

'That smile on his face, it isn't for the camera, is it?'

'You know him so well, Carla.'

'Well?'

'Well – yes.'

'*Did* you!'

Was it better than Tom?

'He never really fancied me, we both know that.'

'Not by the look on this face.'

'I think he did get some respect, when he saw how I worked. Maybe he realised not everyone has to be a dancer to be creative.'

'Or an "artist".' Carla ticked her fingers in the air.

'Still, I got what I wanted,' said Elle with distant whimsy.

'*Did* you?'

'It was a bit cold at 6 in the morning,' she smiled serenely, 'but worth it!'

'And what about Otto, is he still seeing that girl?'

'You know, I don't know for sure if he ever really did.'

'So, he's not got anyone then?'

'As far as I know, no one but his faithless wife.'

Carla turned back to the calendar.

'You know I love Otto, don't you.'

'Yes, of course.'

'You know, Carla, I think if every woman had her way

she'd have one man for his body, but another for his mind.'

'You'd better find yourself another body then.'

'Who says it's Otto's mind I love? But don't you worry, Palermo's a pretty good place to look for minds, I can tell you.'

Carla took another bite of her pastry and smiled.

Perhaps it was working out better for them this way. There'd been not a hint of any of Otto's explosions like there'd been on previous trips.

'He does seem a bit sad though, Elle.'

'Otto? Oh he's all right, you know what a pragmatist he is.'

Carla turned back to the calendar. 'Now, when am I going to get my shopping in? Tom'll want to go to that ghost town but it's too far.'

'How are things with Tom now? He seems very happy.'

'Stressed. But happy, yes, I think so.'

'So I was right in the end.'

'You were right.'

'Any time you need help in the future, just let me know.'

Carla laughed. A laugh with echoes of her old, phoney laugh. 'In seven years' time, maybe!'

Elle closed her eyes and stretched out.

The children emerged from the hut and jumped in the pool again.

Carla watched them for a while, blacking out the niggle, niggle thoughts which threatened to surface, and sighed deeply before going back to her list.

'How does this sound?'

'Go on,' said Elle, without opening her eyes.

'Thursday, Carla and Elle – Palermo shopping and relax at home.'

'Sounds good.'

'Or, Carla, Palermo, Tom, Otto and Elle and kids, take the speedboat to Marettimo beach ferry. I'll stay at home and cook. Then Friday, all to Mount Etna, lunch and dinner out.'

'You know, Carla, I might give the volcano a miss this time.'

'You can't!'

'I'm feeling a little bit been there done that about it.'

'But it's always different every time we go.'

'I'm not stopping anyone else going. I'll stay here with the kids. Tallulah's carsickness hasn't got any better. I think I'll have a better time, really.'

Carla chewed her pen thoughtfully. 'I suppose we could take just the older ones.'

'After their beach day they'll probably want to stay by the pool again.'

'OK, whatever they want to do. Then, Saturday, I've got us morning at home, Tom and Otto fishing, and Margarita babysitting and cleaning up the house while we go on the Godfather tour.'

Elle laughed. 'Do you think you'll make it?'

'Tom's determined . . . But it is so tempting just to stay here.'

'That's the problem, the week starts so wonderfully slowly like this at first, but then it gets faster and faster . . .'

'Tom, there's never enough time, why don't we come twice a year?' Carla asked at dinner that night.

'If you hide my mobile one more time we won't be coming once a year,' said Tom, still smarting.

'There weren't any important messages, were there.'

'There might have been, Carla. You mustn't do that. Really. I'm serious.'

'September would be nice. October, what about

October half-term? Or booking for two weeks next year? If we can get them ...'

'We could manage two weeks, Carla, if we stayed in the Sicilian equivalent of the Travelodge ...'

'It'd make us go out more,' said Elle.

'No – Tom, by next year ...'

'Who knows what'll be happening by next year, Carla.'

'How could we stay anywhere else on this island,' said Otto.

'Or with anyone else,' said Elle. 'Carla's put us down for Zingara nature reserve, Otto.'

'Sounds good!'

Elle yawned loudly.

'You don't have to come.'

'Good.'

'I can go on my own.'

'It was only a suggestion,' said Carla meekly.

Otto shrugged and helped himself to the salad. There was an awkward silence. She caught Tom's eye. He looked down at his food, embarrassed.

'There's a good bathing beach at Zingara,' said Carla. 'Maybe Wilf and Jon will want to go with you.'

'I don't think so,' said Elle, 'unless there's a theme park there.'

'You know,' said Tom, putting his glass down carefully on the table, 'I'm disappointed. I really thought you two were a pair again.'

'As I said on the boat, Tom, divorce is never straight-forward, heavy or light,' said Otto. 'So, I don't like to go out alone, but sometimes I have to do this. Now, I can't rely on Elle coming with me just because I want her to. But I know when she does come with me it is because she wants to and that is a big difference. When she does come we will both enjoy it.'

'You're not opening yourself to new experiences, though; I mean, you could not want to go but then go along and find yourself really enjoying it. You're shutting yourself off.'

'Nonsense.'

'It's not.'

'I know what I like,' said Elle. 'I'd rather go back to the markets than search for golden eagles through a pair of binoculars, just as you, Carla, would hate to go out in that boat and catch fish. Tom, do you really want to go and look at that cruddy old church with Carla tomorrow?'

'We'll have a good day,' said Tom defensively.

'He'll love it,' said Carla firmly.

'We are simply being honest, that's all,' said Otto, raising one eyebrow at Carla.

She dropped her eyes away from him immediately, too fast, she should have held that look, held it in defiance but she hadn't, instead she studied her fish, a mesh of white flesh disintegrating into two dead eyes. All that not regretting the past or anticipating the future, what rot that was. Any fool could see that just by looking at her plan on the calendar. Living in the moment meant wasting most of it. It wasn't possible to forget the past, unless you were lying in a coma somewhere; it was all a big, fat, ugly lie. A lie which still lay in her waiting to burst like a sulphurous ulcer. It could lie dormant for years, but it wasn't going to leave her.

Chapter Twenty-Three

'Looks more like a church.'

'Let's just have a quick peek inside.' Carla tucked her hand in his arm as they walked across the piazza.

She'd deliberately played it down, wanting to surprise him. After they'd adjusted their eyes to the dark cool of the cathedral she was as amazed as he to see every wall and every column covered in mosaic.

'Over 2,000 kilos of pure gold ... the second largest mosaic display in the world.'

'Get your nose out of that damned book and look, will you.'

She looked around uneasily; the scale of the splendour disturbed her. She didn't feel she should be in that cool, holy place packed with all those saints and prayers and echoes of goodness. In every glisten from every tiny tile all she could see was the knowing glint in Otto's eye, framed by that blonde, bushy eyebrow.

The look that'd hauled back all she'd let go, that'd tensed her up for the rest of that evening. Losing her calm and trying to pretend she hadn't. Play-acting. Listening out for every word Otto said.

'Hang on, what's this?'

'I think I'll go outside, Tom.'

'You've got to see this, Carl.' Tom dropped a coin into a slot. A panel of mosaic lit up; Tom turned and grinned. If there was a button to push, Tom had to push it.

'I'll meet you in the cloisters.'

Before she went outside, she turned and nodded awkwardly at the altar, feeling she had to do something next to everyone else's sincere curtseys. She stopped for a while, looking enviously at the people praying in the pews. The sound of Tom's phone trilling its loud and ridiculous Dambusters ring tone, sent her hurrying outside into the bright sunlight.

The cloisters were full of trees and cool, refreshing shade. Rows and rows of slender Arabic columns covered in mosaics. Some were plain, bold and contemporary, others intricate beyond understanding. As soon as she started studying them, she had to look away. Interwoven with the plants and saints were all kinds of monsters and mythical creatures popping out at her, and Otto's eye again, shining even brighter in the sunlight.

She pulled out her sketchbook and copied one of the simpler Biba-like candy-stripes. She went and sat on a low wall by the fountain, and waited for Tom. The trickling of the water was soothing. She soon got bored watching the tourists with their mini-rucksacks and stupid hats and began doodling on her sketchpad. The tiny leaves of the tree cast cardboard-cut-out shadows onto her sketchbook. She began drawing round them, filling the page with squiggles. She wrote 'pomegranate tree' and the date in the top right corner, turned the page and went to sit beneath a different tree. Here the shadows were larger, bolder, curtain fabric probably, this one, she thought happily, as the shapes of that Sicilian afternoon immortalised themselves on the page.

She'd booked a table at the Charleston in Mondello. Another surprise for Tom. She liked to arrange days like this for him. It was an extension of what they did at home. Just as Tom emptied the rubbish and bought the booze and she emptied the dishwasher and bought the food, so she organised their holiday outings, sourcing new restaurants and sights to see.

'Carla does it again,' he said happily as they were shown to their table on the Art Nouveau terrace jutting out into the sea. Throughout the lunch Tom's phone kept trilling. She watched him, half annoyed, but then half proud of the way he was dealing with all the business complications so competently.

'Switch it off, Tom, please.'

She went to grab it from him.

He pulled his arm away. 'All right, all right . . . That was the most incredible place, wasn't it. We've got to get Elle and Otto there.'

'They're not interested in churches.'

'Even Otto would have to admire that.'

'Tom.'

'Mm.'

'Have you worked out if they're sleeping together yet?'

'I don't know.'

'I think they are.'

'Why? Why not for that matter?'

'There's none of that – tension between them.'

'I hope so.'

'I don't think Otto's happy though, do you. What did you talk about on the boat?'

'The usual stuff. Why are you looking at me like that?'

'What he said, at dinner, about what he'd told you about divorce.'

Tom looked at her, chewing greedily. 'Oh, that.'

'What did he say?'

Tom shrugged. 'You know as much about it as I do.'

'Otto is sad though, isn't he.'

'Oh, he's fine.'

'Has he got a girlfriend?'

'I don't know, do I?'

'Haven't you asked him?'

'No!'

'Elle says he did but he hasn't now.'

'Then that's how it is, I expect.'

'Why don't you men talk about these things?'

'Because we've got better things to be doing.'

Carla felt herself relaxing a little bit. 'Strange set-up though.'

'Have you noticed, though, they're only together when they're with us.'

'The kids are enjoying it well enough.'

'So are you, aren't you?'

'Yes!'

'Well then, don't worry about it, it's not our problem, Carl, is it.'

Tom's phone rang again.

'Tom!'

'Yeah, yeah, hang on . . .'

She watched him walk out of the restaurant, phone clamped to his ear, walking up and down the jetty past the brightly painted fishing boats bobbing in the breeze. Danielle was the least of her worries now, the whole business was consuming him, mind, time and body. She had to face it, there'd never be a good time to tell him. She should have done it that first morning. The best she would ever get now would be at the end of the holiday. She had to get that trust back, the trust in herself as much as in him. She'd tell him what had happened to her, exactly as

282

it happened. And then her feelings, and about Elle and everything. She'd make him understand. She'd make him.

The only trip they did every year was the one to Mount Etna. They all tried to persuade Elle to go along but she was insistent, and the boys decided to take advantage of another day by the pool.

'I don't know, I think we should have forced the boys to come,' Tom said, climbing up into the front seat next to Otto.

'They're too young for views,' said Otto, turning on the ignition.

'Volcanoes are exciting enough for any eight-year-old, aren't they?'

'I think all they remember is Tallulah being sick all over them,' Carla piped up from the back.

'They're happy with the pool. Let them have what they want; they get pushed around so much at home these days.'

'Thanks!'

'Not you, Carl, all that school stuff . . .'

They soon left the ugly suburbs of Palermo behind them and were driving through open countryside. She stared out at the rolling green wheat fields, half wishing she'd let it be a boys' day out and had stayed behind with Elle. But then it was a luxury to sit and look and not have to change tapes, sing stupid songs, play I Spy, hand out nibbles and be ever alert with the sick bag.

And Etna was always worth it. All the colours she'd ever seen before and more. She felt being in such an elemental landscape would suit her more than the church, would help her get the right words she knew she had to say the next day.

The mountain range appeared on the distant horizon, adding large, impressionist chunks of purples and mauves to the rich blue sky and then, after another bend in the road and rising above them all, the volcano, its peak lashing at the sky in vertical streaks of sulphurous cloud.

'The beginning of the unreality starts here,' said Tom happily. Innocently.

Nearing the foothills, they drove through miles of shining green smattered with thousands of tiny dots of lemon and orange, going on for ever like the world had only ever been one big citrus farm. But gradually, everything turned black – lava houses, lava churches, lava roads, lava walls, lava fields.

'Who'd live in a place like that?' said Tom in his Lloyd Grossman voice.

The villages beneath the volcano were strange with an energy all of their own, an anticipation hung over them, a fear and respect for a power which made the Mafia look like the Richmond Rowing Club.

Otto shifted down a gear as they began the climb up the lower slopes. The smell of sulphur filled the car. The dark colours below made the blue of the sky more intense, like a Springfield sky. There were still houses, ruined houses with pastel walls which always made her want to buy up each and every one and bring them back to their past glories and make their fountains flow again and their marble columns stand proud.

And then all the villages and houses disappeared and they were out in the black fields, smattered at first with forests of poplar and chestnut.

'Welcome to the moon,' said Tom as they reached the end of the driveable road.

Carla got out of the car. It felt odd to think of anything down in the warm below, Elle on the terrace, the children bobbing in and out of the pool.

Otto went off to take photographs.

Carla and Tom sat outside the souvenir shop sipping little glasses of something strong and hot and very alcoholic.

'It would be wonderful to come here for longer than a week though, wouldn't it, Tom?'

'Maybe one day, who knows,' said Tom, 'in a few years when the orders are rolling in ...'

'And the kids have finished school ...' said Carla.

'And we're too decrepit to want to move far.'

'I'd just stay on that terrace for a month, that'd do me.'

Tom's phone trilled again. He looked at her and smiled guiltily. 'They've got phone masts everywhere these days, haven't they!'

'Tom, I'm going to chuck that thing in the pool tomorrow and I mean it.'

The way his face dropped made hers drop too.

'It can wait another day, surely. Yes, yeah, OK, yes, I understand, all right, yup.' He looked at his watch. 'I'm on top of a fucking volcano! No no, not right at the top - it'll have to be tomorrow now, all right, yeah, yeah, I'm sure. We'll work it out, don't worry ...'

He looked at her and shrugged.

'Oh, Tom ...'

She put her arm around him and gave him a squeeze.

'No one ever said it'd be easy, did they.'

Chapter Thirty-Four

Carla and Otto followed a little distance away from a young tour guide trailing a pair of crew-cutted marine-like Americans, an elderly English couple and a young, smiling Japanese couple.

'It's just as well Tom had to go back early, he'd never have seen this lot out.'

'It's because of Tom we're here,' said Otto, 'and beside, he knew it would be a guided tour.'

'Yes, but he'd be moaning like anything by now, like if I start reading a sign in an art gallery.'

'They can be very relaxing – depending on the guide.'

'I agree,' she said.

Depending on the company.

She was glad Otto was wearing his sunglasses. Round silvery reflective ones she could see herself in, hiding that glint which said he knew something. He definitely knew.

'I didn't think you liked being told what to do, Carla.'

'I like to know what I'm looking at. And, I have to say, after years of saying do this, do that, it's a luxury to be made to sit, and taken places and told when to go where and when and where to eat. I'm even getting fond of coach trips.'

'Since when did you start going on coach trips?'

'Only when I'm helping the school outings, but there again I could see myself in years to come trotting off to Victoria coach station with my little packasack ...'

'You make yourself sound old, Carla.'

'I can't see it'd be Elle's idea of fun.'

Otto stiffened slightly. 'Who knows what Elle loves or hates these days?'

The group had come to a halt on the steps of an old flat-fronted church.

Carla smiled cosily at the Japanese girls as they obediently gathered around the intensely bright and over-chatty guide.

'So, ladies and gentlemen, we are in movie number one, *Godfather 1*, and here we are, outside the church where Michael and Appolonia were married.'

'Doesn't do much for me,' Carla said quietly, amidst the mutters of recognition and camera clicking. She stepped back and looked up at the façade. The same as the façades of any of the other hundreds of churches on the island.

'I have to ask you this,' asked the American. 'Are they still around today, these – Mafia?'

The guide smiled to himself and nodded his head. 'They are everywhere.' He lowered his voice. 'Just like her.' He gestured and raised his eyes overdramatically towards the volcano and beckoned. They all leaned forwards.

'You can feel their power even when you can't see them. But,' he perked up, making them all stand up a bit straighter again, 'it's not for you to worry, you will never see them. They want the tourist to come here; all you will find is the friendliness from the normal Sicilian people.'

'So we don't get to see any?' said the American disappointedly.

287

'Don't they have special bars or club-houses?' asked the Englishman.

'Yeah, family mansions, there must be some of those.'

'The Mafia is divided by area, not by family, their names are after the districts they control. The nearest you will get to seeing them is the *posteggiatori*, the car parkers, if any of you are driving cars? No? Very wise. Next time you are in Palermo or the big towns you can see them. They have police whistles and American baseball hats and wear the money pouch belts. The parking is free of course but you must pay them your "pizzo", your protection money.'

'We have the same in London, it's called the NCP,' said the Englishman.

His wife laughed.

'How much pizzo do you have to pay?' asked the American.

'One euro.'

'A bargain!' The Englishman and his wife shook with laughter.

'So those guys are mafia?'

'Three away. Half his takings go to the middle man who will take his cut before giving to the local boss.'

'Who controls your patch here?' asked one of the Americans, 'Do you have to pay to do this?'

His eyes slid shyly to the floor. 'This I cannot say.'

They all looked at each other. Oooh.

'Why hasn't it been gotten rid of?'

'The Sicilian name for the mafia is *piovrra*, the octopus, its tentacles getting into everywhere. Sicilians like to be secretive, like all the Italians we hate the authority, we know it is corrupted; we take it for granted that our politicians are greedy for power and for money, that business is corruption, that in marriages there is infidelity . . .'

288

Carla kept her stare straight ahead.

'So.' He turned and waved his arm. 'Here we have the church of the famous wedding; you can go inside if you wish but what you see in the film is only the outside.'

'Not much point then,' said Otto, settling himself down sideways on a wall.

Carla hovered for a while, unsure whether to follow the group or stay where she was.

They all disappeared inside.

It was still and quiet.

Too quiet.

'I need some shade,' she said at last, 'I think I'll go inside.'

'No,' Otto stood. 'Come on, let's get away from them.'

'I thought you said you liked guided tours?'

'It's a tiny village, we can find the café on our own. They'll catch us up soon enough. And now, ladies and gentlemen,' he changed his voice to a mock Italian accent, 'we are making the same famous walk to the café as Appolonia and Michael with all their family and all their friends.'

'Are we?'

'Yes.'

'Do you really remember it?'

'Yes.'

'Next year you can be Tom's guide.'

'If there is a next year.'

She glanced at him quickly and looked away.

He walked on in silence.

The road led to the edge of the tiny village. Across a wider lane, nestling in open hilly countryside, a crumbling terracotta villa faced sideways to the road. In the centre a beaded curtain covered an open arched doorway with a sign above saying 'Bar'.

'Now, that does look like something out of a movie,' said Carla. 'Tom would love this.'

'I can smell the beer from here,' said Otto.

They crossed the road.

'It does feel familiar, does it to you?' Carla scraped a dark green metal chair back and sat down.

'Yes, yes, it does.'

'You did see the films though?'

'Of course.'

'Tom loved those films, he's happy with *The Sopranos* now, though . . .'

There was a rustle of beads and a young waitress appeared.

They ordered their beers.

'So when did you see them?'

'What?'

'The films?'

Otto leaned back and crossed his legs. 'I can't remember, the first when it came out, in the cinema; the second on video, I think.'

'I can't remember much about them.'

'You'll have to get them out again when you get home.'

'Yes. Yes, that'd be good.'

She sipped her beer.

Otto sipped his beer.

She wiped her brow.

'Do you want to go inside?'

'No – no, I'm fine.'

She held the cold beer glass to her forehead. The air was thin and warm, the dappled shade of the trees as still and fixed as stone.

'No, I'm not fine really, Otto. Look, I know you two have been through real problems, well, the truth is, so have Tom and I.'

Otto pushed his glasses onto his forehead and raised the eyebrow. There it was. She'd imagined it so many times it was a relief to see it, and, at last, to find out what the that glint was all about.

She rallied herself. 'Tom must have said something to you about it?'

His eyes dropped into a frown, he shook his head slowly, his mouth fixed, his chin firm.

He took a long gulp of beer.

'Look, I know Tom is your friend and all that. Tom and I, we haven't, well, I haven't, and, well – you may know this already.'

He was just looking. Staring. Not encouraging her to continue or to stop.

'Elle knows all about it!' she piped up as a final shove.

'Does she?'

That was genuine, the astonishment that Elle should know, but not the astonishment that something had been up. Had Tom said something on that boat, if not before? Had Elle kept her loyalty to her intact? She had to think fast, rearranging the words she'd rehearsed so well for Tom.

'The truth is, I've been unfaithful to Tom, Otto.'

'I'm surprised, Carla.'

'You don't sound surprised.'

'Why are you telling me this?'

'I was going to tell Tom today – after what you said when you came back from fishing that night, I knew you knew something. It seems everyone knows something about it. Except Tom. I can't live with you all knowing and he not knowing . . . it's destroyed the trust between us.

'Knowing – *what* exactly?'

'That's what I need to know from you. I need to know if Tom knows . . .'

'That you are having an affair?' He shook his head disdainfully. 'I don't think so, Carla.'

She looked at him sharply. 'No, no! It was a one-night stand. A, erm, zipless fuck, as Elle calls it.'

Otto threw his eyes in the air. 'Does she? And ...?'

'What do you mean and ...?'

'Is that it?'

'It – *that* – has been tormenting me – you know what a jealous guy Tom is ...'

'You want me to be honest?'

'Yes!'

'I think you feed on that, Carla, if you want me to tell you the truth. I think you want him to be jealous.'

'I do not! That's how he is. How he's always been. Oh, he's a flirt, I know that, but I've always lived with that quite comfortably and ...'

'Maybe you don't see it in yourself, Carla, but there's always been an – air about you when you are with Tom, like he is one of your children who needs looking after ...'

'That's because he does need looking after.'

'And where is he now?'

'Sorting out a cock-up with the agents about floor space somewhere or other, you know that. What I need to know from you, Otto, I'm sorry, but I have to know this. Has he said anything to you?'

'About?'

'Us!'

'Carla, have you been blind?'

'What do you mean?'

'Haven't you noticed something about your husband these past few months?'

'It's you who bangs on about honesty, Otto, and now it's my turn. I'm going to be honest with Tom, I'll tell

292

him, I was going to tell him this evening. At least now I've blabbed to you it'll mean I have no going back on that . . .'

'You've been a good support for Tom, Carla. And so you had a one-night stand.' He shrugged. 'Maybe you needed to do that.'

'That's what Elle says.'

'You've got to stop seeing everything in black and white, Carla. Tom *needs* this challenge he has now.'

'And I'm seeing him through it!'

'Haven't you noticed how much he's grown up the past few months, as he's taking responsibility for himself? Making this business is the best thing he's ever done; now, don't go and ruin it for him.'

'How can I stop these feelings then?'

'The child in you is the soul in you, we love Tom because of that but, I have to say, I think you are being a little childish in the wrong way, Carla.'

She felt herself flushing. 'All I want is to get this all out into the open and carry on. To restore the trust between us. What's so wrong with that? You two are being honest with each other, that's what you believe in, isn't it?'

'I had to let Elle go to keep her, Carla, that is what is happening; surely you can see that.'

'So it's not all about houses and grannies and children and . . .'

'No . . . If there was any real problem it was with the sex. After the children – it changed. It wasn't only Elle, after she began rejecting me we were both looking elsewhere, it only made sense to bring it up all in the open. We had to do that.'

'Exactly!'

'Carla. Has Tom been flirting with any of the Italian girls since we've been here?'

'No.'

'In the restaurants?'

'No.'

'On the beach?'

'We haven't been on the beach.'

'Not once have I seen him looking at a girl.'

'That's because he's always talking into his bloody mobile.'

'I think you have already broken through, Carla. You must forget about your, your *zipperless* thing, that is something for you to grow out of yourself. Maybe it is you who needs to be growing up a little bit here.'

'Letting go, you mean,' she said sarcastically.

'Sometimes rumour grows deeper and louder than truth, Carla.'

'What do you mean?'

'So – you make a mistake once in your life! Mistakes are how you learn.'

'But I never make mistakes!' Carla raised her voice.

'Maybe this is your mistake,' said Otto, even louder. 'We all make mistakes, including myself, I am not excluded from that.'

'So, how are things – erm - between you and Elle now?'

'A lot lot better.'

'A lot *lot* better?'

'A lot lot lot better!'

'So you are really together again? Ah, Otto – I'm so pleased!'

'She's been teaching me some new techniques and I have to say we are rediscovering each other's bodies again in quite a new way. You know how I hate all her hippy holistic nonsense, but I have to say this Tantric sex is rather an interesting thing. If you like I have a book, I could quietly pass it on to Tom . . .'

'No! No! Otto! Don't do that!!'

You little bugger, Tom, you little bugger!

'Come over here everybody now *please*!'

They both looked up slowly as the tour group surrounded their table. One of the Americans sat down with them, the other pulled up a chair. Cameras started clicking.

'Here we see our friends have chosen their table very good. This is the table where Michael, Calo and Fabrizio sat for the famous scene ... And then every day of the filming you would find Coppola was here, drinking their famous lemon granita. If you haven't had one of Maria's lemon granitas you haven't lived, ladies and gentlemen ... Please, please, sit down, take a seat ... The actress who played Michael's second wife, she also is from this village, and Maria the same bar owner. As you can see, it doesn't change at all since that time.'

The beads rattled, the waitress hovered.

'I guess it's lemon gratinas all round?' said the American.

Everyone except Carla nodded.

He leaned forward and rested his hand on the back of her chair. 'Hey, I hope we weren't interrupting anything between you and your husband there ...'

Carla smiled. 'No – no, of course not.'

Chapter Thirty-Five

They drove back to the villa in silence. Feeling stung, Carla pretended to sleep.

Otto could be cold. So cold.

Did she really come across as such a fusser? No, not only a fusser, a childish fusser, he'd called her. That was awful. That was terrible. And yet, he was right, he was definitely right about some things. She hadn't noticed Tom not noticing the girls. She'd grumbled often enough about him talking on his mobile all the time, though. Did she really only react when things weren't right? When he was doing something she didn't like?

When they got back to the villa, Elle was busy in the kitchen, the children were bathed and tucked up in bed, the wine was chilling in an ice-bucket and the fish marinated and ready to grill.

Elle's cosy hausfrau mode made Carla feel even more uncomfortable.

Otto took the plate of fish outside to the barbeque.

'Anything I can do, Elle?'

'No, no, everything is under control.'

'There must be something. Really, I'd rather be doing something with my hands.'

'No, you relax. Tell me about the trip.'

'It was fine.' Carla folded her arms and leaned her side against the fridge. 'We saw all the things we were meant to see. I wasn't that interested in all the Godfather stuff but Savoca is a very pretty village ...'

She spoke brightly and cheerily, taking Elle through the tour, watching her back as she moved around the brightly tiled kitchen, wondering. All the doubts had returned. All the absolute certainty that of course Elle had been making it all up. That to suggest she went with Tom had been a crazy idea of Carla's, and Elle had just strung her along, helping her to get over her own guilt. Nothing had needed to be said, even. She'd become so convinced of it. Tom wouldn't have been able to behave so normally afterwards. When he and Elle were together, like she'd seen them together all this week, there wasn't a hint of any past naughtiness, and, heavens, she'd studied every glance and twitch and every word exchanged closely enough.

She leaned forward and looked outside for Otto.

He stood stiffly but, she could tell somehow, contentedly at the end of the terrace by the barbeque, looking out to sea, tongs in one hand, a beer bottle in the other.

Elle was taking French beans out of the colander and chopping the ends off one by one. Carla latched on to the neatness of it, fascinated by the way each bean received Elle's equal, undivided attention. It would have been quicker, she felt like saying, to bunch them together and do a handful at a time, but she let if pass . It was one thing to pump up the courage to ask another woman about her marital sex life, quite another to interfere with her bean-trimming routine.

'We had an interesting talk together, actually. Your husband and I.'

'Oh.' Elle glanced over her shoulder, quickly turned

297

back and took another bean. Carla remembered the look. The same one she'd had in the supermarket. It gave Carla the courage to speak on out.

'He says you've discovered some interesting new – techniques.'

There, she'd said it.

Elle turned and grinned at Carla. 'That's right!'

Carla waited for her to say more but she'd turned back to her chopping.

'I have to say,' she said eventually, not turning round. 'It's good stuff, Carla. It has sparked up our relationship again.'

'So – did you, I mean ...' She checked on Otto again. The barbeque was fizzling now and she could smell the fish. 'I know we promised never to talk about it again but I've long been taking it as a joke, that you and Tom ever ...'

Elle put her knife down and turned around.

What was going on in her mind, Carla could only guess at. Her mouth felt dry.

They both looked out at Otto.

Elle put both hands on Carla's shoulder.

'We didn't, Carla. Is that what you want to hear?'

'As I said, I'm sorry, I feel embarrassed at bringing it up. It was just that Otto was saying ...'

'And you thought. Yes, yes, I see what you're thinking. Understandable. It's understandable.'

Carla didn't know what to make of the definite clippedness to Elle's tone.

'I did what you did, Carla. I bought a book.'

'Well, I'm glad, Elle. I'm really glad you've sorted out –'

'I didn't give it to Otto though!'

They both shut up as Otto appeared at the door. 'We need the salad on the table in three minutes.'

Carla moved away from the fridge to let him open it.

'Smells delicious, Otto.'

Carla followed him out onto the terrace and settled at the table, the candles already lit and flickering in the night air.

The chit-chattering easy flow of conversation soon started up again as they sat down to eat, in the sultry warm air, with the taste of the sea on their plates and the sound of the sea lapping gently against the rocks below them.

One thing was for sure. She'd never know, and she'd have to let it go. Just as she'd never know about Danielle or any of the others. As Otto said, she must learn by her mistakes. Mistake. It was too late now, she had to accept that. Far too late for up-front honesty. She still felt her conversation with Elle hadn't concluded. She felt the need for them to all talk about it together. To clear the air one final time.

'And I promise, I'll never bring up the subject again.'

'Not for at least another seven years!'

'Seven years. Will we still be coming here?'

'I hope so.'

'With two great burly teenagers and Dyl and Tallulah ten . . .'

'And refusing to have anything to do with the opposite sex.'

'Very wise,' said Otto.

'This is going to be one of those nights I shall always remember.' She ate her ice cream slowly, letting each spoonful melt fully in her mouth, staring out at the evening sea, feeling grown up, sophisticated even, like she was someone she could live with again.

'You know, I think we learn more about each other by not knowing everything about each other.'

She caught Elle grinning at her, warily. She gave her a secret half-smile back with her eyes.

'Secrets exist for a reason, they protect us,' said Otto.

'My only worries are those jaunty elbow nudges from Bryony, and I can still hear ...' she hadn't mentioned the en-suite moment; now she told them about Hazel's voice outside the bathroom. It felt weird telling Otto a girly detail but she'd had a lot of wine. They'd laughed till the whole episode seemed as light as a feather, a flicker of the past that could float away and be forgotten about.

'Don't worry about her. You've only got another year of the playground and Wilf'll be going to school on his own.'

'I can't imagine it. What'll I do in the mornings when I don't have the school run any more?'

'I thought you hated the school run!'

'Well, you get used to it, don't you.'

'You still have Dyl to take to nursery.'

'It's not the same. As much as I hate it, I do quite like to see everyone, see what they're wearing, who's hanging out with who, who's still in pyjamas ...'

'I'm going to get some this summer,' said Elle.

'Pyjamas?' Otto looked shocked.

'Not for bed, Otto. People have started wearing them out now.'

'You could get away with it, Elle; I'd look like I'd just rolled out of bed. Or with my make-up on, maybe a character from Gilbert & Sullivan.'

She waited for Elle or Otto to deny it. But they didn't. Suddenly, she felt lonely. She wanted to go home now. She'd had enough. Quietly, she tiptoed off to bed, leaving them canoodling like teenage lovers beneath the stars.

Chapter Thirty-Six

Richmond Hill Juniors and Infants Parent Teacher Association
Bromyard Road, Richmond TW9 2LM

PTA Newsletter – April 2003

Thanks to all the parent helpers (and the staff!!!) on the sponsored run last Sunday. What a fabulous day it was! We couldn't have been luckier with the glorious April sunshine.
Thanks too for all Elle Ollson and Carla Alexander's efforts on the (rather unusual!!) school calendar this year. I'm sure you all agree:

A little late!
but well worth the wait!!

With the Easter holidays already two weeks behind us it seems like only yesterday we were all getting used to our new classrooms and now we find we are fast approaching the time for change once again! But not before plenty of fun events and a wealth of enter-

*tainments to take us through the long summer days
ahead! Not least, it is time to put our heads together
for the Summer Fair which is fast approaching!
We're delighted to welcome* Fat Chance *back to the
stage and all the usual stalls will be there as well as
some fabulous new events. One of the highlights this
year will be the year 1 maypole dancing, thanks to
Angela Walker's marvellous generosity once again;
if you have any raffle prizes to donate please see
Sarah Calvert or Deborah Brewster; Chris and
Simon Wilde will (again) be running the barbeque,
but we need more volunteers – especially from
amongst the dads out there!!*

Hmm, fat chance Carla thought, snapping the notice onto
the newsletter bulldog clip and hanging it back on its
hook. She underlined the last bit in red felt tip, more as a
joke to herself than anything else, adding a few more
exclamation marks for the hell of it. She'd barely seen him
since they'd returned from Sicily, as they found themselves in the world of self-employment turnover hell.

She hadn't really believed everything would slip into
place neatly, but even so, the realities of independence
were far from anything to do with the freedom Tom had
so hoped for. Any idea that Tom would be spending more
time at home working on his character chairs and achieve
his greatest ambition of being there at 6pm every night to
watch *The Simpsons* with Wilf, soon seemed like a distant
dream. He had, as Ant put it, joined the 9–5 club. On a
good day arriving home at 9 and leaving again not long
after 5 the next morning.

Once the contracts had been signed, Bruno all but disappeared. As did Danielle, handing over all business
dealings to be sorted by the fearsomely bureaucratic

Brussels-based offices of Gilbert and George. Even with the heavily vetted contracts signed and sealed, every request for cash had to go before legions of committees, each of which only met on certain dates of the month. The first rent on the Stockwell factory couldn't be met and had to be topped up out of their personal account.

It was no wonder Tom's laughter lines had turned to worry frowns. Whether there was anything good about this, as Otto seemed to think, she didn't have time to consider; her efforts were channelled into helping as much as she could with the dreaded economics of the whole enterprise.

It was still with some trepidation she made her first foray back into Cyn's coffee mornings to offer her services for the summer fair, though not before quietly looking up Scud's tour dates on their website. She was concentrating hard on not feeling so wrong about everything. She did have the right to exist there. She did.

'No sign of the pyjamas yet then?' she said, sitting down next to Elle.

'You're looking very smart for a Tuesday morning, Carl? Even for you.'

'I'm going out for lunch.'

'Where?'

'Up in town.'

'Get you, do you want me to collect Dyl?'

'It's OK, I've got Zita for the afternoon.'

Elle looked impressed. 'A serious lunch then?'

Carla nodded.

'Out with it, Carla, who, where, why?' said Ant.

'My husband, if you must know.'

'Oh yeah!' laughed Cyn.

'You didn't tell me!' said Elle.

'That's because I didn't know. He called me from the factory this morning. I told him not to be daft, he hasn't

303

got the time to comb his hair these days, but he was very persistent so... it will be the first time we've sat down together properly since Sicily, really ...'

'What about the weekends?' asked Bryony.

'What are they?'

'Where are you going?'

'Tate Modern?'

'Oh, that'll be lovely!!' said Bryony.

Oh no it wouldn't. She sat through the meeting as in a dream, knowing whatever it was Tom had to say, it wouldn't be pleasant. Why else when they were so time and cash poor?

With just time for a couple of forays in the galleries tempting her all the way up the escalators, she arrived at the top floor at 11.45 as arranged. Presumably so she could grab a table. She was surprised to see him already there, sitting at the third table in, next to the window, looking tired but smart in his crumply, baggy beige jacket and open-neck white shirt. She felt proud but a little shy as she bypassed the small queue already forming.

His seriousness was a little daunting, making him look like the distinguished designer he was. Like a face she'd never seen, almost. It was only then and in that moment that her shoulders dropped and her guard went up. The evening on the terrace with Elle and Otto, all that laughter, all the sophisticatedness of lies revealed itself for what it was again. The evening had been a sham. A shabby sham. She deserved whatever she got.

For all her resolutions to put everything behind her, it was all going to come up like a freak wave out of the sea to grab her and pull her under. What if he wanted to tell her what happened with Danielle? What then?

'Looks like Legoland, doesn't it?' she said, gazing out over the City of London laid out below them as she pecked him on the cheek and took her seat. Over-jollily. As if to say, you *dare*, husband dear, throw any unpleasantness on top of this.

She looked him coyly in the eye. 'Well, this *is* a surprise!'

'And why not?'

'Because you don't do surprises, Tom.'

He shrugged, smiled and sipped at his wine.

What was *that*? It wasn't his pre-argument ironic smile but it wasn't his jolly-joke daft smile either.

'I have to say it's good to see you in the daylight hours once more.'

He chinked her glass. 'And you.'

The waiter was back already to take their order.

'I'd recommend the chips,' he said not looking up from his menu.

She ordered a salad with extra chips on the side for when Tom had finished his. Unsure what was going to happen next, she launched into their once-routine meal-starter Wilf and Dyl updates.

'They've concocted these disgusting names for Winders, I think I'm going to have to ban them like everyone else. Red ones are blood, green ones are bogeys, and orange ones are, wait for it, ear wax.'

Tom didn't laugh, but nodded approvingly. 'Sounds good.'

He was listening but he wasn't taking it in. She could tell.

'Tom, could you stop sounding like you're approving a new office routine.'

She felt sorry as soon as she'd said it. She pushed on quickly.

'Has Dyl told you about his invisible friends?'

Tom shook his head.

'Sadler and Nick.'

'Where'd he get them from?'

'I called them pretend friends and he ticked me off, he said no, they're not pretend friends, they're invisible friends.'

'A bit like our invisible friends.'

'Otto and Elle?'

Tom nodded.

'They understand, they know what we're going through. Though we must get them round for supper sometime, when you get some time, I mean.'

Tom laughed ironically. 'Yeah!'

'It can't go on for ever like this, Tom. It'll settle, when the premises are sorted properly; it's teething problems, it must happen to everyone . . .'

'How do you think they're getting on?'

'Who?'

'Elle – and Otto.'

She swallowed.

'I think they're as together as they've ever been.'

'Do you?'

'I hope they tear up those daft divorce-lite papers. I think they will, don't you?'

'They won't have to.'

'Why?'

'They were never legally married, were they.'

'I didn't know that. Why didn't you ever tell me that?'

Why didn't Elle ever tell me that?

'I'm telling you.'

'How long did you know?'

'I – can't remember exactly . . .'

That night?

'Elle might have told me.'

Or Otto, that day. She shook her head slowly.

'Don't worry about it, Carl.'

'It's funny, isn't it, I think all we ever really know about people is there's always stuff we'll never know. Like this, today. If you'd told me six months ago we'd be sitting here on a school day, having lunch, and it was something you'd arranged, without my nagging or hinting at anniversaries or anything I'd have been totally shocked. I still am, actually. One of the things about you, Tom, has always been how predictable you are. I mean, I even know what socks you're going to pull out of your drawer first every morning.'

'So, it won't be a surprise ever again, will it?'

They smiled at each other.

What was it? She unfolded her napkin and put it over her white skirt. *What was it?*

'Are you sure you've got time for this? We could always go to the snack bar on the third floor.'

'I've made time, Carla, like I have to make time for everything else at the moment.'

Go on, get it over with.

'But why?'

'To say sorry.'

'Sorry? What for?'

'I've been so busy.'

'But you've been busy for months, Tom, I'm more than used to it and I know why. I'm learning to live with the new routine, much like the old really, except you're never there.'

'That's why we're here.'

No, it's not. Was it going to be a good reason or a bad reason? There weren't any good reasons she could think of but there was one very good bad reason.

Once the food arrived she decided the only way was to chill it out of him. She didn't offer up any more Dyl and

307

Wilf stories. She thought about how she should respond. With tearful apologies, with relief, with the old accusations about Danielle ...?

They ate in silence until, halfway through the main course, 'Carla, there is something serious I need to talk about.'

Her stomach lurched. As soon as he said it a new thought struck. Was he going to tell her about his evening with Elle? That it did happen? She wouldn't be able to bear that. She wouldn't. She'd have to tell him in return. New news he wouldn't be able to cope with right now. He wouldn't like it. He wouldn't like it at all. No. She couldn't tell him. Of course she couldn't tell him. Her secret would just have to get a bit bigger, that's all.

'You know all that fuss about factory space and –'

She laughed.

'It's not funny!'

'Nothing, carry on ...'

'And we went for the Stockwell space even though it was a bit on the big side ...'

'Yes.'

'Which is what's causing all these headaches from Brussels.'

'Yes, yes...'

'I was wondering if you'd be interested ...'

'What?'

'In taking over some of it.'

'What on earth *for*?'

'It'll have to be in a small way at first, but, you know those shadow designs you did in Italy, well, Danielle saw them ...'

'How did *she* see them?'

'I showed them to her!'

'When?'

'I'd pinned some up in the office, she noticed them . . .'

'You pinned them up? And I thought she was never there!'

'She's not! She called in yesterday though.'

'Did you have a go at her about Brussels?'

'Of course I did. Now, shut up and listen. The thing is, she loved them. And that's not all. I do want to say I'm sorry, Carl, it made me realise, they are fantastic; I've been taking your talent, your many talents, for granted for too long.'

After a long pause, she finally spoke again.

'How could I ever find the time! Apart from which, how could I ever get to Stockwell every day? Who'd look after Dyl?'

'You wouldn't need to go every day. You could sort something out with one of Cyn's cousins. It'll make your life more interesting . . .'

'I'm not interested in being interesting, Tom, you're plenty interesting enough for both of us. And besides, there'd be a mountain of stuff to do, colours to source, fabrics, machines, printers, collators . . .'

'You'd be brilliant at it. It's what you wanted to do. I've been so lost in my work Carl, I've been selfish . . .'

'That's because you've had to be.'

'There's no big rush, so long as we get the proposal accepted it'll keep them sweet. You could target Dyl's starting school next year, if you want, but, more importantly, well, there's something else . . .'

Carla swallowed hard. She remembered Danielle in her garden, with Tom, the smoke mingling together. His lack of flirting. Was that the beginning of Tom taking life seriously? Was that all it was?

'I just realise how much I've taken you for granted, Carl. You've been like, like another object in my life –

309

like, I love you to bits, you know that, like I love my work.'

'Your chairs, you mean, not all this scrapping for premises and deadlines ...'

'I do love you Carla, you know that, but I've just been accepting you've been there, like Out of the Blue and all it brought us.'

She smiled. 'Knowing you so well, Tom, I take that as a compliment.'

'Or a table, maybe. A very *good* table.

'A Prouvé table maybe ...'

He reached out for her hand, 'Now, *there's* a table. But still ...'

'It's still a table ...'

'It's time for us to do a little bit of shifting the furniture around. Like you know, before we had the kids you remember how you went along with my spontaneity? Taking off at a moment's notice, not booking anything in advance?'

'And how, after the kids, you went along with my orderliness? I don't think we can change that, Tom. That's how it is when there are children around.'

'I don't want to change that ... but you've supported me for so long, it's time I ...'

Carla watched the love in his eyes glaze over. As one they withdrew their hands from each other. She didn't need to turn around. The voice was audible across the whole, vast restaurant.

The sculptural form and function of elemental shapes, that's what we have to get through. They must show the integrity, the playful but minimalist aesthetic without betraying the geometric form within the framework of the theatre of play, never forgetting the authenticity and simplicity of the materials ...'

310

'You didn't tell me this was the works canteen!'

'You know now.'

'Yup, I know now.'

'Welcome to Supernatural, my partner, my sleeping partner.' Tom picked up his glass. 'Let's say we flourish as two unique halves.'

She chinked his glass. 'To two unique halves.'

Chapter Thirty-Seven

Treyarnon Bay, Cornwall
April 2004

Dear Elle and Otto

The beaches here are
unbelievable and hotel
spa something else.

Elle and Otto Olsson & family
91 Onslow Road
Richmond
TW9 3LM

Hmm, what to write next?

Something about the weather. They'd been bloody lucky with the weather. But, as the boys kept on pointing out, the rain never stopped anyone surfing.

Weather perfect...

Corny but still, they were in Cornwall.

Sorry I'm being corny, but still, we are in Cornwall!

Oh dear, I'm beginning to sound like Bryony.

Oh dear, I'm beginning to sound like you-know-who ...

Why hadn't she written in larger letters? There were still two-thirds of card space to fill.

What about – *the boys have made loads of new friends at the surf school.*

or – *thank heavens we didn't book Sicily!*

No, that wouldn't do. Even though they'd know she was referring to Wilf and Jon's spectacular falling-out, which had been going on for months now. It wasn't quite the right note she was looking for. On the other hand, she couldn't write 'wish you were here' because she was really glad they weren't. She had known, as soon as they'd returned last year, that she never, ever wanted to sit on that beautiful terrace again.

They'd long given up grinding Wilf and Jon's faces together to get them even to acknowledge one another, but Dyl and Tallulah were closer than ever, which meant she and Elle sometimes met up in the daytime, though rarely after school. Or at weekends, even, since Jon had changed from football to rugby.

They still saw each other for coffees sometimes. At the Bon Appetit, not Dickens and Jones. Though finding a day when both of them weren't working wasn't easy.

Tom and Otto saw more of each other. As the business found its feet, Tom had finally started getting home by *The Simpsons*. He'd even been giving himself some time off lately, disappearing with Otto on Ryanair fishing weekends to Sweden, Scotland and wherever else was last minute and available.

The boys are learning to bodysurf. They love it! Dyl's even better than Wilf!
See you soon!
Love from us all,
C,T,W & D

She put the card to one side. Then picked it up again.

She'd fallen in love again. They both had. They all had. Should she tell Elle? Should she write it now? Why not? It was one of those loves that wasn't going to go anywhere, they all knew it. And it made such practical sense too, that was the joy of it. She picked up her pen again.

PS – We've found a new house – we've decided to relocate, workshop and all! You must come down.

She paused and thought for a moment, before changing the full stop to a comma –

,for a weekend –

and adding three exclamation marks

!!!